Always Hayden

Always Hayden

This book is a work of fiction. Names, characters, businesses, organizations, places, events and incidents either are the product of the author's imagination or are used fictitiously. Any resemblance to actual persons, living or dead, events, or locales is entirely coincidental.

Printed in the United States of America

Editing by Teri@editingfairy.com
Book Formatting by Derek Murphy@Creativindie.com
Bookcover image@pixabay.com

Paperback ISBN: 978-0-9991169-5-1
Ebook ISBN: 978-0-9991169-6-8

Library of Congress Control Number: 2018907925
First Edition: 2018

10 9 8 7 6 5 4 3 2 1

Always Hayden

A Cloverly Wolves Novel

B. S. TODD

One

Hayden

Hayden ran the mountainside in an attempt to work off the excess stress and tension that had consumed him since returning home from Cloverly. He held fond memories of the small Kentucky town and visits with his uncle's pack when he was younger. It was a yearly vacation he always looked forward to. Usually, he, his siblings and their mother made the trip. Of course, his dad would have visited more often but being the alpha of the Smoky Mountain Pack in Tennessee, he didn't always have the opportunity. His last visit to Cloverly, however, the one Hayden hadn't planned, was anything but enjoyable.

Frustrated and tired after his strenuous midday run, he entered the cabin that Tucker and Jesse vacated earlier that morning, their scent a reminder of everything he didn't have. The oldest of the Wilson siblings, Hayden should have been the first to find his mate, but little brother beat him to the punch. Seeing Tucker and Jesse together, his wolf stirred with the notion that maybe he, too, should find a mate and settle down. But Hayden belonged to the Tennessee pack and his female did not.

He paced through the cabin as shadows stretched along the mountainside, guessing the time to be four-thirty or thereabouts in the afternoon. His mind was a muddled mess and his inability to quiet it only added to his frustration. He and Lori should've been planning their own bonding ceremony and subsequent celebration in that very cabin, but boy, how quickly things changed.

Explaining the bond to Lori sounded simple enough, even if he thought her to be somewhat fickle. And after what Tucker went through with Jesse, there was no way in hell he would deny their bond and walk away. Plus, it wasn't unheard of for a mountain wolf to bond with a human, although it was quite rare. Granted, he hadn't known Lori as long as Tucker knew Jesse, but that didn't mean their bond wouldn't be equally as strong. He was determined, Lori was a challenge, and together, they complemented each other perfectly.

His wolf growled in agreement.

As he stared out the cabin window, his thoughts turned to the day when he first set his eyes on the feisty brunette. She was Jesse's best friend who drove in from Cloverly with Jesse's family to attend the bonding ceremony scheduled for later that night. After Jesse's introduction, Lily, his youngest sibling, was over the moon at learning Lori was a human. She threw her arms around Lori's neck, knocking her off balance and she landed on her ass. *And what a nice ass it was!* He silently chuckled. Seeing Lily straddling the guest, he had no clue what happened so he rushed across the room to offer his assistance and then, BAM!

The connection between him and Lori sent a surge of electricity to the most inappropriate place, causing his eyes to flare. His breathing grew rapid and his face burned hot by the time he realized she had mesmerized him with her smile. Then Jesse snorted, bringing him out of his stupor and he rushed out the front door. There was no denying the bond between them was strong, if only based on the tightness of his jeans! Shoving his hands through his hair, he rushed around the house to the trail that ran along the mountainside. In order to clear his mind and douse the growing fire that threatened to consume him, he had to put more space between them.

Hayden enjoyed his fair share of female attention over the years—and reveled in being a true alpha male—but never in his dirtiest, wildest, uncensored dreams did he believe his body could respond to a female's touch the way it did to Lori's.

A wide grin spread across his face when he thought about Lori exposing her spunky-as-hell attitude at the bonding ceremony. Fisting that little hand on her hip and glaring up at Katherine, whom she perceived a threat, he wanted to grab her and have his dad perform their ceremony right there on the spot. Just thinking about it ignited a fire so deep in his soul that if he dwelled there too long, he would explode. But because she was a human, he couldn't force her into the bond. Naturally, the thought crossed his mind more than once when he realized she was just as tenacious as he was proud.

So for three days, Hayden courted the little beauty and those were the happiest three days of his life. Her bright smile and chestnut hair matched the color of his sister's, and hell, she already blended right in with the family. She was thin, athletic in build—not too tall, not too short—about the right height to rest her head against his chest. And her long, slender legs were the best of his fantasies; he could imagine them wrapped tightly around his waist. He squeezed his eyes shut. If only he could push her out of his mind until he could figure out some way to get her back to the mountains, but that wasn't likely to happen anytime soon.

Memories of them sitting on the front porch swing haunted him. Shivering as her teeth chattered, Lori didn't want to go inside. The night air was too cold for her and being the gentleman he was, he offered her his lap. As he wrapped her tightly in his coat, she snuggled against him, and he never wanted to let her go. Her warm breath grazed his chin as she rested her head on his shoulder. Everything about her tugged at his heart and he instantly fell in love. She was funny, smart, and way too trusting, but he could also see some sadness that swirled in her soft, blue eyes. He wanted to kiss the sadness away, but had to restrain the urge.

Then Katherine showed up. Expecting to have everything her way, she was beyond pissed when Tucker bonded with Jesse—but she got over that quick enough. Katherine knew she didn't stand a chance against a new blood but never considered Lori, the little human, a threat. She followed them around town, always flirting, or making suggestions that she knew were inappropriate.

Spurring sneers and jeers from her friends, she was about as desperate as they came, but in the end, she crossed the line. And Hayden had to put a stop to it before she provoked his wolf.

He and Lori had just finished their walk and were standing in front of the alpha house when he pulled her into a kiss. It was a bold move for him, but he was unable to hold back any longer so he took the plunge.

Low and behold, out of nowhere came Katherine. Talk about bad timing! Demanding his attention, Katherine got exactly what she wanted even if it was more than she expected. After practically growling at Lori and making threats, it was high time she learned her place in the pack. Hayden grabbed her arm hastily and marched her back down the road to her house.

In hindsight, perhaps it did look like he was choosing her over Lori, but his intent was merely to keep Lori safe and far away from all the hatred Katherine spewed. When he ran into Katherine's parents, he explained what was going on. Her threatening the future alpha's mate was an unacceptable act of disobedience that would not be tolerated.

Hayden returned home just in time to catch Lori loading the last of her things into Tucker's car. He had no idea how to handle the mixed emotions that saddled his heart, but clearly, he was in the wrong. Trying to do what he thought was right, he inadvertently hurt the one person he only sought to protect.

A fresh layer of snow fell overnight, and Hayden feared Lori would slide off the road, so he had no choice but to drive her home. She straddled her bags and crawled into the backseat, refusing to sit beside him, or even look his way. When he glanced at the rearview mirror, she pulled earbuds from her pocket, determined to ignore him for the entire drive. Within fifteen minutes, she fell asleep to the music. *She looked peaceful, beautiful, like an angel,* he thought. She was definitely his mate and he had to figure out a way to tell her—if only she would listen.

By the time they arrived in Cloverly, she had woken up a couple times, but he knew that sleeping was just her way of avoiding him. "Where do you live?" he asked, but being the stubborn female that she was, she refused to allow him to take her home. Instead, he took her to the side door of the Lucky Leaf something-or-other—a large brick building on the corner of Main Street. Once he unloaded her bags, he reached for her arm and she glared back at him. He just wanted to explain their bond, but she wasn't having any part of that. Yanking her arm away, she quickly stopped him in his tracks.

"You can't shove your tongue down my throat and then walk off with another girl and expect me to be waiting when you get home! That will never happen. So scurry your butt back to the mountains where you belong and leave me alone!" That was the last thing Lori said before she stormed into the building.

His wolf grumbled a reply, and he had every intention of going after her until he realized how many humans were in the area. He cursed. It wasn't a risk he was willing to take so he waited in the car for what seemed like hours. Growing restless, he was bound and determined to have it out with Lori right then and there. But when he got out of the car and walked over to the door, he found it locked. He growled in frustration, *so this is how you want to play!* Storming around to the front of the building, he was more than annoyed that she would actually lock him out, and he peered through the window. Recognizing her scent at the door, his frown deepened when he realized the lights were off and she was actually gone. There was no way she could've left without him being able to track her. He sniffed the air, but her scent was no longer there. Again, he growled in frustration while hurrying back around the building to his car.

After driving to his brother's cabin, he slept on the couch until the sun came up before heading back to Tennessee. Passing by the boutique on his way out of town, which was closed, he noticed the lights were still out. He could have kicked himself for allowing her to give him the slip. She was a crafty female, but his persistence would eventually find her.

The drive home was quick and no surprise that he made it back in record time. His wolf, however, was furious that he failed to explain the bond he had with Lori. So once he was back on the mountain, he had no choice but to let his wolf run off his frustration. That was earlier that day, and after a cool-down, he walked into the kitchen where his mother was sitting at the bar, sipping coffee.

"Thank the moon. Are you okay?" Lucia asked.

"I'm fine, Mom." He poured a cup of coffee and took a seat across from her. The rich aroma drifted to his nose, and he licked his lips. "I just needed time to sort things out." He ran his fingers through his hair as he stared down at the cup.

"Hayden, what's going on between you and Lori? I've heard Jaylee's version, now I'd like to hear yours." She cocked her head and waited.

"I don't know. Everything happened so fast. One minute, I was running across the room to get Lily off Jesse's friend, and the next minute, I was staring into the eyes of my mate." He rubbed his hand over his face and picked up the cup.

"You have a bond with Lori?" she asked and he nodded. "Did you tell her?"

"I tried. We'd just finished our walk around the mountain and I kissed her. Then Katherine walked up and she was pissed. She started threatening Lori, as well as our whole family. I know there's nothing she can do, but she thinks because Jesse is a new blood, and Lori is a human, she could sway the pack against us."

"Please! That's the craziest thing I've ever heard. We have humans in our pack! Not many, but we do have them. As for Jesse, she is a member of our family whether Katherine likes it or not," Lucia said, her voice tightening.

"I know but Katherine likes to run her mouth in front of an audience, and well… she pissed me off so I took her home and set her parents straight." He swallowed the rumble that worked its way up his throat and glanced back at his mom.

"Good. After the way she acted at the bonding ceremony, I don't think we need her stirring the pot. But that still doesn't explain what happened with Lori." Lucia was persistent, and Hayden knew he had no choice but to tell her what she wanted to know. He loved his mother dearly, and no matter how badly he thought he screwed up, she would always be there to help guide him in the right direction.

"She thought I chose Katherine over her, so she refused to speak to me. Her feelings were hurt and after thinking about it, I totally understand why. I shouldn't have walked away with Katherine, but I needed to keep Lori safe. By doing that, Katherine got exactly what she wanted."

"So, what now? You can't just let her go. You saw what your brother went through when he denied his bond with Jesse," Lucia reminded him.

"You know me better than that." Hayden flashed a lazy grin. "I have no intention of letting her go. I've been out there on the mountain, trying to figure out what I'm going to do and… she knew what I was when she crawled into my lap. She just doesn't know we share a bond."

"Then you're headed back to Cloverly?" He almost chuckled at the excitement he heard in his mother's voice.

"As soon as I know Dad and Sawyer can handle things here, I'm going to call Alpha Cooper." This time, he did chuckle at her widening eyes.

"No, I'll call my brother. You get things arranged and pack your bags."

Hayden was relieved that his mother was on board with his plans to go after Lori, and his mood shifted when his thoughts wandered back to the chestnut beauty. If only he'd taken her down the mountain to a secluded area and demanded that she listen to him. But being forceful would have only made matters worse, he assumed at the time. Now he wondered if he should have at least tried.

That night at the supper table, he and his dad and Sawyer worked out a schedule. It shifted the off-mountain responsibilities to Tony, his dad's beta, and Sawyer was assigned to pick up the slack. Hayden didn't like going off and leaving Tony to cover for him, but if everything worked out as he planned, he would be back in Cloverly before mid-winter.

He gazed up at the waning moon as he walked across the front porch and sat down in the swing. It was another cold, snowy night as he rested his head against the back of the swing and closed his eyes. With Lori consuming all of his thoughts, he could still smell her scent, which lingered on his coat. Brown sugar and cinnamon was always a favorite flavor, and now he knew why.

Picturing her in his lap and remembering the way her body melted against his, he sighed. She had sparked new life into his wolf, something that was woefully missing for years, and just having that little taste of heaven, his wolf could never settle for less.

"I'm coming for you Lori," he whispered, enjoying the quietness of the night.

Two

Lori

Groggy from lack of sleep, Lori sat on the side of the bed and stared out the back window. The dreary winter day did nothing to boost her mood, and the chill in the air reflected the iciness that gripped her heart.

It had been years since her mother brought a date home, and based on their conversation, Lori assumed he stayed there all night, but she had no right to complain. Steve had stayed over plenty of nights after her mother took a swing shift job in the neighboring county. Because of that, her senior year was spent secretly expecting that she and Steve would always be together.

Since September, after celebrating her eighteenth birthday, her mother began spending more time away from home with her newly divorced boyfriend, Dean. Dean didn't seem like a bad guy, but her mother tried way too hard to impress him, and Lori didn't know why. So when he invited them to spend Christmas at his house, Lori declined, hoping her mother would as well. That's when everything went downhill—quickly. After accusing Lori of being selfish and unreasonable, her mother stormed out the door leaving her to spend her Christmas Eve alone.

Lori fell asleep on the couch that night, staring at the gift she bought for her mom, still wrapped and under the tree. It was the worst night of her life, which was saying a lot considering she could vividly remember the day she stood at the front window holding a large, pink valentine she had made for her dad. He never got his gift either. So when Tucker called and invited her to Tennessee, she nearly jumped at the chance. She was eager to escape the nightmare that had become her life. Big mistake.

She swiftly dressed as the bedroom walls closed in around her. Not wanting to confront her mother in front of Dean, Lori headed out the door without bothering to look back when her mother called her. Bundled in layers, she soon found herself standing in front of Gramma's house—only two doors down. She'd made many trips down that sidewalk over the years, but now that Jesse no longer lived there, tears stung her eyes. Jesse was the last of her friends to move on in life, and maybe it was time she did as well.

Confused and depressed, she needed someone to talk to, and anyone at that point would have sufficed. She glanced across the street at Brian's house, and decided maybe she wasn't that desperate—before she turned her attention to the woods. *What do you have to lose?*

Looking down at her boots, she thought she was

slightly overdressed, considering the light dusting of snow on the ground, but at least her toes were toasty warm. Then she glanced back to make sure no one was watching as she edged her way around Gramma's house to the oak tree in the backyard. She was well out of her comfort zone, admittedly, but since Megan was the alpha female of the Cloverly Pack, she felt fairly safe and would dropped names if necessary.

Entering the woods, she listened as overhead branches creaked in the chilly breeze. Without the foliage, the woods seemed lonely, like the gaping hole that festered in her heart.

She puffed out an icy breath, wishing she could erase everything that had happened in the past week. After her trip to Tennessee, she had stopped at the boutique to let Megan know she was home and picked up a bottle of Scent-Begone—the name she would now label her bottle of Fortuity. Megan wore the perfume when she was hiding from the pack, and since she was only half wolf, if it worked for Megan, maybe it would work for Lori as well.

Hayden was waiting outside the building, and judging by the position of the car seat, he wasn't leaving anytime soon. How touching. He was extremely good-looking, even taking drool-worthy to a whole new level, but Lori wouldn't fall for his pretty boy smile. She had no intentions of hearing him out, and the sooner he was gone, the better.

Once she confirmed he was still in the car, she hurried out the front door with a cunning grin on her face. She may have been from a small town, but he was clueless, which worked in her favor. Dousing herself with enough lavender fragrance to smother a cow, she swiftly ducked into the cafe.

Taking a seat at the corner booth, and nearly starved after skipping lunch, she ordered a large bowl of chili and an ice cold soda. Eating alone had become the norm for her, and she glanced over at a group of teenagers who were goofing off at the counter. She longingly frowned, remembering a time when her mother waited for her to get home from school. It was only the two of them after her dad died, but once her mother hit the dating scene, that all changed.

Lori had just finished eating when she noticed Hayden standing on the sidewalk in front of the boutique. He looked confused but gorgeous, and as her stomach roiled, she covered her mouth with a napkin. Knowing he was a badass wolf, she held her breath and hoped Hayden wouldn't detect her scent. She scrunched her nose and sneezed. The lavender fragrance was not something she preferred, but a small sacrifice on her part as was hiding out until Hayden was gone in order to escape his wolfish charm. She inhaled a deep breath as he turned and walked away. The pain in her heart filled her chest and she slumped over on the table as beads of sweat appeared on her brow.

That was yesterday, and although her indigestion was finally gone, she still felt the ache of a lonely heart.

"Thanks a lot, Hayden," Lori whispered, and continued along the trail. It wasn't fair to blame him for her actions, but she could blame him for her not being in Tennessee.

Lori loved winter and touring the snow-covered mountains with Hayden was by far the best day of her life. Not because of the white-blanketed hills or the pink sheet of sunset cast over top of the pines. But gazing out over the mountains, she realized if she stayed in Cloverly, she would never fully experience what life had to offer. It was a sad realization when she thought about it, and once again, something she could pin on Hayden.

Hayden was a foot taller than her five-foot-five. His rich, brown hair touched his shoulders and his dreamy, brown eyes sparkled like gold dust in the full moonlight. Everything about him was magnificent—when she compared him to her book boyfriend.

Lori scowled, knowing her world would never include him, especially with Katherine still in the picture. The tall blonde that reeked of money flaunted her looks anytime he was near. How could he resist the temptation of her flirtatious personality and brazen sex appeal? Observing the way the busty bimbo drooled over him, she half expected Katherine to mount his leg and mark her territory. *You just wish you were that ballsy.* That thought made her angry and she clenched her fist.

Flexing her fingers as she walked into the clearing at Sallee's Rock, she looked up at the boulders. From where she stood, the rock looked higher than she cared to climb although it was not nearly as tall as the mountains that tugged on her heart. She took a seat on the first boulder she came to and leaned against another. The hint of snow that wafted in the air tickled her nose, and she closed her eyes, remembering how Hayden gently lifted Lily Rose from her snow angel. Lori imagined she probably looked like a giddy school girl when she admired the snug fit of his jeans. *Only you would go there.* That was truer than not, but if she remembered correctly, the gleam in

Hayden's eye when he straddled her angel, he had gone there as well. Enjoying the calmness that washed over her when she thought about the prettiest man that ever graced her sight, she dozed off.

Snow flurries drifted to the ground and Lori opened her eyes when a shiver rocked her body. Sitting alone on the boulder, she wasn't afraid to be there, but it wasn't exactly the place she wanted to die. She covered her face with her gloved hands and blew out a breath to warm her nose. The temperature had dropped by at least five degrees, and she glanced up at the gray clouds floating overhead. Realizing she wasn't alone, she shivered again and jumped down off the boulder—noticing the sun had dipped behind the treetops.

"Lori, isn't it?" a male voice asked as he walked over to where she stood.

"Yeah, and you're Nigel, right?" Something about his stance bothered her, and she took a step back.

"Whoa! I come in peace." He smiled and shoved his hands into his pockets. "I didn't mean to disturb you but it will be night soon, and the woods always get darker before the sky does."

Lori glanced over at the trees. She didn't consider that, but since he mentioned it, it did make sense. "I lost track of time, but I should probably get going."

"I can walk you out if you'd like." His dusty blond hair peeked out from beneath the black sock cap he wore. He was older—but by how much, she didn't know—and a nice looking man. His eyes reflected an unusual color when the light caught them, a teal or a greenish gray, maybe.

"Thank you, but that's not necessary. I can jog back.

It's not very far."

"Well, could you call me when you get home? It would save me from worrying, knowing you made it out of the woods before dark," Nigel explained. He pulled out his wallet and handed her a business card.

Lori rolled her lip to keep the grin off her face as she took the card he offered. "Sorry, I'm not trying to laugh, but you're a wolf and you carry a business card? That's just too cute."

"Yeah, I consider the wolf my better half," he chuckled. "But I'm a man first." She glanced up and he winked. *Take that Hayden.*

"So-o-o, Stonewall Security. That's your business name?"

"It's a play off my name," he said as she looked back down at the card.

"Nigel Stone. Nice."

"Thanks, and your name is?"

"Lori Mayfield." She looked up and grinned.

"Not Jared Mayfield's daughter, are you?" His forehead creased as he thought about the question. "No, I don't think he had any kids."

"You knew my dad?" Her grin sagged, feeling a bit surprised to hear someone outside her family mention her father's name. Since her dad's death, her mother never discussed him and if it weren't for the picture on her dresser, she could have almost fooled herself into believing he never existed. She drew in a sharp breath, causing her lower lip to tremble.

"I didn't mean to upset you," Nigel said, lifting her chin with his finger. "I'm sorry." The sincerity in his eyes and sad smile on his face oddly enough comforted her.

"No, I'm fine. It's just… I was only six at the time. I barely remember him."

"Yeah, he was gone way too soon." Nigel seemed troubled, and again, his brow creased. "He was a bit older than me but he had a unique ability to read people. He saved my hide on more than one occasion. It was a tragic loss when he died."

"Yeah," she said and looked down at the card to hide her misting eyes.

"If it makes you feel any better, you look a lot like your dad." He nodded when she looked up. "He also liked walking in the woods."

"I don't really like the woods," Lori admitted. Looking over at the trees, a pain shot through her head and she squeezed her eyes shut. An image of Jesse walking into the clearing flashed in her mind. She opened her eyes. "I just needed to get away."

"I see. Well, I practically live in these woods so if you ever want company, I'm usually around here somewhere."

"Thanks, I'll keep that in mind."

Nigel smiled and shoved his wallet back into his pocket. "Well, Lori, as fascinating as it was to see you again, you really should be heading back."

"I know. Jesse's probably looking for me as we speak. But it was nice talking to you. It's not often I run into someone that knew my dad."

Nigel glanced across the clearing and then back at Lori. "Your dad was a good man. Anytime you care to discuss him, let me know. I could probably tell you a story or two."

Lori waited until he disappeared into the woods before heading for home. "Nigel Stone," she said as Jesse suddenly walked out of the woods, startling her.

"What are you doing here?"

"I could ask you the same question," Lori said, shaking off the déjà vu. She didn't intend to sound gruff but Jesse's tone suggested she were trespassing in an area that was off limits to anyone without fur. Brushing past her best friend, she rolled her eyes.

"I saw your footprints by the oak tree and got concerned. Okay?"

"Right, because you recognized my footprints. I get it. The wolf mojo thing," Lori sneered over her shoulder. It was another reminder that she would never be able to compete with the blonde flea-bag that was probably propositioning Hayden at that very moment.

"Lori, stop! What is wrong with you?"

"Nothing!"

"Nothing seems like a whole lot of something, considering you've never spent time in the woods alone. Stop lying and tell me what happened in Tennessee! And don't say nothing happened because Lucia told me you insisted on having Hayden bring you home." Jesse grabbed her by the arm, halting her retreat.

"I didn't insist no such thing! I was fully prepared to drive myself home. It just so happened the big baboon got back before I could leave," Lori griped as she shoved Nigel's business card into her pocket.

"Calling him a baboon sounds serious." Jesse grinned, and that was all it took to send Lori into a full-blown rant. "Slow down, and start at the beginning."

"One minute, he practically sticks his tongue down my throat, and the next, he's walking away with Miss Highfalutin'. Men are just a bunch of pansy-ass cowards.

Too afraid to be alone, yet when they're with someone, they're always sniffing around for something better." Not wanting to relive the embarrassing moment, she turned and headed down the trail. Waves of heat climbed up her neck and Jesse snickered behind her.

"Was he a good kisser?"

"Hell, yes, he was," she hissed, shooting a glare over her shoulder and Jesse struggled to keep a straight face. "But I'm not willing to become another notch on his bedpost just because he's an expert at tonsil-teasing."

"Lori! I don't think that's what Hayden was doing. Did you even give him a chance to explain? I find it hard to believe he would kiss you and then walk away like it was nothing," Jesse said, running up behind her.

"Oh, it was something, all right! He jumped away from me like someone lit his tail on fire and then he took off down the road with her. I lost! Why else would he leave me standing there like a fool? And to make matters worse, Katherine looked back and winked at me! How was I supposed to take that?" Lori sat down on a log and tears filled her eyes.

"It was a misunderstanding. I'm sure of it," Jesse said, wrapping her arms around Lori.

"I have nothing to offer a guy like Hayden, but I still believe in happy endings. Funny, isn't it? You and Megan both found your Romeos, I only read about mine."

"Does this have anything to do with Steve? I know you thought he abandoned you when he left for Oklahoma, but it wasn't like he hadn't been planning to go to college. You knew it would happen; maybe it was sooner than you thought, but still. He's following his dreams, and doing what makes him happy, so you should do the same."

"Yeah, I know, and that's why I'm going home," Lori said, wiping her nose on her glove. Steve had nothing to do with her foul mood, but she was too embarrassed to tell Jesse that. She hoped to find in Hayden what Jesse found in Tucker, but apparently, he was only using her to make Katherine jealous.

So why did she desperately want to talk to her best friend, and now she couldn't get away from her fast enough? It wasn't fair to Jesse if she got jealous of her relationship with Tucker, but dammit! She had experienced happiness for three days. Three solid days, Hayden made her feel worthy. Not only for being on that mountain, but also being with his family, who embraced her with open arms—and she was no more than a mere human. But who was she kidding? Everyone who meant anything to her eventually walked away in the end, and fate being her cruelest of friends, liked to kick her in the teeth just to see her cry.

Knowing Jesse still trailed her gave Lori some comfort since the woods were quickly growing darker, and the shivers that assaulted her body, she didn't think was because of the cold. By the time she reached the oak tree, a steady stream of tears was flowing down her face and she refused to look back. She waved Jesse off and continued around the house before running into a roadblock.

For a split second, the arms that kept her from landing on her ass felt somewhat familiar. She looked up and her heart shattered at the sight of Tucker, whose brow was wrinkled with worry. Pushing him away, she took off down the road to avoid his pity, as waves of nausea roiled her stomach. Tucker would probably tell Hayden she was crying over him, so she swore at herself. She didn't cry over guys! At least, not so often that anyone knew, but Tucker looked so much like Hayden. In that brief instant, through heavy tears, she thought Hayden had actually come back for her.

Choking on a sob, she raced up the stairs to her bedroom, glad her mother was not home to witness her meltdown. More than likely, her mother was spending the night at Dean's house, which meant Lori could sulk without any interruption. It took two months for her to get used to being alone in the house at night, and to her surprise, now she preferred it. Flinging her coat into the corner, she kicked off her shoes and threw herself across the bed as her phone vibrated in her bra.

Three

Jesse

Nothing ever went as planned, Jesse was starting to believe. After arriving home with Tucker, any plans of spending the rest of the holiday curled up with him in front of a roaring fire were dashed when she found Lori at Sallee's Rock. She understood why Lori was pissed at Hayden, but to take it out on her was ridiculous. There was something else bothering Lori. And although Lori acted as if it were nothing, Jesse would eventually get her to talk.

That night after Tucker fell asleep, Jesse pondered the conversation she'd had with Lori earlier that afternoon. Lori was usually optimistic and the one person that never seemed to take life too seriously. Always upbeat and happy, people couldn't help but be drawn to her, but now, she'd changed and that troubled Jesse the most. *Some best friend you are!* She kept kicking herself for not noticing the little telltale signs before now, like how Lori kept drooling over Hayden and not eating, which spoke volumes. Then she just snapped for no reason… Working her bottom lip between her teeth, Jesse glanced around the room.

The small bedroom was cozy, even more so since she was now sharing Tucker's bed. His massive arm tightened around her, his woodsy scent soothing to her soul. She glanced over at the alarm clock on the dresser. It was five in the morning, but no matter how hard she tried, sleep eluded her. Snuggled in his warm embrace, she lay there staring at the ceiling. Right after sunup, she quietly crawled out of bed. As she tiptoed around the room, she peeked over at the bed and found Tucker watching her.

"Sorry. I didn't mean to wake you. Are you hungry?" His eyes flared with her question as she moved around to his side of the bed and he grinned. Of course, he was hungry. He was always hungry.

With one swoop of his huge arm, he pulled her down and growled against her neck before rolling over and pinning her beneath his thigh. "Is that an offer? If so, I like my breakfast warm, soft, and sinfully delicious." Her body hummed as his hand drifted down her side, and she arched against him. His dirty bedroom talk and velvet-smooth, chocolaty voice melted her to a pulpy mush. He would be her undoing if she allowed him to continue down that path. Shrugging against the nip on her ear, every single nerve ending ignited and there was no turning back.

"Yes," she squealed. Her panting breath excited him and within seconds, everything turned to a deep royal blue when the large, plush blanket engulfed them, hiding them from the rest of the world.

"Welcome home!" Megan said when Jesse walked into the boutique later that morning. "I can't believe you got hitched! I want all the details. What was it like? What's his family like? What about the pack? Did you love the dress? I bet you looked beautiful."

"Hold up, Lizzy-bop! My brain doesn't function that fast without caffeine," Jesse said as Megan shoved a large Styrofoam cup into her hand. If nothing else, Megan could surely lift her spirits and probably her attitude in general.

"I know. I came prepared. Alpha Cooper called Jack last night so I expected you to show up here today," Megan said as she pulled Jesse over to the lounge area. "What's wrong? For someone that's newly bonded, you don't seem too happy. Why are you here? We're closed, you know, until after the New Year."

"It's not that. Tucker has been wonderful through everything, and I would love to spend the rest of the week just hiding out with him." *Pinned beneath the blanket!* She took a sip of the steaming coffee and blew out a breath, remembering their early morning make-out session.

"Well, at least you had a good start to the morning." Megan grinned as if she were reading Jesse's mind.

"It's definitely something to look forward to, that I'll give him," Jesse said, failing to hide her blush. Their early morning romp eased the tension in her body but did little to calm her sleep-deprived brain. Swatting at Megan who rolled over on the sofa, laughing, she giggled.

Once the laughter died down, she sighed, her frown now back in place. "I'm worried about Lori. Have you talked to her?" Jesse couldn't figure out why Lori wouldn't answer her calls, and it hurt her feelings. Was she that upset? Lori was usually an open book, but lately, she kept to herself. Jesse knew Lori and Hayden shared a bond—which Hayden confirmed when he called Tucker late last night—but Lori's reaction seemed to be fueled by something besides jealousy, although she didn't have a clue what it might be.

"About that." Megan's eyes went rounder and Jesse set her cup on the table, bracing for what she expected would be bad news. "I wasn't going to say anything because I figured I was reading more into it than what was really there, but I talked to her the day she came back from Tennessee. Did she tell you she stopped in here?"

"No! And that's the problem. She's mad at Tucker's brother, but for some reason, she's taking it out on me. Maybe she was embarrassed that I followed her to Sallee's Rock, but it was getting late and starting to snow." Jesse nodded when Megan's lips contorted into a frown. "Why would she go into the woods alone? That's not the smartest thing to do." She took another sip of coffee as Megan tapped her chin. It was a nervous gesture she picked up after Travis attacked her on Hunter's Ridge.

"Well," Megan fanned her hand out and continued, "Maybe she figures the worst thing she could encounter in the woods would be us, and she already knows the pack. She would feel safe, I think. I mean, she attended your bonding ceremony and except for your dad, how many other humans were there?"

"That's true, and..." Jesse waggled her brows, "from what we were told, a sassy, little brunette spent a lot of lap time with a hunky, big brother late at night on the front porch swing. I had no clue about it, being so new to the whole wolf bonding phenomenon, but apparently, it happened right before my eyes. She was most definitely comfortable with the family, and they felt the same with her."

"So Lori shares a bond with Tucker's brother?!" Megan gasped and Jesse nodded for confirmation. "There's no way..." Megan's voice trailed off as she stood and paced back and forth behind the sofa. "Lori came barreling in here the other day like the devil was on her tail, but she didn't say much; she just zipped in and zipped out. I thought it was odd that a girl who never wears perfume suddenly decided she had to have a bottle of Fortuity." That got Jesse's attention and she paused mid-drink. "I assumed she was picking it up for her mom, maybe as a late Christmas gift, until she walked out the door and drenched herself in a perfume bath right there on the sidewalk."

"She used Fortuity? That little sneak!" Jesse looked toward the front window as if she could see Lori standing there. "I can't believe she did that." Placing her cup back on the table, she leaned against the sofa pillows and massaged her forehead.

"Oh, wait! It gets better," Megan said, and Jesse looked back with a scowl on her face. "She took off toward the cafe, and I thought with it being the holidays, maybe Steve was in town and she was meeting him there. No big deal. It's Steve, right? Anyway, after I locked up and shut off all the lights, I came back inside to get my purse. That's when I noticed a dark-haired man looking through the front window. He didn't see me because of the plants sitting on the dividing wall." She motioned with her hand. "At first, I thought it was Tucker, you know, because he had dark hair and a burly build. But when he turned, he didn't have the bulk that Tucker does, and it kind of freaked me out. Now thinking about it, I'm going to assume it was his brother."

"That explains everything! Hayden gave Lori a ride home after she blew up at him and threatened to drive herself. And when Tucker talked to him last night, he said Lori gave him the slip. I thought he meant she left the store and went home. I didn't realize she deliberately masked her scent."

Megan chewed her lip and looked to the front of the store, her forehead creased with concern. "Could you help me for a minute?" She hurried over to the perfume display without waiting for Jesse to follow.

"What are you doing?" Jesse asked when Megan shook open a plastic bag.

"Recalling Fortuity. Do you know how dangerous this could be if it got into the wrong hands?"

"Until you, I never even knew it was possible."

"Yeah, me either. I guess because I've used it in just about everything, it comes natural. Shampoo, body lotion, body spray, Fortuity; heck, if I'm not mistaken, I think I ate lavender pudding once." Megan chuckled. "I only hope none of the ladies wearing Fortuity gets into trouble. We'd never be able to track them."

"I know, right? If only we were criminals. Imagine the things we could get away with right beneath Officer Riley's nose." Jesse laughed, although nothing about it was funny.

"What I imagine is eventually getting caught and having to deal with Daddy Cooper." Megan pulled a face. "Pack laws are similar to human laws except their punishment is twice as bad. I've seen Alpha Cooper pissed, and he's not anyone I want to cross. Which is why I'll tell Mom to change the formula. We could use artificial lavender without anyone being the wiser. Until then, I think we should keep this quiet, and definitely not breathe a word about it to Lori. She doesn't need to know we're onto her."

"True. I suspect this probably won't be a onetime event. When Hayden returns, she'll pull the same stunt. She needs to realize we're her friends first, and if she doesn't want anything to do with him, we can serve as the buffer between them." Jesse had no intentions of interfering with the bond, but if Lori didn't want to bond with Hayden, it was clearly her choice to make. Then she remembered how she felt when Tucker denied his bond. *It sucked.*

"Can't we at least give him time to sway her? You know, the bond is there for a reason, and without it, his wolf will never accept another mate. I would hate to see them make the same mistake Tucker did. You know how hard that was on both of you."

"Yeah, I guess we could give her a little nudge in his direction," Jesse said, "considering he's making a special trip back just to see her."

"So he's the cousin Jack said was coming to visit?"

"That would be him. He's hoping if he gives Lori time to calm down, maybe she will let him explain what happened in Tennessee. But I don't think she'll give him the time of day. He's already pissed her off and you know how she is. It'll take a miracle to get them together."

"And staying at the alpha's house in Kinsley can't help matters. I'll talk to Jack and see if we can get him a place over here in Cloverly."

"Or he could stay in my apartment! I was going to suggest we offer it to Lori, but for now, Hayden could use it. He can earn his keep by working here at the store. I'm sure we can find small handyman jobs to keep him busy. That will give Lori more time to get to know him without feeling obligated. What do you think?"

"It sounds good to me, but you'll have to move your stuff out first. We could do that today if you want. Plus, I can't wait to see Lori's face when she realizes he's here," Megan said, placing the bags of Fortuity in a large box.

"That's actually the part I dread most. Their reunion may not be all rainbows and butterflies. She is majorly ticked." Jesse looked up at the apartment door.

"Then... what would you suggest?"

"Honestly, there's not much we can do but stand back and count the bodies." She frowned and glanced over at Megan. "I hope it doesn't come to that, but after seeing Lori in the woods, I wouldn't rule it out."

Trudging up the stairs, Jesse started to laugh, which made Megan giggle. "You know what the funniest part is? Hayden and Tucker are a lot alike, but Hayden has a harder edge about him and smelling lavender everyday will probably annoy him."

"That'll be the least of his problems. Knowing Lori, she could barricade the door just to get back at him. I wouldn't put anything past her," Megan said as she followed Jesse into the apartment.

Four

Lori

Lori faked a smile as she pulled open the front door of the boutique. Swallowing hard as her stomach churned, she braced herself for the signature fragrance that would soon fill the air. The lavender scent didn't usually bother her, but after dousing herself in Fortuity a week ago, she couldn't seem to shake the odor. She glanced up at the overhead bell that announced her arrival. As soon as she found the time, that noisy gadget was coming down.

She walked through the door dressed in baggy jeans that were getting baggier by the day, and her thrift store army jacket, which covered a faded sweatshirt. She looked a mess and didn't quite fit the store's fashion image, but it was Cloverly, and nothing about the town was truly fashionable except for the boutique.

"It's about time you got here," Jesse greeted her, wearing black slacks and a navy, button-down sweater. She was all about fashion and eternally the picture of perfection. She tapped the toe of her boot against the tile floor. "Why didn't you return any of my calls? I've been worried sick about you." She narrowed her brows when Lori smirked.

"Well, don't put yourself out, sister." Lori's snarky reply didn't go unnoticed, based on the quick glance exchanged between Jesse and Megan. She walked into the warehouse while shedding her jacket, and hung it on a hook next to the door before returning to the store. "I need coffee," she said, adjusting her gray sweatshirt.

"Megan's got you covered," Jesse said but Lori ignored her.

"What's with the sunglasses?" Megan asked, offering her a cup. She was dressed in black jeans and a dark-blue, button-down shirt; apparently the two had coordinated their outfits.

"I have a migraine. I celebrated the New Year a little too hard and now it's come back to bite me in the ass." Lori took a sip of coffee before heading to the lingerie section.

"Yeah, that's another thing. We even stopped by your house to invite you to the New Year's party at Megan's."

"And let me guess… I wasn't home." Lori smiled bitterly. "Yes, I know. I found the note you tucked between the doors. But Steve stopped by and I went out with him to a friend's house. Sorry." She stooped down and busied herself with sorting through the leftover Christmas items to avoid Jesse's skeptical stare. She wouldn't give her the gratification of knowing she spent the holiday alone; no one needed to know about that. They also didn't need to know she was keeping company with Nigel because that wouldn't have gone over well at all.

"But I thought you told Megan you were out of town for the holiday." Jesse set her coffee on the counter and turned toward Lori.

"We were. Mom was with Dean, and I was in Berkley with Steve. That's out of town, the last time I checked." Lori tossed the lingerie back in the bin, intending to straighten it later.

Her head throbbed when she stood up and walked over to the lounge area. Why she didn't just call in sick until the headache-from-hell went away, she didn't know. Taking a seat on the sofa, she rolled her eyes when Jesse sat down catty-corner from her, but since they were hidden behind the dark glasses, Jesse didn't notice. Lori bit the inside of her jaw to keep from smirking at the annoyed look she saw on her friend's face.

"You were really with Steve?" Agitation flashed in Jesse's eyes, and Lori hid her grin behind her cup.

"Why not? I didn't have anything better to do, and we've been a couple for how many years?" Lori asked as if she didn't remember.

"But I thought... do you really think that's a good idea? Just the other day..." Jesse jumped when Lori shot up off the sofa.

"If you think for one minute that I'm going to sit home and pine over some flea-bag that doesn't give two shits about me, then you've wasted that minute. Hayden had his chance and he blew it." Lori's jaw clenched and she gripped her head. "And if I'm not mistaken, I don't recall anyone telling *you* what to do. I mean, who gets hitched to someone they've only known for how long… a month?" Moving the sunglasses down her nose, Lori glared and added, "Even your ceremony was barely a nine-hour notice, right? Is there something you'd like to share? Bun in the oven? Pup in the pouch?" Lori sneered and Jesse frowned. She knew that wasn't the case, but apparently, she hit a sore spot.

"Stop being ridiculous. It's not the same thing, and I'm not pregnant," Jesse retorted.

"Sure it's the same. You're an adult and you've claimed your independence. Well, it just so happens that I'm a month older than you, so I should have the same right without you or anyone else prying into my business," Lori snapped before finishing off her coffee in one large gulp.

"Lori, you know that's not what Jesse was doing. We've just been worried about you," Megan cut in as she moved over to stand beside Jesse.

"News flash: I don't need you or anyone else worrying about me. I may not be like you, but I'm perfectly capable of taking care of myself." Lori spun on her heels and walked to the front door.

"Lori, wait!" But Lori was out the door before Jesse could say another word.

The brisk morning breeze sent a shiver up her spine, and Lori wrapped her arms around her body to hold in the heat. Thankfully, the café was right next door. Except for a few goosebumps, there was no chance she would freeze to death. The cafe was a safe place that she previously used to avoid Hayden, and now she was using it to avoid her friends.

She pushed her glasses up on her nose as she walked through the door. The place was lively with customers, but most of them were already seated so she continued to the counter. Her mouth watered when Ester pulled out a large tray of biscuits from the oven and then waved. Not to seem rude, Lori waved back, turning as the waitress walked over to take her order.

"Hey, Lori. What can I get for ya this morning?" Mallory asked, readying her pen.

"A large breakfast to go." Lori handed her a ten dollar bill and leaned against the counter as she stifled a yawn. She was irritable from lack of sleep, which was probably why she had such a headache.

Ever since leaving Tennessee, she felt annoyed, angry, and lost, all of which she blamed on Hayden. *You miss him.* She covered her mouth to hold back the nausea that climbed up her throat. Deep down, she did miss him, which was the reason she lied and said she was in Berkley with Steve. Hayden was probably at home enjoying his time with Katherine, so she would pretend to do the same. She looked up at the calendar on the wall.

Her mother spent the past two weeks with Dean, only returning home for a change of clothes, so no one noticed Lori hiding out in her bedroom. Watching every sappy movie she could get her hands on—some of them twice—she practically wore out her DVD player. *You are so pathetic*, she snarled. It didn't really matter what she did in the privacy of her bedroom as long as a certain baboon believed she had already moved on.

"Here ya go," Mallory said, offering a wide smile with her change.

Lori dropped the money into her pocket and lifted the

food box off the counter—flashing a tight-lipped smile in return. As she walked to the door, she mumbled, "Frickin' bubbly waitress."

Once she was back at the boutique, she took her food and sat down on the bench next to the dividing wall that separated Lori's Lingerie from the lounge area. The sixteen-by-sixteen-foot room was small compared to the rest of the store, but how much space did a person need to sell underwear? Resting her head against the wall, she shoved a piece of bacon into her mouth. She was starving after eating nothing but noodles and beef jerky all week, and the bacon was delicious. She made a mental note to stock up on real food the next time she decided to hide herself from the world. Shoveling a fork full of eggs into her mouth, she groaned when her stomach reeled. And just like *that*, her appetite was gone.

Lori got up and tossed the food box into the trash as Megan cheerfully announced, "I think we need a girls' night."

"Sorry, but I work the night shift this week," Lori said. It wasn't a bald-faced lie, but not the truth either. During the winter months, they shortened the hours at the library and usually, if Lori were working at night, it was by her own choice.

"She didn't mean tonight, but if you're free, maybe the three of us could get together this weekend," Jesse suggested.

"Already got plans."

"What is so important that you can't spare one night for your best friends?" Megan asked as she walked over and leaned against the wall.

"I have a date, if it's any of your business, which it's

not." Lori gathered a stack of lingerie in her arms to avoid their questioning stares. Telling outright lies and knowing she wasn't good under pressure, Lori fully expected to get caught but decided she would deal with the fallout later. All that mattered now was that her friends stop looking at her like she was a wounded animal and just let her move on. That's what she fully intended to do, however hard it might be.

She walked into the warehouse, her attitude a bit brighter since her stomach was calmer. She removed her glasses and placed them inside her jacket pocket. "So how does Tucker like living in an apartment? It has to be a far cry from the cabin," Lori yelled through the door, her headache easing from her caffeine intake.

"He assumed we were going to live at the cabin, so I didn't suggest the apartment." Jesse laughed.

"I can't say I blame you. I wouldn't give up my cabin to climb those steps every day. That just wouldn't happen." Lori counted the seventeen steps that led to the upstairs apartment and then dumped the lingerie she was holding into a box marked *sale items*—she would retag them later. She walked back into the store and chewed her lip to keep from smiling. "I think we should do a girls' night, but at Megan's cabin. I hear it's a pretty nice place, and maybe Whitney and Tracy could join us. Surely the guys won't mind hanging out with Tucker for a night."

"I think that's a great idea," Megan said. "Wanna do it this weekend?"

"I already told you, I have plans, but maybe next weekend." That was all it took to ease their minds, and even Lori found it easier to breathe.

"Fine, next weekend it is," Megan said and went back

to her area at the front of the store.

The rest of the morning passed without any snide remarks or biting comments and Lori was glad. She hated acting like a snotty bitch to her friends, but she needed more time to think through her own problems without their interference. When the lunch hour came around, Jack and Tucker showed up, and Lori happily volunteered to watch the store while the four of them went out to lunch.

"We could lock the door and you could join us, you know," Jesse suggested, again with the wounded animal look.

"I couldn't eat another bite. I'm still stuffed from breakfast," Lori reminded her, and although hesitant, Jesse nodded.

"Fine, but if you change your mind, we'll be at the cafe."

Lori waved as they walked past the window, her fake smile back in place. Every time she saw Tucker, her heart raced with thoughts of Hayden. He and all the Wilson men looked alike, a constant reminder of what she tried to ignore. Picturing Hayden's arms wrapped around her as she sat in his lap made her belly flutter. What she wouldn't give to be back on that front porch one more time... Another reason she needed to avoid Tucker. He stirred up way too many memories of Hayden. And for some odd reason, her heart couldn't handle it. *Stop pining over him; he's a jerk!* She stomped into the warehouse, looking for something to keep her occupied. After they returned from lunch, she intended to avoid Tucker. Staring down at the box of lingerie that needed retagging, she opted to use that as an excuse to stay out of sight.

Thirty-five minutes later, the front door opened and happy laughter filled the store. Lori peeked around the door and her eyes instantly fell on Tucker. *It's not Hayden.* The biggest difference between the two was their personalities. On one side of the coin, Tucker was easygoing and soft-spoken. On the flip side, Hayden was firm and straightforward.

"Oh, you're back. Good, I need to make a quick run to the flower shop. I'll be back in a few minutes."

Without waiting for anyone to respond, Lori grabbed her jacket and headed out the side door. Squinting to avoid the glaring sun, she pulled her sunglasses out of her pocket to shade her eyes. *The flower shop? You don't even like flowers.* That was another lie she often told over the years. Unlike Jesse and Megan, she was a late bloomer and most of the guys considered her one of the boys. She was envious of girls with boyfriends that showered them with flowers, and the primary reason she hated them.

She rushed across the side street and walked into The Flower Pot where she was greeted by a warm smile. "Come in, dear," Brid said, and instantly, Lori's stress melted away. "Is there anything specific you're looking for?"

Lori shoved her hands into her pockets and inhaled the soothing, floral fragrance. "Honestly, I don't know why I came in. I just..." Her voice lagged as she scanned the flower arrangements that were beautifully displayed around the shop. "They're so pretty," she whispered.

"Yes, they are," Brid said, coming to stand next to her. "I find it very rewarding... tending to the flowers."

"I'm sure it is, and I'm sorry. I didn't mean to take up your time."

"Think nothing of it. It's been a slow day, actually." Brid patted her arm, a comforting gesture that made Lori blink back tears. How many times had Jesse's grandmother greeted her that way? "Stop by anytime you need a temporary escape." She smiled as she walked back to the counter and busied herself with counting the money in the till.

It was an odd statement, but at that moment, it was all Lori needed to hear. As Lori headed out the door, she gave the little shop one last glance.

"You are the voice he protects."

Lori turned back as Brid licked her thumb and continued counting the stacks of bills. *Now you're hearing things. Great!*

She slowly walked back to the boutique, her emotions weighing heavily on her mind. Why couldn't she be as content with her life as Brid seemed to be with the flowers? *Because this is not where you want to be.* She looked up as Jack and Tucker drove past. It would be a long five days but if she played her cards right, she could fly under the radar, and possibly survive the week.

Five

Hayden

The old brick building mocked Hayden as he waited outside for Tucker and Jesse to arrive. The memory of Lori ditching him still galled his wolf, and he found it somewhat disturbing. He knew there were ways for wolves to conceal their scent. That was one of the first things taught in alpha training, believe it or not, and something Lori shouldn't have known anything about. Humans covered their tracks, their fingerprints, and even colored their hair, but at no time did they use their noses to get from A to B.

With his elbows on the steering wheel, he rested his forehead on his fist and closed his eyes. It was a flurry-filled day with the temperatures hovering in the low thirties as the sun struggled to push through the clouds. He smiled at hearing the roar of pure muscle, but eventually, Tucker's car slowed down and turned off Main Street. Exceptional hearing was another feature that separated wolves from humans. He opened his eyes when they pulled over and parked behind his truck.

"Sorry it took so long," Tucker said as he walked around the car to open Jesse's door.

"I haven't been here that long myself." Closing the driver's door, Hayden walked over to meet them on the sidewalk. His arrival earlier in the day allowed him to actually check in with the regional alpha—his uncle—since he was in their territory. "Thanks for letting me stay in your apartment."

"You're welcome. It's fully furnished so you should have everything you need," Jesse said, handing him a key to the side door. "In case you want to leave after hours."

Hayden nodded. It had been weeks since he last saw Lori and knowing she worked at the store part-time, as well as at the library, he wondered how hard it would be to get her alone. And if he did, how would he explain the bond? It wasn't like she didn't know he was a wolf, but since she was human, he wasn't sure she would want to be with him. He walked through the warehouse and waited behind Tucker as Jesse peeked into the storeroom.

"Can we come in?"

"Coast is clear. She's been at the library for at least an hour," Megan said.

Jesse motioned, and Hayden followed Tucker into the

store. "Megan, this is Hayden, Tucker's brother."

"It's nice to meet you," Hayden said, his eyes alternating between Megan and Jesse. Even wearing blue jeans and sweaters, they both looked polished and appropriate, the image that the store intended to project, he assumed.

"Now I understand why Lori is in such a tizzy," Megan said as the front door swung open, startling her.

"Well, now, I see I'm late for the party, yet no one bothered to invite me. How rude," Tracy said, sashaying through the door. Her olive green poncho hung open, revealing a peach cashmere sweater that stopped two inches shy of the low-waisted jeans she wore.

"Hey, you, get over here! I want to introduce you to my brother." Tucker motioned with his hand.

Hayden sucked in a breath when Tucker pulled Tracy into a hug and kissed her on the cheek. With Jesse just an arm's length away, he expected her to latch onto the redhead the way she grabbed Katherine the night of their bonding ceremony.

"It's okay," Jesse laughed, apparently noticing his curious gaze. That wasn't something he expected from her, and a perfect example of how fickle females could be, in his opinion.

"This is Hayden, my older brother." Tucker looked between the two and grinned. "She's my best friend."

"Well, isn't this a nice surprise," Tracy said, flashing a brilliant smile that danced in her eyes. "You would not believe the things Tucker has told me about you over the years."

"You're probably right, considering when my brother talked about his best friend, he failed to mention you were a female." Hayden chuckled and winked at Tucker when Tracy elbowed him in the ribs. Little brother seemed to be a big hit with the females, and oddly enough, even Jesse didn't seem to mind.

"Shame on you!" Tracy scolded, teasing Tucker for his discrepancies. "So what are you doing in Cloverly?" She looked back to meet Hayden's smile.

"I was passing through and thought I'd stop in for a visit before heading home. An extended vacation," he lied.

"I'm sure Tucker is thrilled. I know how much he misses his family." Tracy turned towards Tucker who instantly leaned away. "And you said he wasn't good looking." She winked at Hayden as she walked over to the counter, which put a huge grin on his face, causing Jesse to roll her eyes.

"Come on and I'll show you around before you get yourself in trouble," she said, pulling Hayden in the opposite direction while Megan waited on Tracy.

"So what does Lori do here?" Hayden whispered as he glanced back, amazed that Tracy was actually a female, and a sexy-as-hell one at that. He chuckled when Tucker put his hand up in front of Tracy's face, causing her to laugh. There was no sexual tension between them, none at all, but if he'd had a best friend like her, there would definitely be benefits. *You would know.* He rolled his lip. That thought had his mind veering on the dirty side, a place he visited much too often.

The last time he was with a female friend was three days before he met Lori. Funny, but now, he couldn't even recall the details of their fleeting romp; and if you asked him how Lori's ass felt when he held her in his lap? Now that, he could remember like it was yesterday. Heat rose from his core and he blushed. The grip Lori had on him was not only painful at times but downright embarrassing. He stepped around the small dividing wall and a twinge of excitement rushed through his veins.

"Welcome to Lori's Lingerie." Jesse fanned her hands out. "This here is Lori's exclusive area and specialty."

Picturing Lori wrapped in the lace she sold only intensified the heat from within. *Naughty and nice.* A jolt of electricity shot below his belt, and he suppressed a growl. He walked to the back wall where silk slips and camisoles hung neatly in rows and wondered how Lori fit in with the boutique. Then he remembered her talking about taking a job at the library to help her mother pay the bills. She wasn't used to having money and nothing about the way she dressed suggested she'd ever spent a dime on herself. *That's gonna change.* Picking up a pair of black lace panties, he looked over at Tucker who was now standing beside Jesse. "These wouldn't last long at all."

"No, they don't make lace like they used to." Tucker laughed when Jesse swatted his arm. "I think we should head up to the apartment before you get me in trouble." Hayden grinned and followed Tucker into the warehouse as the overhead lights clicked on. "We should probably turn those off, at least, temporarily. So you may want to watch your step," Tucker said as he began walking up the stairs.

The heavy metal staircase was far from soundproof, even when Hayden tried to step lightly. A creak here and a pop there soon had him wondering if there was a weight limit. He pictured Tucker and himself climbing up together on the steps before crashing to the floor. He grinned when he imagined the spectacle it would be.

"Oh, and another thing," Tucker said as they walked into the apartment, "you may want to keep the lights off as much as possible, or at least the bedroom light." Leading Hayden into the bedroom, he cracked the blind and pointed toward a two-story brick building on the opposite side of the park. "That's the library; and just one block down and one block over is where Lori lives."

"Got it," Hayden said, hiding his smile. He knew how he would be spending his nights, and it wouldn't be watching television. "Are you sure Lori doesn't know I'm here?" He glanced around the small apartment as they walked back to the door.

"For now, I'm positive; but come Monday, you're busted." Tucker laughed as they descended the stairs, meeting Jesse and Megan in the warehouse. "I'm switching off the emergency lights. We don't want to tip Lori off that Hayden's here," he said.

"Well, aren't you the brilliant one?" Jesse flashed a goofy grin, which made him chuckle.

"Yeah, I believe I proved that just this morning." Tucker waggled his brows as he walked across the warehouse and shut off the lights.

"The honeymoon phase. Gotta love it," Megan said as she pulled open the side door.

Hayden preferred to stay right there in the apartment now that he knew where the library was. Through the large front windows, he expected he could easily see Lori moving around if he watched long enough. But since the pack was nice enough to let him stay there, he opted to humor them for one night.

Six

Hayden

Following Tucker down Cabin Run to where the pavement stopped, they turned right and drove along a gravel road until a large cabin came into view. Hayden parked beside Tucker and got out of the truck. "This I don't remember."

"Wait 'til you see the inside. It's nice," Tucker said as they walked up to the door.

Hayden glanced over at the other two cabins that were still in the finishing stage. He liked the seclusion the trees offered, as well as the view of the river. He cocked his head, listening to the lapping river water as the front door swung open.

"Aw, man, you are a sight for sore eyes! I was wondering when you would venture this way," Jack said, pulling Hayden into a big hug. "It's been way too long."

"Yeah, it's been awhile, but judging by the looks of things, you've done really well," Hayden said as Jack opened the door wider for them to enter the cabin.

"It's been a big job, and we're just getting things moved in, so ignore the mess." Jack motioned them through the cabin to where the others waited.

Despite walking into the strange room, Hayden was with Jack and Tucker, so he instantly felt at home. Spending the evening watching Friday night football with his family and friends, Hayden was finally able to relax. It was a nice change. A break from his younger siblings and the luxury of having an adult conversation without all the usual interruptions. Once the game was over, they all moved into the dining room where Whitney served chicken soup and his favorite salami sandwiches. Jack and Mason talked about old times, stirring up memories Hayden had forgotten over the years—and he couldn't help but grin.

"It wasn't often we put anything over on the alpha, but when we did? Oh, man, we strutted around like peacocks." Hayden laughed, forgetting his troubles for the time being.

"And when we got caught, we tucked tail and ran," Jack added before they were all rolling with laughter. Then, silence descended over the room and everyone seemed lost in their own memories.

Hayden glanced around the table, instantly wishing Lori were there. It sucked being a third wheel, but being a third wheel-times-three was ten times as bad. He coughed to clear his throat. "So what does Lori do when she's not working?" he asked out of curiosity without missing the look that passed between Jesse and Megan.

"We don't actually know. We were supposed to have a girls' night tonight, but every weekend something comes up with her and she can never make it," Jesse said.

"Is she still with Steve?" Judging by the astonished looks on their faces, they weren't expecting Hayden to know about him. Jesse wiped her mouth and Megan moved her chair closer to the table.

"What makes you think she would be with Steve?" Jesse finally asked.

"Nothing. It was just a question." Hayden looked over at Megan. Maybe there was more to Steve and Lori's relationship than Lori let on, based on the way everyone seemed to suddenly avoid eye contact.

"He was a friend she dated during high school. If he were still here, then yes, that would be the first place we would look, but he's attending college in another state," Megan said.

"So it wasn't a serious relationship?" Hayden stirred his soup; like the others, he waited for one of the two to answer. He looked over at Tucker who merely shrugged.

"They were close, but he has nothing to do with Lori. She just disappears," Jesse said.

"What do you mean disappears?" The memory of Lori ditching him was still fresh in his mind and saying he wasn't a little ticked would have been an outright lie. He knew she was avoiding him because she was angry, but there was no reason for her to ditch her friends too. Concern creased his forehead.

"Just what it sounds like. She's masking her scent the same way she did the day you brought her home. One thing about Lori, if she doesn't want to be found, you won't find her." Jesse wiped her mouth and sat back in her chair.

"That's not totally true," Jack spoke up. "I found Megan by using our bond."

"Yeah, but Lori isn't a wolf," Megan said.

"Maybe not, but Dr. Stevens said the bond was the same for a human."

"Really? Is that before or after the bond is sealed?" Mason asked and Jack shrugged.

"He didn't seem to think that would matter when I was looking for Megan."

Hayden didn't like where the conversation was going and he stared down at his food to avoid meeting anyone's eyes. Lori may not have been a wolf, but that didn't mean the bond they shared wasn't equally as strong. He would have sworn he could even pick up on her moods, which was why he returned to Cloverly so soon. Through the bond, Lori seemed upset, dejected, maybe annoyed, and he found it hard to believe it centered solely on Katherine.

He finished the rest of his meal in silence, listening to the surrounding conversations, but there was something nagging at the back of his mind, something that was gradually chipping away his hope.

He came there to offer Lori his bond, but not knowing where she was only agitated his wolf. He wondered if her persistent absence was her way of saying she didn't want anything to do with him. A low growl echoed around the room and he looked up. "You'll have to excuse my wolf," he said, and they nodded, understanding.

It was getting late, and all Hayden wanted to do was go back to the apartment and crawl into bed. He was exhausted from the six-hour drive and consumed with worry. He needed downtime to unwind and settle his thoughts. He also needed to sleep. Excusing himself, he said goodnight and headed out the door to his truck.

"Don't forget, we're meeting for breakfast," Tucker yelled from the porch, and Hayden nodded as he backed out of the drive.

Hayden was all about family, so when Tucker moved to Cloverly, it was hard for him to adjust. They were supposed to be the alpha and the beta. They were supposed to run the Smoky Pack. They were brothers by blood and best friends by choice, but fate had a way of disrupting even the best laid plans.

Parked beside the boutique, he glanced over at the side entrance when a familiar aroma teased his nose. Of course, he would pick up the one scent that never failed to set his heart racing. He rubbed his hand over his face as he got out of the truck and walked over to the door. It was eerie to be entering the warehouse in complete darkness, and he couldn't imagine a female choosing to live there alone. With all the overhead pipes and rattles of an old structure, even he found it hard not to shiver.

After climbing the metal stairs, Hayden unlocked the door and walked into the apartment. He kicked his shoes off next to the couch, and headed straight to the bathroom where he undressed, keeping the lights out. With a towel wrapped around his waist, he walked into the bedroom. He wasn't sure he could sleep in the apartment because Lori's scent seemed to be everywhere, and it wasn't Fortuity. Reaching over to open the blind, he stopped and stared across the darkened room. His wolf stirred as he scented the air. He wasn't alone.

Quietly, he walked around to the opposite side of the bed and his heart raced when he saw Lori curled up beneath the blanket. His first instinct was to wake her and pull her into his arms. He longed to beg her to give him a chance but decided against it. Just having her there was enough to ease his mind, and come morning, they could talk. Moving back to his side of the bed, he dropped the towel and slipped beneath the covers.

Seven

Hayden

Heavenly. That was the only way Hayden could describe the feeling that consumed him. With Lori safely at his side, he listened to the soft rhythm of her heart beating until he drifted off to sleep. *Sitting in his lap as his hand wandered over the round contours of her ass, his wolf purred.* His eyes snapped open. His wolf *did not* purr and he would argue that point with anyone!

He glanced down to where his hand was firmly planted on Lori's backside, and slowly, without waking her, peeled his fingers back. *What were you thinking?* He held his breath and she snuggled closer. With her head resting on his shoulder, her warm breath caused goosebumps to appear across his chest. She was flawless in his eyes: smooth skin, tousled hair, and a smattering of freckles across her nose. His pulse raced with her nearness even though he had no clue why she was there. Or why the thought of crawling into bed with her was a good idea. He was exhausted and not thinking straight, he told himself. Which was partially true, but not completely. He wanted to feel her body next to his; he *needed* her there with him. Plus, from what he could tell, she was wearing sweats, and he was careful not to slip beneath the same blanket she was under. He did give her that.

Tucking a silky strand of hair behind her ear, he held his breath when she stirred. Just to see her dreamy blue eyes, the thought of yanking the sun above the horizon to make her wake up crossed his mind briefly. Instead, he held her as she slept, keeping his hands in safe zones while wishing he could open his eyes to find her in his arms every morning.

An hour later, she stretched her body next to his, slipping her knee between his thighs and he sucked in a sharp breath. Covering her yawn, she snuggled back against him, and it took everything he had to keep from rolling her over and kissing her awake. He closed his eyes and told himself, *her touch wasn't intentional*, but that didn't stop the desire from… His eyes shot open when she suddenly jerked away.

"What the hell!" Lori yelled just before she fell backwards off the bed.

Hayden couldn't contain his laughter when he rolled over on the mattress and found her in a rather compromising position. He took hold of her ankles and arched an eyebrow, but when he saw the glare she aimed his way, he had no doubt she was pissed.

"Stay away from me, you big baboon!" She extracted herself from his grip by kicking him wildly, and then backed up against the wall, her eyes darting around the room.

"Wow. I haven't been called that since... elementary school."

"Do not insult my vocabulary or I will unleash the sailor." The warning glint in her eyes sent a surge of electricity to his core and he briefly blinked his eyes shut to will away the heat. Damn, she was fiery and he couldn't wait to douse her flames.

"I've met a lot of sailors in my day. So I hope you have a life vest; given the chance, I will rock your boat." His cocky half-grin had her rolling her eyes and when he raked his teeth over his bottom lip, she scowled.

"What are you doing here?"

"Since the first time I laid eyes on you, I've wanted you in my bed," Hayden said, unable to hide the desire that shimmered in his eyes.

"Are you always this forward?"

"What can I say? You bring out the best in me." He reached out to her with his open hand and she smacked it away. *What did you expect?* He had no clue when it came to Lori. Unlike most females, who begged for his attention, she insisted on throwing it back in his face.

"Too bad. I'm not interested in you or your bed." She grabbed her shoes from beside the nightstand before making a beeline for the door.

"Lori, wait! I was just teasing." Hayden jumped off the bed, following her with a huge grin on his face. She was faster than he expected for someone who just woke up. *And sexy as hell*, he thought as she pulled open the front door, aiming an irritated glare his way.

"You're naked!" she screeched before hurrying down

the stairs as that awareness hit him like a sledgehammer to the gut, halting his chase.

"Oh, shit!" he murmured, racing back into the bedroom, with an impish smirk on his face.

Trying to remember where he left his clothes the night before, by the time he was actually dressed, Lori was long gone. Rushing down the stairs, he didn't waste time looking through the store, not after seeing the side door standing open. *Great, just great.* He walked over and slammed the door, spitting curse words along the way.

"Really... that's the best you've got? I expected more from a big, bad mountain wolf than a string of dirty words. You give up way too easily." Startled by her gutsy voice, he turned to see where Lori was and found her perched atop a stack of pallets in the corner of the warehouse.

"You didn't leave." It wasn't a question but a statement that filled him with renewed hope. The early morning light that filtered in through the overhead windows exposed her hideout and she jumped down to the floor.

"I'd stick around any day to see a man running naked through a warehouse." Her teeth raked over her bottom lip. *She was teasing*, or was she trying to provoke him? With a sparkle in her eyes, she slowly stalked towards him, her half-smile suggestive as hell.

Unsure of what she was doing, and wondering if she changed her mind about him, he was willing to bet she wouldn't go back to his bed. Fire burned in his veins, setting his body aflame with a longing so deep, it trailed down to his toes—and his wolf stirred. He lifted his nose as her scent flowered around him. She wanted him, and craved him as much as he did her. His eyes traveled down her body and for once, he was glad his shirt wasn't tucked in. She was right there in front of him, so close to touch. And if he'd had his way, she would never look at another male, naked or not. He flashed a sly grin as she stepped around him to the door.

"Too bad you're not naked," she smirked, instantly dousing his fire.

Hayden yanked his shirt over his head and tossed it to the floor. "That's an easy fix." He didn't miss the longing gleaming in her eyes, which caused her to blush. Holding the door shut did enter his mind, but his little vixen was fighting the bond, and also playing hard to get. He groaned inwardly as he lifted his hands to surrender, his muscles flexing with the movement.

Lori stared, wanting to say something, but instead, she grabbed hold of the doorknob. As soon as she stepped out onto the sidewalk, the door closed behind her and he chuckled. She would find out soon enough; he loved to play games.

"I'm coming for you," he whispered as he raced back up the stairs.

After a cold shower and a change of clothes, Hayden stood on the sidewalk next to an older house—one-and-a-half-stories—that blended well with the rest of the neighborhood. Recognizing the area from his frequent childhood visits to Cloverly, his breath caught as he recalled the memory. *He and Tucker snuck out of the cabin with Jack and Mason late one night. Being the rowdy bunch they were, any chance that arose for them to run meant they were gone. The alpha didn't usually mind as long as they followed his rules and stayed clear of the neighborhood. They could only phase after dark, and only when they were deep inside the woods. Normally, that was exactly what they did, but on that night, their rebellious natures took over and they dared to make a mad dash through town, ending up in the neighborhood behind the cabins. It was early morning, and everyone was still sleeping. That was the story they told when Alpha Cooper caught them red-handed. Hayden, however, knew better and kept his mouth shut. Passing through Lori's backyard, the pack tackled each other to the ground in good, old-fashioned horseplay. Everyone but Hayden failed to notice a pair of blue eyes that were watching them from an upstairs window.* They were the prettiest blue eyes he'd ever seen in his sixteen years, and a night he would never forget. He'd often thought about those eyes, wondering what happened to the young girl they belonged to, and now he knew. Glancing toward the upstairs window, he wasn't aware that a vehicle pulled over to the side of the road, or maybe he just didn't care.

"Can I help you?" a husky voice called out from the curb. Hayden turned and stared at the blond male, his wolf bristling. "Do you know them?"

"If you're talking about Lori, then yes," Hayden replied and a low growl rattled his ribs. If he was Steve, Hayden would gladly defend what he considered his, whether Lori liked it or not. Unlike his brother, he would never let anyone interfere with his bonded mate, especially another male. "And you are?" Hayden braced himself for what he knew was to come.

"I'm Brian. I live right down the road, across from Jesse. But if you're a friend of Lori's, you probably already knew that."

Whoa! That was not at all what Hayden was expecting. Brian sounded every bit the arrogant ass Tucker often described, and Hayden instantly went on defense. "I know for a fact Jesse doesn't live on this street, so if you're the neighborhood watch, you suck at your job," he retorted loudly, causing Brian to frown.

"Well, you're partially right. Jesse has an apartment now, but she stays with her grandmother from time to time." Brian flashed a knowing grin.

"And you know this because you're friends with Jesse?" Hayden's jaw ticked as Lori's footsteps sounded on the sidewalk behind him. His hackles rose, and he wondered how friendly her relationship with Brian was.

"Of course we're friends. Sometimes we're a bit more than that." The smirk on Brian's face had Hayden moving forward with his fists clenched at his sides.

"I'm staying in the apartment above the store, and Jesse and my brother have bonded. I know what you say isn't true." Hayden's tone thundered a warning.

"Go beat your chest somewhere else, Brian. It's over," Lori said, joining both of them at the curb. Hayden stepped forward, shielding her from the nosy neighbor, but she wasn't having any of it. "Would you stop already?" She pushed around him and leaned against the Jeep. "Jesse and Tucker got married Christmas day. Did you not get an invitation?" She smiled, and for a split second, all Hayden could see was that beautiful, smartass mouth. He slowly blinked, his mind erasing all the dirty thoughts she initially triggered.

"What? He knock her up? That's the only way she'd marry—" Before Brian had a chance to finish his sentence,

Hayden's fist connected with Brian's jaw and Lori flinched.

"Do not talk about my brother as if he is beneath you," Hayden growled. Thankfully, Brian had quick reflexes and managed to avoid the full impact of the punch.

Lori shoved Hayden back and stepped between him and the Jeep. She didn't seem the least bit worried that she was standing in front of a very angry, very irritated wolf, which surprised him. Why she would put herself in that kind of danger, he didn't know, but it was an issue they would most definitely discuss once their bond was sealed.

"Are you coming with me? Or would you prefer to stay here and trade love taps with the locals?" Lori flipped her hair over her shoulder and walked away without looking back.

Hayden turned and glared at Brian. "This isn't over," he warned, before hurrying down the sidewalk after Lori.

"You're not in the mountains, wolf-boy. You need to control your temper before you hurt someone," she said over her shoulder.

"I'm no boy!" Hayden snapped, making Lori chuckle.

"Did I bruise the big, bad wolf's ego?" she teased and when he growled, she snickered.

"My ego is just fine. It's the boy-part we need to clear up."

Lori lifted her hand to dismiss him, but instead, she found herself staring at his chest.

"If proof is what you need, I'll gladly give it to you." Again, his thoughts veered to the raunchy side as he inhaled her dizzying scent. He didn't normally tolerate mouthy females, but with Lori, it was one hell of a turn-on. Touching her from his chest to his knees, his body hummed with the heat they shared. And whether she admitted it or not, she was definitely affected by his touch.

Lori's face flushed as she looked up through a fan of brown lashes—sparks of mischief glowing in her eyes. "Been there, done that, still not interested." She placed her hands on his chest. "Maybe you should retreat to the mountains, lover boy. I'm sure Katherine will greet you with open arms…" She lifted up on her toes, her lips just shy of touching his, and then pushed him away.

"Are you always such a hard ass?" Hayden ran his fingers through his hair as she continued down the sidewalk. At least she had finally changed out of those baggy-ass sweat pants and was wearing an attractive pair of jeans that defined her hips nicely.

"What can I say? You bring out the best in me." She smacked her rear and then flipped him off.

"Is that an invitation?" He grinned, but she ignored him.

Their walk continued in silence, but the images she conjured up in his mind, she was anything but silent. He kept pace one step behind, watching her hips sway and suspecting she did that simply to taunt him. He groaned when she added a little more sway to her walk as if she could read his mind. It was apparent she was still pissed about Katherine, but if she would give him two minutes without opening her sassy mouth, he would gladly explain. Crossing Main Street, he looked up at the apartment. It was just thirty degrees outside, yet the need for another cold shower consumed his thoughts.

Eight

Jesse

The boutique was not where Jesse and Tucker planned to meet Hayden for breakfast that morning, and the longer they stayed there, the more agitated Jesse became. Biting her tongue was her way of dealing with her best friend, when in reality, she was pleasantly pissed. She forged a smile as she looked around the store, her eyes stopping at Lori's Lingerie.

Since Lori started masking her scent, Jesse never saw her on the weekends; and how odd that Hayden suddenly returned and poof! Lori magically appeared. It was rather suspicious, but considering Hayden and Lori did share a bond, maybe he could tap into that. *Good for him,* although that didn't devalue the issue at hand.

She glanced back at Tucker and Jack, who were standing at the front window as if it were just another day. With a subtle roll of her eyes, she strolled across the store and stopped beside the dividing wall.

Lori was sorting through a new shipment of lingerie that arrived late Friday afternoon and humming a tune Jesse didn't recognize. Her stomach rumbled and she snarled. It was bad enough she missed breakfast to intervene in a situation that should have never taken place. But now to have that stupid tune stuck in her head? Oh, that was the last straw! "Since when do you work on weekends?" The sneering grin on Lori's face when she looked up, made Jesse scowl.

"Well, it wasn't my intention, but I am eager to see how the scolding plays out." She arched a brow before going back to work, but that just proved to Jesse that she was hiding something.

"Lori, do not instigate. You know how jealous their wolves are."

"I, unlike you, know nothing of the sort. I may be surrounded by a bunch of fur-hounds, but I'm certainly not one of them. So there."

Through gritted teeth, Jesse whispered, "Look, if you're trying to make Hayden jealous, stop it. It's way too dangerous. He's not used to being around so many humans."

"Sorry, sister, but it wasn't a streak of jealousy that caused him to punch Brian. We're not that close, even if I did wake up to a very naked, very much aroused Hayden this morning," Lori sneered, her eyes flashing a hint of anger.

Jesse glanced to the front of the store to see if Tucker or Jack could overhear their conversation. They couldn't. "What are you talking about?" she asked, turning back to

Lori.

"As if. You know damn well what I'm talking about. Hayden didn't just mysteriously appear in your apartment this morning. If I'd known we were expecting company, I would have dressed for the occasion. Now stop trying to play innocent when the look on your face says you're guilty as hell!" The hiss in Lori's voice warned Jesse to tread lightly because she too was pissed.

"You've been staying at the apartment?" Jesse asked, narrowing her eyes when she realized that was where Lori had been sneaking off to on the weekends. "Ever hear of karma? Get used to it because I see a lot more of it in your future."

The thought of slapping some sense into her best friend was appealing after the way she'd been acting, but before she could act on that thought, Hayden walked into the room. Wearing a pair of jeans and a long-sleeved t-shirt that matched his eyes, his hair was damp so Jesse assumed he'd just gotten out of the shower. She turned to confront him. "The man of the hour, care to explain?" She pressed her hands on her hips and tapped the toe of her shoe against the tile floor.

"Me?" Hayden asked as his eyes homed in on Tucker and Jack. "What would you like me to explain?"

"Brian called. He wasn't very thrilled that you got pissy and punched him," Jesse said, which made Hayden grin.

"First of all, I don't get pissy, I get mad. And second, if he has a problem with me, he needs to deal with me," Hayden said as Tucker walked over and joined them.

"He said you punched him. Did you?" Tucker asked.

"Hell yeah, I did. He's a jackass." Hayden looked

down, hearing Lori snicker.

"Hayden, you can't go around punching humans. We're stronger than they are," Jack said, walking over beside him. "And Brian, jackass or not, happens to be a respected member of the community."

"I can't imagine why," Hayden sneered. "The guy is a pig."

Jesse scowled at Tucker, who was trying very hard not to laugh. It was evident he didn't care for Brian, but he wasn't helping the situation. She jabbed him in the ribs and turned back to Hayden. "Look, I don't know what happened between you two, but I do know Brian wasn't flirting with Lori."

"Then you should also know that I'm not my brother, and if I honestly thought he was flirting with her, he wouldn't be breathing right now," Hayden said, and Lori chuckled while Jesse palmed her forehead.

"Then why did you hit him?" Jack asked.

"He hit him because he was talking smack about Tucker," Lori said. Jesse didn't expect her to be so defensive, but when she jumped to her feet, it was more than obvious she was ticked. "He deserved the punch. Too bad it was no more than a grazing." Lori flashed an angry glare towards Jesse as she stomped into the warehouse.

"Lori, get back in here!" Jesse ordered.

"Did you need something? Or are you just trying to piss me off?" Lori asked from the doorway. This time, it was Hayden who chuckled. Jesse pursed her lips, looking between the two. *The bond. Of course, Lori got defensive.* "It was a tap on his chin, okay? And he was lucky that Hayden hit him and not me."

"Calm down, Lori. We're not taking Brian's side. I'm

sure he deserved the punch, but he did call Jesse. And because Hayden is a wolf and I'm the alpha, we had to question him," Jack added before Lori walked back into the warehouse.

Throwing her hands up in dire frustration, Jesse looked back at Hayden, who shrugged. "So, what are we doing today?" she asked, turning to Tucker.

It was too early in the morning, and she was exasperated with trying to make sense of the situation, especially when Hayden and Lori kept feeding off each other's energy. *A very naked, very much aroused?* She blushed at the thought.

"I was hoping to round up some volunteers and maybe spend the day at the cabin. There are a few things I need your input on before we can finish." Jesse's face lit up and Tucker grinned.

"Lori, are you coming with us?" Jesse couldn't hide her excitement as she yelled into the warehouse and hurriedly slipped on her coat.

"I can't. I told Mom I wouldn't be gone long." Lori grabbed her coat off the wall hook beside the door and looked back at Jesse. "Maybe some other time."

Jesse started to object but Lori's mood instantly shifted and there was no mistaking the hurt in her eyes. She wanted to pull her into a hug and tell her things would get better, but she wasn't so sure now. She turned back to Hayden. "Give her more time and she'll come around, but you need to tell her about the bond as soon as possible." Hayden looked back at the door but Jesse placed her hand on his arm. "Not today. Wait and see how she responds tomorrow. She can feel the connection to you; she's just confused over why. I know. I felt the same way about Tucker." Jesse felt bad for Hayden. Normally, a guy wouldn't have to work so hard to capture Lori's attention. A flexed muscle, a sexy smile, even a misplaced wink in her direction was more than enough to have her drooling non-stop. *So why not him?* Jesse sighed but followed Tucker and Hayden out the front door.

The drive to Berkley took all of fifteen minutes, and from where Jesse stood in the front yard, the two-story cabin overlooking the river was surreal. With her head resting against Tucker's chest, she whispered, "I can't believe this cabin actually exists!"

"It doesn't. It was just a dream," Tucker teased, and she smiled up at him.

"I'd like to think it was destiny showing us what could be."

"I hope you're right, because I have a very fond memory of a certain dark-haired beauty tempting me with wet kisses. Maybe later, after the others leave, we can role play where we left off."

Her body buzzed as his breath grazed her ear, and she leaned into the soft kisses trailing down her neck. She loved it when he made her all giggly, but dared not spur him on. Drawing in a deep breath, she began willing the effects of his touch away. "Sorry, Romeo, but your kisses will have to wait. We have too much work to do," she reminded him, and he groaned.

"Do you really think they would miss us?" His voice vibrated against her ear, sending a shiver to her toes.

"Positive," she said breathlessly.

"Hey, what are you two doing out there?" Tracy called from the front porch and Jesse snickered.

"Nothing; go away!" Tucker pulled Jesse into the shadows of the tree line.

"No sense playing hide and seek, I have excellent eyesight." Tracy laughed when Tucker grumbled and he and Jesse turned and walked her way. "And if this is what you get for being an alpha, I may have to slide my name into the mix. It's amazing."

Upon entering the cabin, Jesse instantly fell in love with the massive stone fireplace, and hardwood floors. It was bright and airy from the large windows that faced the river. Picturing herself snuggled against Tucker in front of the fireplace as fresh snow fell on the ground. Or in the summer with the babbling river relaxing them into a deep sleep… It sounded wonderful. She wrapped her arm around Tucker, her left hand sliding into his back pocket. "It's beautiful. I love it."

"So you don't mind leaving your dad and grandmother in Cloverly?"

"It's just a fifteen-minute drive at most. I think I can handle it." She laughed when he poked her ribs. "I would live in a cave if that's what it took to be with you."

"That's nice to know, but totally unnecessary." Tucker rested his chin on top of her head and pointed, showing her where the two rivers came together.

"I hope someday to have a place just like this," Tracy said, interrupting them with a hug.

"There's no doubt in my mind. You've got biker-boy wrapped tightly." Tucker jumped away to avoid Tracy's swat. "In a good way." He winked and strutted to the back of the cabin where the other males were gathered.

"Have you decided when you're having your ceremony?" Jesse asked. "You know, I've already started designing your gown. It's my way of thanking you and Randy for the wolf portrait."

"I would like to have it as soon as possible, but we've been putting it off because we didn't want to bring any unwanted attention to his family. After Travis and Viv... and they had friends, all of whom I expect are gunning for me. Not to mention the whole issue of bringing Randy's parents up to speed. He doesn't want to keep secrets from them, especially since he's already started picking out baby names. He wants a large family." Tracy rolled her eyes. "Can you imagine a little Randy running around here growling?" Jesse smiled, imagining a little Tucker doing just that. "You don't think they will shun me when they find out what I am, do you?"

"Not on your life. Being a wolf doesn't make you a bad person, just different. Randy's parents can see the way he adores you. We all can. I don't think you have anything to worry about," Jesse said and motioned Tracy out to the front porch. "Can I ask a favor of you? It's kind of a secret so...."

"Oh, I love a good secret. What do you need?" Tracy followed her across the yard and stopped at the water's edge.

Jesse glanced back at the cabin before she whispered, "I need help to make Lori jealous."

"Make Lori jealous of me?" Tracy's brows furrowed and she frowned.

"No, no, no!" Jesse laughed. "I wish it were that simple. I need some girls to flirt with Hayden, right in front of Lori." She put her finger to her lips. "I'm not supposed to say anything but Hayden's going to need all the help he can get. They share a bond, but Lori won't give him the time of day."

"Go on..." Tracy grinned, and when Jesse saw the sparkle in her eyes, she knew Tracy was in.

"I know Lori better than anyone, and she's crazy about Hayden, but her confidence is in a bad place right now. I need her to get pissed, angry even, to snap her out of her own head. She doesn't think she's good enough for him, especially after meeting Katherine." Jesse fluttered her lashes, irritated that Lori could actually fall for Katherine's mind games.

"Who is Katherine?"

"She's this wannabe rich chick from the mountains, who fully expects to bond with Hayden. She's a nasty, vindictive, little number."

Tracy lowered her eyes, the toe of her shoe working a mud hole at the river's edge. "Unfortunately, I know all about those females."

"Honey, you have nothing on this girl. She's vicious. She actually confronted me and Tucker after our bonding ceremony. Demanding to know why he chose me over her."

"She didn't! I would never do that."

"No one in their right mind would do that. She truly believes she's better than everyone around her, and somehow, she managed to convince Lori of that."

"Say no more," Tracy said. "Without a bond, and being next in line to rule the Tennessee Pack, Hayden's practically royalty; and females can smell royalty from a mile away. Where do you want this to happen?"

"It has to be at the store. Anywhere else and Lori won't stick around." It was funny that she turned to Tracy for help, considering how they used to despise each other.

Now they laughed about Jack being the primary reason for their dispute when in reality, Megan held his bond.

"Well, then? Let's get the ball rolling." Tracy rubbed her hands together and flashed a cunning grin. "Maybe I could stop by and let you take the measurements for my gown. I really liked the one you designed for Megan. Is Monday morning okay with you?"

"That sounds perfect. I'll see you then." Jesse fist-bumped Tracy as they headed back to the cabin.

Lori

Monday morning came too soon, and dragging herself out of bed took every ounce of energy Lori could muster after her mother returned to the house. And haunting thoughts of Hayden sleeping bare-ass naked just a few blocks away kept her mind reeling in the gutter for most of the night.

Since waking up in bed beside him, accidentally of course, his raw image had been permanently seared into her brain. He was the manliest guy she'd ever met, and considering Brian lived right down the street, that was saying something. Even Tucker, whose build was slightly larger, couldn't compare with the sheer maleness that seeped from every pore of Hayden's beautifully sculpted body. Seeing him naked, Lori certainly knew what he had to offer, but he was virtually royalty and she was no more than a peasant that plowed his fields. *I'd plow his field, all right!*

He was direct and knew what he wanted, which confused her. How did she manage to attract the attention of such a strong man? A man that given the chance, she knew could make her world sizzle. She shook off a shiver and pushed her sunglasses to the top of her head.

"Morning, sunshine," Jesse greeted when Lori walked into the store. "What has you so bright-eyed and bushy-tailed?"

Lori fluttered her lashes as she pulled off her coat. "I swear, my mother is worse than a hormonal teenager that can't keep her legs together. Talking and laughing until all hours of the night. She's completely lost her mind. I have to crank up the stereo just to drown out the cackling, if I intend to get any sleep. The neighbors probably think all we do is party but I guess it's better than thinking we're having an orgy every night."

"I'd like to think you weren't participating in an orgy," Hayden said, his booted footsteps following her into the warehouse. "And I'd also like to think Steve wasn't your boyfriend."

"Well, now, he is a boy, and yes, come to think of it, he is my friend. Let me guess, you've been talking to Jesse," Lori replied, hanging her coat on the hook next to the door.

"Actually, I was speaking to both Jesse and Megan. They said you and Steve dated all through high school. Sounds pretty serious." Hayden arched an eyebrow when she chuckled.

"Serious? As in, did we have sex?"

"I didn't ask that, but since you brought it up." Hayden crossed his arms over his chest, his muscles stretching the seams of his long-sleeved Henley. He leaned back against the wall, patiently waiting.

"Well, since you think you need to pry into my business." Lori cocked her hip and smirked. "I may talk the talk, but I've never walked the walk." He grinned, and she pursed her lips. "Don't pull that pretty boy smile on me. I'm not walking with you either."

"Oh, but you will, and when you do, you'll know I'm no boy."

She swallowed hard when she saw the gleam in his eyes and said, "Any trouble buying hats with an ego as big as yours!?" Pulling the sunglasses off her head, she swiftly shoved them into her coat pocket, trying to banish his naked image from her mind.

"Facts speak for themselves." His intense gaze caused her heart to pound madly in her chest, and had they been anywhere else, Lori might have shown more interest. But Katherine's words reminded her why she never would. *You are not good enough for a Wilson male.*

Hayden stole her heart the very first night on the mountain. He was kind, considerate and treated her the way she felt an actual boyfriend would. And the two of them sharing the porch swing was by far her best memory. *His large arms held her tight, keeping her warm.* Never had a guy showered her with so much affection. Even Steve couldn't hold a candle to him.

Her heart dropped to her stomach when Hayden pushed off the wall and walked back into the store with a satisfied smirk on his face. Deciding she wouldn't let him have the last word, she trailed after him only to be intercepted by Jesse.

"We have a sale running this week, so expect to be

very busy. And Valentine's Day will be here in less than a month. I hope you ordered the red lingerie?"

"I hate Valentine's Day," Lori mumbled as Hayden followed Jesse to the back of the store.

"What did you need me to do?" Hayden asked, looking back to wink at Lori. Her blue eyes narrowed and her face flamed red.

Straightening the silk slips that hung near the back wall next to the mirror, Lori expected it to be a long day based on her attitude alone. Hearing the overhead bell chime, Lori glanced up when Tracy walked through the door, followed by a dark-haired girl. Lori waved and started marking down the items she knew would sell first. New inventory was something she always looked forward to, but in order to get the new stuff, she had to sell the old stuff first.

"Just the person I wanted to see! I was telling Jasmine why this has become my favorite place to shop," Tracy said, and Lori grinned.

Tracy was probably her best customer, and if the boutique ever put out a catalog, she would expect to see Tracy on the cover. Tall and slender, she looked like a supermodel, and her friend was equally gorgeous. "Well, you know the ropes, and if you need any help, just holler. It was nice meeting you, Jasmine," Lori said before she excused herself. She knew she had to keep busy with Hayden in the building. If not, she feared making a total fool of herself by peeking around counters to catch a glimpse of his muscles flexing whenever he moved. "Megan, do you need my help with anything?"

"I sure do. Could you go inside the warehouse and bring out the box of lavender shampoo that came in

Friday? Just put it on the shelf. I would greatly appreciate that."

Lori nodded and headed into the warehouse, which made her instantly happier. From there, she couldn't see Hayden. But overhearing Jasmine talking to Tracy, she paused just inside the door.

"... I'd have gotten here sooner if I'd known the eye candy was so delicious! Why didn't you tell me Tucker had a brother?"

The dark-haired mophead needed to mind her business! Lori gritted her teeth and leaned closer to the door.

"I can introduce you, if you like. You know, he's next in line to be alpha of the Smoky Mountain Pack," Tracy bragged and Lori scowled. "Hayden, I have someone I want you to meet." *Traitor!*

Lori slipped back into the store and ducked behind the dividing wall. It was childish, sure, but what-the-hell-ever?! She peeked between the shelves as Tracy made the introductions but Hayden just nodded politely. He didn't seem the least bit attracted to the girl, not like what Lori expected. But that didn't stop Mops from touching his arm for absolutely no reason. Lori smirked when Hayden casually dismissed them before he continued rewiring the light switch.

That's my man. Choking on that thought, Lori rushed back into the warehouse to cough. *Just do your job and ignore them.* That's exactly what she planned to do just as soon as she caught her breath. She straightened her shoulders and found the box of shampoo before heading back into the store. Helping Megan was a great distraction; and fifteen minutes later, she forgot about

Hayden, almost. The doorbell chimed again.

"Beth!" Tracy said, stopping in her tracks. "What are you doing here?"

Lori glanced at the newest customer and saw that Tracy clearly wasn't a fan. Hidden beneath her knee-length, red coat was a short, black skirt and a tight sweater that hugged her flawless figure. Lori bristled and looked at Jasmine, who had still not taken her eyes off Hayden.

"Same thing as you, I assume," Beth replied, placing her coat over the arm of the sofa. Beth browsed the store, talking to Megan about her body lotions before moving around to Lori's Lingerie. "Oh, I simply adore these," she said, picking up a pair of dark purple lace panties. She found a matching bra and turned to look in the mirror.

"Those are on sale today," Lori said.

"I'll take them, but first, I need a male opinion." Beth turned and sashayed back to the dressing area. "Hello there."

Hayden was startled and then surprised by the tall blonde who was standing behind him. "Can I help you?" he asked, looking confused and preparing to bolt for the door.

"I'm sure you can." Beth licked her lips as she held up the hanger with the purple lace undergarments. "Do you think these complement the color of my eyes?"

If that weren't a desperate attempt for attention, nothing was. Beth, who was all smiles, glimpsed Jasmine and then smirked. Seems Moptop didn't like all the attention Beth was giving to Hayden and Lori couldn't wait to see them take each other out. It could turn out very entertaining as long as she restrained herself from clawing both of their eyes out for visually undressing him. At the rate they were going, she'd have to stand guard just to let Hayden finish his job. Distracted by her thoughts, Lori didn't catch Hayden's reply. Obviously, he had blown so much hot air up the blonde's big butt, she was virtually floating.

Beth glided over to where Tracy and Jesse were deep in conversation and said, "Is it okay if I wait here?" Her hungry stare was fastened on Hayden's backside, causing Lori to bristle.

Determined to escape before her head exploded, Lori stormed into the warehouse as fire pumped through her veins. Pacing back and forth, she glanced over at the darkest corner, a secret cubby and the perfect hiding spot. When she was sure no one would see her, she ran over and jumped up on the stack of pallets and backed up against the block wall. *He made his choice, and it wasn't you.* Hearing the doorbell chime, she pulled her knees to her chest—listening harder.

How could one guy totally ruin her life with just one kiss? She rested her head on her knees. She should have never gone to the mountains that night. She would have never met Hayden, and could have been satisfied living her life in Cloverly. As it was, ever since meeting him, he invaded her thoughts morning, noon, and night. Her simple life in Cloverly didn't seem so appealing anymore. But she couldn't blame it all on him. Everything around her was changing: relationships were being built, and both of her best friends were hitched and happy. She was the odd man out. It totally sucked that even Steve had already moved on.

"Mind if I join you?" Propping his arm next to her on

the pallet, Hayden rested his head on his hand and Lori looked up.

"What?! And miss all the drooling?" She arched an eyebrow before returning to her original position, resting her head on her knees.

"Oh, yeah, the she-wolves. They're such a pain in the ass," he said rubbing his hand over his face. Lori looked up again. "It's just the title that attracts them."

"What do you mean?"

Hayden shifted his feet and rested his head on his arm. He looked exhausted, his eyes were heavy, but that didn't stop the gentle smile that tugged at her heart. "Becoming an alpha female is virtually royalty to them. It's all about the power to control." He lifted his hand to stifle a yawn.

"Is that what an alpha female does?" She smiled when he closed his eyes. The sudden urge to push the hair off his face had her locking her fingers tightly in front of her knees. *If only.*

"No, that's not what a *true* alpha female does. They share the authority and control of the pack as much as the alpha, but only when necessary. Mostly, they support the alpha and oversee the daily matters of pack life. Nothing too major or complicated; more like keeping the peace between squabbling children."

Lori leaned her back against the wall, her breath shaky. She was on the verge of tears. Her heart longed to be with him, to touch him, but she was only kidding herself. How could she compete with an alpha female? "I'm afraid the pallets will fall over if you climb up here." Her delayed answer to his original question was unexpected, and he opened his eyes.

"You're probably right. I'm not sure it's safe for you to be up there either."

"As if that matters to you!"

"I'm here, aren't I?" He stood up and moved closer to where she sat.

"Why? When there are so many girls like Jasmine and Beth who would kiss your feet to get a speck of attention from you? Not to mention Katherine! I'm not like any of them. I don't have that wolfy sex appeal." She chuckled silently. "There's nothing extraordinary about me."

"If only you knew." He glanced down as she rolled her bottom lip. "You fascinate my wolf." A low growl reinforced his statement, and he looked up and winked.

"As much as I enjoy your wolfish charm, I'm mainly concerned with the man."

The rumble grew louder and he closed his eyes, inhaling through his nose. When he reopened his eyes, a golden flare sparked in the dim light, causing her heart to thump in her ears. "This is what you do to the man." He placed her hand on his chest, and she felt the pounding of his heart, keeping rhythm with hers.

A lone tear rolled down her cheek.

"Lori!" Megan's voice shattered the moment and Lori wiped the tear away.

"It's just me, Megan." Hayden kissed Lori's hand as he flipped a switch behind her head before stepping out of the corner.

"If you see Lori, would you please tell her she has a customer waiting?"

"Will do." Stepping back into the shadows, he closed the breaker box a little harder than necessary, solely for her benefit. Once Megan exited the warehouse, he lifted

Lori off the pallets and pulled her into his arms.

“Thank you,” she said, her voice muffled against his shirt. She glanced up through damp lashes, hoping he would kiss her, while praying he would walk away. She inhaled his intoxicating scent. Mountain air, smoke, crisp cold nights. Her body trembled and her breathing grew shallow.

“Don’t thank me. It’s my job to protect you.” His words confused her as he lifted her chin and drew her into a kiss. His lips were soft, but demanding, drinking her in, the same way he did on the mountain. Then a picture of Katherine flashed in her mind and she pulled out of his arms, struggling to catch her breath.

“I’d better go.”

Ten

Lori

"Front counter, ladies," Lori said, motioning with her head. After assisting another one of her favorite customers, who thankfully was not there to drool over Hayden, she was ready for a group pow-wow. It was still early, and there was no way she would get through the day without snapping if she constantly had to defend Hayden. He admitted not liking the attention, and after he actually covered for her, she thought it was the least she could do. "Look, I really appreciate everything you do for me, but back the hell off."

"What are you talking about?" Megan asked, shooting a confused glance at Jesse.

"Yeah, Jesse, what am I talking about?"

"I have no clue. Here, take another shot of caffeine." Jesse tried to shove her coffee into Lori's hand, but she pushed it away.

"I don't need more caffeine. What I need is to open a can of whoop-ass. And the next girl that comes through that door lusting over Hayden will be what opens that can. Now call off the slut brigade, or hell's gonna break loose in Cloverly, and it ain't gonna be pretty."

"Like I said, I have no idea what you're talking about." Jesse's eyelashes fluttered and Lori practically laughed in her face. Jesse sucked at lying, much more so than she did, so it was nice to watch her squirm.

"You're not making me jealous, if that's what you think, but you are thoroughly pissing me off by sticking your nose where it doesn't belong. Now call off the brigade or else."

"Fine, have it your way! I was just trying to help," Jesse huffed.

"That's what I'm trying to tell you. I don't need your help, but your support would be fantastic. Hayden's a good guy, but I'm not what he needs." Lori leaned in and whispered. "I'm just a novelty and once the thrill is gone, he'll go back to what he knows, which is waiting for him on the mountain. I can't put myself out there like that! Everyone always leaves, and he's no different."

"He's here now. Give him a chance," Jesse whined. "You might be surprised what he's looking for."

"I don't want to discuss this right now, so back off and let me breathe. Okay?" Lori rubbed her forehead as she turned and stared out the front window.

"I'm not..." Jesse paused and Lori waited for her to get defensive again, but instead, she said, "I'm sorry. I promise not to stick my nose in your business if you promise you won't go MIA again."

"Fine, whatever." Lori walked out the door, clearly done with the discussion. Inhaling a refreshing breath, she turned to the window. "This is what I'm talking about." She smiled when Jesse grinned. The brisk cold sent a shiver down her spine and she zipped up her coat. She had no idea what she was doing or where she was going, but she needed a little privacy to think through the ruffled mess in her head. And fresh air to clear her mind.

As she crossed the side street, she paused for a moment in front of the flower shop. Looking through the window, Brid waved. *You are the voice he protects.* She frowned, remembering those words. She'd been doing a lot of that lately, hearing other people's voices in her head, saying words that were more rhyme than reason. *More like confusion and chaos.* Even her dreams were all over the place and starting to affect her attitude.

Crossing Main Street, she circled back through the park as unseen eyes followed her. Was it Hayden from the upstairs window? She wouldn't look. Or Jesse and Megan from the store? She didn't care. Instead, she just laughed and sat down in the first swing she came to.

Holding tight to the chains, she pushed back with her legs, and then lifted her feet, setting the swing into motion. The higher she swung, the wider her grin grew as her body relaxed with the movement. Her heart felt lighter, and she attributed that to her previous conversation with Hayden. She closed her eyes as she soared through the air, her mind taking her to a favorite place her heart instantly recognized. The mountains, so peaceful and serene and packed with snow, were beautiful. She breathed in the crisp mountain air.

When she stopped pumping her legs, and the swing

slowed, she opened her eyes and looked to the left. Her feet dropped to the ground, practically jolting her from the seat. She could imagine how silly she looked, but a guy as big as Hayden? She glanced up to see if the chains could hold his massive body. "Are you crazy?" she yelled, and he flashed a grin as he swung past.

"I forgot what it felt like to be a kid," Hayden said, slowing down.

Lori tightened her grip, if only to keep from jumping out of the swing and crawling into his lap. She'd never seen Hayden let his guard down and just have fun. On the mountain, when he entertained his siblings, he was always on the alert, or watching out for trouble. But this was a relaxed Hayden and a bright smile beamed across his face… *Shoot me now.*

"Race you to the slide." Hayden was out of the swing and gone before Lori could untwist the chains.

"No fair," she yelled, jumping out of the swing. She raced to catch him as he sprinted up the metal steps in three bounds. "Ever heard of ladies first?" She looked up as a sliver of sunlight broke between the clouds, casting a bronze halo around his head. He was dangerously sexy, wickedly appealing, and definitely no angel.

"By all means." He jumped over the rail, landing beside her on the ground. Wrapping his arm around her waist, he carried her to the top of the ladder as she beat on his shoulder and squealed.

The tornado slide had always been her favorite at the park. Going down the slide with a friend usually meant twice the fun. But sitting in Hayden's lap was way more fun than she remembered. After their seventh trip down the winding canal, Hayden pulled Lori against his chest and laid back on the slide, both of them giggling like kids.

Staring at the grayish clouds overhead, "That was amazing," Lori said, her nose red from the cold.

"Are you sure you're not part wolf? Because your tolerance for the cold is pretty unbelievable."

"This is my favorite time of year. I love winter." She stretched her arms out as light flurries drifted in the air, sticking out her tongue to catch a flake or two. It was the most fun she'd ever had, giving a whole new meaning to hanging out at the park. She snorted when he groaned.

"What's so funny?" he asked as she rolled over and looked up, her body dropping down between his thighs. She squeezed her eyes shut as her face glowed with a blush. Peeking up at him, his wolfish grin suggested he liked her new position.

"Are you trying to get us kicked out of the park for indecency?" She smacked his leg, and pushed up on her knees, but that position wasn't much better so she fell back on her rear. "At least, close your legs. I feel like a pervert just looking at you." Her body heated substantially with her confession, but even then, she couldn't pry her eyes away. She quickly unfastened her jacket to cool down as Hayden sat up and rested his elbows on his knees, his grin nearly as wide as his legs.

"I like it when you look at me." His eyes flared, and holy cow cakes! The sizzling heat that burned through her body was back with a vengeance. She drew in a shivery breath.

"We really need to go before we draw an audience," she said, holding out her hand.

"Too late for that. Your friends have been plastered to the window ever since I got here." He stood up and pulled her to her feet, dusting off her pants.

"Stop it. Now, you're being a pervert." She slapped his hands when he slapped her backside.

"It's only fair." His laughter joined hers as they walked across the park, but Lori didn't miss her meddlesome friends as they scurried away from the window. And she could have been mistaken but based on the quick arm swipe over the glass, she wasn't the only one feeling the heat. "She-wolf alert," Hayden whispered when the door of the boutique opened.

The huge lipstick frown was the first sign that Beth didn't like what she saw; the second, she wasn't carrying out a bag. "Guess I just lost a customer."

"That's okay. Purple was definitely not her best color." Hayden wrinkled his nose and Lori grinned as he took hold of her arm before they crossed Main Street together.

"Well, I guess I'll see you tomorrow," Lori said. Stopping in front of the boutique, she rubbed the toe of her shoe over the light dusting of snow that coated the concrete.

"You're leaving?"

She looked up and instantly wanted to kiss his frown away. "Yeah. I don't want to witness the drool fest Jesse planned for today."

"So, my dear sis-in-law was behind that." Hayden glanced into the boutique before turning back to Lori. "Well, maybe we could foil her plans. I have coffee and homemade chili upstairs if you're hungry." He flashed a naughty grin. "Or else we could play checkers?"

"Checkers?" The unbelieving smirk told Hayden she wasn't buying his story, and that made his grin wider.

"Yeah, you could king me."

"Umm, I'm not really into checkers," Lori said, her head slowly shaking from side to side. She glanced through the window at Jesse who was nodding her head furiously, and looked away to hide her grin.

"How about Scrabble? You could spell out all the dirty words that I know you've been dying to whisper in my ear."

Again, Lori couldn't help but smirk. "Well, now, that *is* tempting, but it's probably not a good idea. My mouth tends to get me in trouble." His eyes dropped down to her lips and thoughts of their kiss earlier in the warehouse sent a hoard of butterflies to her belly. Her face heated.

"Twister?"

"You play Twister?" She pursed her lips, growing curious now. Clearly, he was enjoying their banter, based on the gleam that sparkled in his eyes.

"No. But the thought of getting tangled up with you sounds pretty damn appealing to me."

Unable to hold back, Lori burst out laughing. He was so much fun to be around, and it was lunch and nothing more. Or at least, that was the reasoning in her head. "Chili sounds great. I skipped breakfast this morning."

"Really?" he asked, and she glanced back at Jesse who was motioning her to come inside.

"As soon as you walk through that door, they'll be all over you like a duck on a June bug. But if you can distract them for five minutes, I'll sneak in the side door and wait for you upstairs."

He rolled his bottom lip and set her plan into motion. She turned and walked away as he ran his fingers through his hair—utterly rejected. Now, if only her friends would buy the act.

Glancing through the window, angry eyes glared back at her and she blew a kiss, causing Jesse to stomp her foot.

Eleven

Lori

Her plan worked perfectly and as soon as Hayden walked into the boutique, her friends emerged to comfort him. Of course, she had to give props to Hayden for his performance. Once he displayed those puppy dog eyes, they were soft putty in his hands. She giggled and fell against his side. "That was way too easy."

"It was, but they were more concerned about you. They seem to think you're acting out of character," Hayden said.

"I'm not acting out of character; they just need to stop hovering. I have a mother, granted at this time, she's reverting back to her teen years, but still." Lori took another bite of chili and groaned as the spicy heat warmed her insides. "So what are we doing today?" She kicked off her shoes and tucked her feet beneath her legs.

"I know what I'd like to do, but with your guardians downstairs, I'm not sure I'd escape with everything intact. So maybe we could talk about what happened on the mountain?"

"I don't know what came over me. I guess that's the character issue Jesse and Megan were referring to. Normally, I don't back down without a fight, but... what right did I have to stop you? I heard the rumors and automatically assumed you might secretly be into Katherine." Lori wiped her mouth with a napkin and set her bowl on the coffee table.

"It was nothing like that, I promise you. Katherine has been a running joke between me and my siblings for years. She's very bratty with a nasty attitude to match. I didn't like what she was saying, and I didn't want you to witness that." He looked up through thick lashes, and Lori's heart melted.

"But you were gone... for so long, and I thought..."

"I know, but I wasn't with her alone. She's twenty-one, which is old enough to do as she pleases, but the threats she made couldn't be tolerated. She still lives with her parents, who are respected members of the pack, so I had to at least give them a chance to set her straight. Next time, I won't be so lenient." Lori smiled, hearing his normal tone change to what she assumed was the alpha coming out.

"Maybe, but that doesn't excuse how I made a fool of myself. I'm sure your family thinks I'm just as bad as Katherine." She looked down, ashamed of the part she played in the ordeal.

"We share a bond."

Lori's eyes shot up to his. "What?!" Her heart

drummed in her chest and she turned and stared across the room. *We share a bond.* His words echoed in her head as she tried to remember everything Jesse and Megan told her about their bond. At the time, she was only interested in the naughty tidbits; now, she wished she paid more attention to the boring stuff.

"Does that scare you?" he whispered through her hair. His nearness made her lightheaded but his confession made her giddy.

"Your eyes. I noticed them when we first met, but at the time, I thought it was only a reflection from the fireplace. That was when it started." She looked up, not actually answering his question.

"Yeah, at the time, I didn't know you knew about us, and I didn't want to frighten you, so I rushed out of the house, hoping you didn't notice." He laced his fingers with hers.

"After everything that went on here, you couldn't scare me if you tried." A slight blush tinted her cheeks. She wasn't afraid of him; at most, she feared making another fool of herself. The attraction she felt anytime he was near made her fight with all she had to resist the urge to strip down and straddle his lap.

"Are you sure?" His mischievous grin told her he accepted the challenge and he scooped her off the sofa and carried her to the bedroom. "Scared yet?" She laughed when he tossed her on the bed.

"Hell no!" She pushed up on her elbows. "Not yet." How far was she willing to go? She wasn't sure, but as her body heated up with the thought of sharing a bond with him, she giggled nervously.

Every nerve ending tingled beneath his gaze, and

when he pulled his shirt over his head, she bit her lip, encouraging him. His eyes flared, and her heart raced as she stared at his oh-so-naked chest. *That should be illegal.* She smiled shyly and looked away, but an irresistible intrigue had her glancing back when he unfastened the button on his jeans.

"You talk tough, but your eyes say otherwise." He crawled across the bed, his body hovering over hers as his scent drifted in the air. She drew in a long breath as her mind revisited the mountain. The images he incited made her fingers draw a trail across the hard lines of his chest, tempting her to taste. Wanting him, and needing him to want her, she wrapped her arms around his neck and pulled herself up off the bed, moaning when he nuzzled the crook of her neck.

As he sat back on the bed, she straddled his lap, and his arms wrapped around her tiny frame. If only she could stop time! That moment was where she longed to stay forever. She arched against him as his hand roamed her lower back, causing goosebumps to spread all over her body.

"Hayden," she panted as he leaned down, drawing her into a kiss. Soft, gentle lashes of his tongue sent her body spiraling out of control until his breath became hers.

Too soon, he pulled out of the kiss and said, "I want so badly to show you how much you mean to me. The man, not the wolf." His words made her mind whirl and a soft quiver moved through her body.

She wanted to be with him more than she wanted to breathe, but it was all so new: the feelings, the desire, *a bond?* She looked up as he closed his eyes, his breathing slower now, and she did the same.

Remembering the first night Steve stayed over at her house, she fully expected him to make a move and was more than ready to kick his butt out the door if he did, but when he didn't, it was just as insulting. She chalked it up to him not being interested in her. She was a tomboy and unlike most girls her age, flat-chested with very little curve to her hips. She opened her eyes and looked down at her shirt and baggy jeans. Not much had changed in the past three years; compared to her friends, she still had the figure of a boy. "I'm afraid," she whispered, and he tightened his grip.

"I would never hurt you, nor push you into something if you weren't ready," he said as she searched his eyes. She could lose herself in those beautiful, brown eyes, but if he walked away, it would destroy whatever was left of her self-esteem. "This is as new to me as it is you." He eased off the bed and set her on her feet, tucking a loose strand of hair behind her ear and she flinched. "Are you okay?"

"Stress headache," she said, touching her temple as the room spun and her vision blurred. Blinking the black spots away, she stumbled and appeared disoriented.

"Lori?" Hayden said, gripping her arms.

"I'm okay, really." She smiled, but Hayden intently watched her straighten her shirt. She wanted to be in a relationship like her friends, but fearing he would reject her once he returned to the mountains, she pushed him away. "I'm sorry. I..." She looked down as Hayden grabbed his shirt off the floor and slipped it over his head.

"It was me. I shouldn't have teased you that way." He pulled her into a gentle hug and lightly kissed her hair. "I love you."

Her breath hitched with the possibility, but when he turned and walked out of the room, her heart deflated. Everything she ever wanted was right there within her grasp, and then she decides to admit she was afraid? *What an idiot!* She swallowed hard, trying to hold back the pain of rejection until she could escape again, but as with everything else in her life, she failed miserably.

Twelve

Hayden

Aggravated by a bout of insecurity, Hayden couldn't believe he was walking away from Lori. She was in his bed, urging him on, willing to surrender to him. But when he looked down at her hesitant smile, his own self-doubt kicked him right in the balls. Was there such a difference between making love and getting a quick screw?

Looking back, he was appalled by the number of females that so eagerly satisfied his sexual urges in the past, sometimes even up against a tree. They appeared in droves, meeting him in the woods, jumping at any chance to snag an alpha male. But after years of searching, he gave up on ever finding his mate and reluctantly settled on remaining a bachelor for life. Now he mentally kicked himself for lacking Tucker's restraint when it came to the lustful she-wolves.

Irritated by his human actions, his wolf objected to leaving Lori behind. With the full moon approaching, he knew he had to keep a level head. *She's not like us,* he reminded his wolf, although he might as well have been talking to a tree. A low growl rumbled in his chest. His wolf was lonely. Although Hayden never suffered from a shortage of females to keep him company over the years, his furry side wasn't that easily impressed. Lori, alone, had managed to capture the heart of his beast. And as difficult as it was to confess, anytime she was near him, his wolf purred.

The image of her straddling his lap made his heart strum with joy. Usually, when a female offered herself, he wouldn't hesitate, but Lori was different. She could see the man he was, not the alpha he would become, and when she dared to admit she was afraid? That almost did him in. He pushed the uncertainty out of his mind. *It has to be her choice* he kept telling himself, which did nothing to ease the stabbing pain that threatened to rip through his chest.

Hearing Lori moving around in the apartment, he hurried down the steps. He was still pondering his motivation for confessing that he loved her. It was much too soon and like it or not, she wasn't ready for that deep of a relationship. *In other words, she was there for the taking and you chickened out.* His thoughts taunted him, agreeing with his wolf, but he refused to take advantage of the situation he inadvertently created.

Would she reject the bond? Being the other half of his soul, a life without her wouldn't be worth living. Still, he wondered what was going on in her mind as he walked into the storeroom, intent on distracting Jesse and Megan so she could get out of the building without being seen.

"Hayden, I didn't expect to see you so soon!" Megan seemed surprised at his appearance, and he narrowed his eyes as he walked over to the counter, unsure why she was grinning. What happened to the pity-eyes she aimed at him earlier? "We were wondering how things were going." Her smile slipped as Jesse stalked towards them with a deep scowl on her face.

"Would you mind explaining why my best friend just ran out the backdoor in tears?" Hayden turned to meet Jesse's glare. "What did you do?" she demanded. A slight growl echoed through the building, but it sounded more like water running through a sluggish drain.

"I didn't do anything! She's not ready to accept the bond," he said, crossing his arms over his chest. The females in Cloverly were a little more impetuous than he preferred, and he had to remind himself he wasn't still on the mountain.

"Ya think!" Jesse snapped as she planted her hands on her hips. He wanted to smirk at her stance, which she adopted anytime she felt defensive.

Megan stepped out from behind the counter and inched her way between them. "Calm down, Jesse. I'm sure there's a logical explanation." This time, Hayden smirked when Megan's short frame struggled to shield him from her best friend.

"There better be. I agreed to help you, but this?" She waved her hands frantically in the air, glaring over Megan's head.

"I would deny the bond before I would ever hurt her," Hayden growled as he walked over to the front window. *Females!* The snow-covered street made him homesick for the mountains, and his mind traveled there. What would he be doing at that very moment? *Running off this frustration!*

"I'm sorry," Jesse said, inching over to stand beside him. "I know you would never hurt her, but seeing her like that... And she's been going through a rough time lately. She's depressed and not thinking straight." She teared up. "I don't know what to do to help her because she pushes everyone away."

"Am I the reason for her depression?" He glanced over and pangs of guilt gripped his heart, squeezing and twisting until he felt nausea turning his stomach. The concern on Jesse's face was proof that she was only looking out for Lori, and for that, he was grateful.

"No, you're the reason she's so confused. Steve and all of us are the reason why she's depressed," Jesse said.

Megan placed her hand on his arm, and he nodded when she said, "It's not like that, so try to keep the wolf at bay." It was a direct order, since she was the alpha female.

"Did Steve hurt her?" His jaw ticked, waiting for an answer.

"No. He was very good to her," Megan said, and although Hayden didn't want to believe her, nothing in her demeanor indicated she was lying.

"Then why is she depressed?"

"Because over the past six months, all her friends have moved on with their lives. She feels left behind. It's just Lori. She is overly critical of herself, and what you see is not always what you get. She only acts tough to keep from being hurt," Megan said.

"Is there something I could do to fix it?"

"I don't know what that would be." Megan shrugged. "We could try talking to her again, but it won't be a quick fix. Once she gets something in her head, she usually runs with it."

"And my being here is basically just making matters worse." He sighed. "What if I went back to Tennessee?"

"You can't leave now! We just told you, she's depressed! How would she handle you leaving? Please don't leave because of me. I tend to overreact where Lori is concerned," Jesse added.

"I'm not leaving because of you. Lori needs time to work things out on her own, but my wolf is very jealous and will become protective of her if I stay. It's very possible it would react by harming any male that gets close to her." He exhaled a heavy breath. "I'll wait however long it takes, but I seriously doubt I can stay here."

"Give us time to talk to her before you do anything rash. We saw her at the park. She was at peace, and happy, because she was with you."

The pleading look in Jesse's eyes nearly brought him to his knees. He understood what she meant; Lori at the park was the same Lori that was with him on the mountain. She was his Lori; the Lori that captured his heart and threw his whole world into a tailspin. If only he could push reset and put them back on the mountain. *She was happy there.* Hayden's eyes locked onto a snowflake and he followed it to the ground. He would give Lori all the time she needed, but he was still puzzled as to why she ran out of the building crying. *Probably overwhelmed, thanks to you.* Having told her about the bond, he went one step further. *Brilliant move.* He pinched the bridge of his nose. There was no way he could go back to the mountains until he knew she was all right.

"I know what you're probably thinking, but it's Lori. She doesn't want more time. She wants to matter enough that someone would fight for her. But the bond between you will never work until she gets Katherine clear out of her head." Jesse stepped to the side as the last customer walked out the door. "Be careful," she called out when the door closed. Flipping the *Open* sign to *Closed,* she slid the deadbolt and locked the door.

"I told her we shared a bond. I also told her I loved her." Hayden huffed, and the window clouded over.

"And?" Jesse asked.

"Here I stand. No closer to bonding with her than when I was on the mountain. And despite what you might think, I do understand her confusion. I also understand depression. Hell, I even understand rejection."

"So you tell her you love her right before you leave? Did you give her any time to respond? Was she okay with it? Those things matter a lot to a girl," Jesse said.

"Well, I wouldn't know. I'm not a girl." There was a reason he stopped seeking a mate, and now he remembered what it was. "Complicated and emotional," Hayden muttered as he turned and stalked across the store to the warehouse. Did Lori want more time? Or did she want him to fight for her? He didn't know what the hell to do so he stood in the center of the warehouse, thinking of Lori sitting on the stack of pallets from earlier that day. She was upset, but talking, and although she didn't come out and admit she wanted to be with him, she did return his kiss. *And look at you now.* He didn't need a mirror to know he was an insensitive asshole, but that was never his intent.

"Where are you going?" Jesse yelled after him when

he pulled open the side door.

"If Lori wants me to fight for her, then I might as well start the battle now." Hayden wasn't one hundred percent sure he was doing the right thing by chasing Lori down, but dammit! If she would just talk to him, and tell him how she felt, things between them would be so much easier. As he pulled the truck keys from his pocket, he noticed Lori's footsteps in the snow, and scowled.

He turned when Jesse and Megan came out the door. "She left in a car," he said, running his fingers through his hair. He should have been the one giving her a ride home after it started snowing when they were at the park. Now the roads were covered. *Way-to-go, asshole.*

"How do you know?" Jesse asked, glancing down at the footprints in the snow.

"Because her footprints stop in the middle of the street right next to the tire tracks." He pointed and added, "And her scent is gone."

"It was probably her mother," Jesse suggested and pulled open the passenger door when Megan started the car.

"Yeah, probably." Hayden waited until they turned onto Main Street before glancing down at the boot print next to Lori's. It sure as hell didn't belong to her mother unless she wore a size eleven shoe! His wolf rumbled low, bristling at the obvious conclusion. It was a male, that he was certain of, but another wolf? That was not expected. His fist clenched as he stormed over to his truck and climbed into the driver's seat. The alpha knew his reasons for being in Cloverly, and to allow another male to sweep in and take Lori away was totally unacceptable.

Thirteen

Lori

It was cruel to leave Hayden at the mercy of Jesse's wrath, but it was better than having him see her cry. Lori hid her feelings behind her snarky attitude and pretended he didn't matter; now, though, he had to know the truth.

When Lori stumbled down the stairs, slipping out the side door, she refused to stop when Jesse called out to her. Jesse was Team Hayden, and she needed someone on her team. She slipped across the sidewalk, her hastening steps slowed by the fresh layer of snow that made every step more treacherous than the last. Glancing over her shoulder, she prayed Jesse wouldn't follow, but based on Lori's previous attitude, she probably knew better.

Distracted by her selfish thoughts, her body pitched forward, and her arms shot out to shield her face from the cold, hard ground.

The unexpected sight of a vehicle fishtailing towards her instantly had her squeezing her eyes shut. *Karma.* She could hear Jesse's voice in her head, but if she were about to die, she sure didn't want to see it happen.

"Lori!" the panicked voice yelled, and she squinted through her confusion. Had the car stopped?

"Nigel?" Her voice sounded winded, and far away.

"Are you okay? I'll call an ambulance." He actually pulled his phone from his pocket and started pushing buttons.

"NO! I'm not hurt. You didn't hit me," she sputtered. Her arm suffered slightly from the impact of her fall, but would be okay. "It wasn't your fault. I was in a hurry and not paying attention." She got onto her knees and used the front bumper to push herself up off the ground. Suddenly, panic filled her eyes and she remembered why she was running. "I need to go. Now!" She hobbled around to the passenger side of the car and got in without wasting time to explain.

"Lori, you need to get checked out at the hospital," Nigel insisted as he climbed into the driver's seat. "I'll give you a ride over there and then take you home."

"No! Just go wherever you were going." Her head hurt like someone hit her with a brick and was probably the reason her vision seemed so blurred. Maybe she landed on her head and was suffering from shock. She couldn't tell because her body trembled so hard, she had to clench her jaw tightly to keep her teeth from chattering. She closed her eyes and sunk lower in the front seat when Nigel turned onto Main Street. "I'm okay, really," she said. When she opened her eyes, her vision was much clearer.

"Maybe, but a head injury isn't something to take lightly," he warned her, but she couldn't risk it.

Small town hospitals were exactly like small towns. Gossip ran through the air vents and by morning, the story would be so exaggerated, Lori would be lucky if she survived the vehicle versus the deer collision on State Route Eighty-one. She nearly rolled her eyes at the thought until she noticed the concern on Nigel's face.

"What were you thinking? I could have killed you! Running out in front of my car like that," Nigel finally said. He glanced over as he waited for the stoplight to change to green.

"I just had to get away." Funny thing when a person faces their own death, they see things in a new light. She stared out the window, but even then, she couldn't stop the tears from filling her eyes.

She didn't usually cry over a stupid ass guy, but Hayden was the source of so much grief that she had to let it go somehow. *So much for the bond.* She blew out an exasperated breath. She wanted him to want her. She wanted to share a bond with him like Jesse did with Tucker. She was willing to jog to home plate, maybe not in a full-out sprint, but her stupid virginity and Nervous Nelly attitude must have scared him away. *It's all good fun until your feelings get hurt.*

"Lori, talk to me," Nigel said with a serious scowl on his face. "Did someone hurt you?" The car rolled forward with the changing light.

"No." It was too embarrassing to talk about, and she didn't think she could ever show her face to Hayden again. "It's nothing like that. Just stupid girl stuff. My feelings got hurt, that's all." Her knee bounced as they sped out the highway.

"I know all about stupid girl stuff. I have five sisters." He was sweet in his efforts to lighten the mood, but Nigel knew that only when she was good and ready would she talk.

"I wish I had a sister."

"You might reconsider that if you ever met mine. They've often been referred to as the spawn of Satan." His laughter filled the car and she couldn't help but grin. Nigel was easy to talk to and the more time she spent with him, the more comfortable she became.

"Now, that is exactly what I would expect a big brother to say." Lori broke into a smile and turned in the seat to focus on their conversation while pushing Hayden to the back of her mind.

"Actually, I'm the youngest, which is why I know so much about females. I got to watch all the things my sisters did when my parents weren't around. I also learned a lot about dating from them."

"Must be nice." She frowned and he reached over and squeezed her shoulder. He was her closest friend these days, willing to listen anytime she needed to talk. Mostly, they chatted on the phone when her mother was out. Occasionally, he stopped by with hot pizza and made sure the house was secure before heading home for the night. It was thoughtful, something Lori thought a big brother might do.

"I promise there's nothing you can say that I haven't already heard. My sisters were very vocal about the males they dated, and when they reached puberty? The stories I could tell you! Sometimes, hearing a male perspective can help you see things clearer."

"It's kind of personal, embarrassing actually." Lori could feel the heat rising up her neck, and when Nigel chuckled, she stuck out her tongue. He was just like talking to a brother, if siblings shared those kinds of details.

"Try me. I might be able to help you, especially if it involves a male friend."

"Okay, but if you breathe a word of this to anyone, my streak of mean is more than a mile long, and I'm not afraid to use it," she warned, making him laugh. "Seriously, though, there's this guy that I kind of like... he's a wolf." She didn't miss his scowl; Nigel clearly was no fan of her getting involved with a pack member. "Is that a bad thing?"

"No, but some pack males have a bad habit of using girls like you, for a good time." He added solemnly, "You need to be careful and not trust people at face value."

She looked out the window and wondered if that was why Hayden said he loved her. Was it to have his way? To have a good time? "It doesn't matter. He'll probably never speak to me again, anyway."

His brow furrowed even deeper. "Is he the reason you were running? If he crossed the line, I'll gladly have a serious talk with him. Just because he's a wolf doesn't give him any right to mistreat you." His throaty growl conveyed his unhappiness about the situation just like she was, which she liked.

"No, he didn't take advantage of me, and that's the problem. Part of me was hoping he would, but he just wasn't interested." She turned back to the window and blinked rapidly when another round of tears filled her eyes.

"It's probably for the best, especially if you weren't his intended mate."

"And if I were, then what?"

"We wouldn't be having this conversation. Very few males could pass up that opportunity, especially if you were offering it so willingly." Nigel clicked on the signal to turn.

That wasn't the answer Lori wanted to hear, but it explained why Hayden didn't take advantage of her. It was all a lie to see just how far she would go. She looked up at the cinderblock building, surrounded by trees. "Is this your office?"

"Not hardly! I run the station for the pack; I need to make sure Josh shut off the pumps. He tends to get excited when he's allowed to leave early. It shouldn't take more than a few minutes." Nigel pulled in beside the building and shut off the car. "You can come in if you want. There's probably no coffee left, but we have other drinks in the cooler."

Nigel insisted on helping her out of the car even though she was perfectly capable of walking. She guessed he didn't want to chance her slipping on the snow and cracking her head open. She humored him and let him hold onto her arm as he led her around to the front of the building. *What a sweetheart.*

Then a familiar voice sliced through her thoughts and she glanced up to see Beth scowling at Nigel.

Lori scanned the parking lot and looked back at Beth, her hands firmly planted on her waist, suggesting she was not happy.

"What is she doing here?" Beth asked, her sneer turning all at once into a frown. It was more than apparent that Beth had a thing for Hayden but really? What happened to sisters before misters?

Lori stepped away from Nigel and leaned against the building, waiting for him to open the door. Trying to ignore Beth was like trying to ignore a large, warm chocolate chip cookie at dinner time. It was impossible to avoid looking her way. She was everything Lori would never be, tree-top tall with generous curves that could make any man smack his mama. Again, she fluttered her lashes.

"I could probably ask you the same thing," Nigel responded and Beth flashed a prissy grin, exposing a large smear of red lipstick on her front tooth. *Not so perfect after all.* Lori coughed into her fist to keep from laughing at the low growl that rumbled the air. It was definitely not an invitation to dinner. She snorted and coughed again, causing Beth to glare even more.

"I'm waiting on a ride, don't mind me." With that, Beth lifted her nose and walked away.

"After you," Nigel said, holding open the door.

As Lori entered the building, she didn't miss the glare he shot over his shoulder. "I don't think she likes me much." Lori looked back to see the scowl on his face.

"Beth doesn't like anyone she thinks is competing with her," Nigel said as he walked past her to the far back corner of the building.

"Me? Competition? Please! Don't make me laugh."

"Sure you are. You're everything she's not." Nigel flipped a few switches before he closed the small panel door. "Most females in the pack are pretty much the same. Looks, killer curves, shitty dispositions. What they generally lack is personality, compassion, and the ability to see past their own noses. Seriously, she-wolfs are so competitive, they can hardly stand each other. Talk about cat fights." Nigel chuckled and Lori grinned. "There are drinks in the front cooler if you want one."

"I'm good, but I would like to use the restroom."

Nigel nodded towards a small door on the opposite side of the room. "Light switch is on the left."

Hurrying into the bathroom, Lori flicked on the light, catching her reflection in the mirror as the door closed. Her hair was tousled, and her face splotchy and tear-stained. She turned on the faucet and moistened a paper towel. *Thanks a lot Hayden.* Yes, she would pin it on him for no other reason than because he made her feel like a cheap floozy. After she took care of business and straightened the snarls in her hair, she exited the room but frowned when she overheard Nigel say, "She doesn't suspect a thing."

The shiver that crawled up her spine wasn't due to the breeze blowing through the opened front door. Lori couldn't see whom Nigel was talking to, or about, but a bad feeling settled in her gut. She couldn't shake the suspicion that maybe he was referring to her. As she moved over to the drink cooler, she reached into her bra and pulled out her phone. Using the speed dial option, she waited for her mom to answer. "Where are you?" Lori asked, feeling glad when her mother said she was almost home. "I'm at the gas station on the highway; can you pick me up on your way?" She knew her mom hated driving in bad weather, but since she promised to spend the night at Dean's, her mother was determined to hold her to her promise. "I'll be waiting." She ended the call as Nigel walked back inside the building, a bit surprised to find her standing there. "My mom gets nervous when the weather is bad," Lori said. Staring out the front window, she relaxed when her mother's car turned into the gravel lot.

"I would have given you a ride home. It wasn't necessary for her to come out in this awful weather," Nigel said, blocking her from going out the door. "You know, I'm always here if you need someone to talk to. Or a shoulder to cry on." He flashed a killer smile, making her feel guilty.

"Actually, Mom just got back into town. She's been raggin' on me to go with her to Dean's and I promised I'd eat supper with them tonight." Lori waved when her mother beeped. "She's probably in a hurry to get back on the road, but thanks for rescuing me earlier." Lori felt really stupid now, just like she felt after everything else she'd done that day.

"Like I said, I'm here anytime you need me." He smiled and pulled open the door. "Have a good night and drive safely."

Fourteen

Lori

Nigel was proof Lori had dropped right over the edge of paranoia. How could she imagine she was so important that he, of all people, would be plotting behind her back? It was totally absurd. She stared out the side window as her mother started the car and backed out of the driveway. A quick trip home, in and out, and they were back on the road, heading to Buffer County.

Lori kept her head down as they drove out the highway, but she stole a glance from the corner of her eye as they passed the gas station. Nigel was still standing beside his car, staring into the trees, and all she could think was *he's your friend and you're an idiot.*

Nigel always kept his word, even when she insisted their friendship remain a secret. Her friends didn't need to know she had another confidante, and to her, it was like eating that damn chocolate chip cookie before dinner, knowing it would ruin her appetite. She sighed.

She was the one that prodded Hayden, egging him on, and because she didn't get what she wanted, he became the bad guy. *Proof if you live in your head long enough, mind games can become your way of life.* Still she couldn't shake the conversation she had with Nigel. If she and Hayden shared a bond, why did he walk away? *Being a virgin doesn't make you anything special.* Granted, she didn't actually go to his apartment to have sex with him, but his teasing smile was more than tempting. She would have definitely gone through with it, had he not allowed her to catch her breath and gather her wits. Now she was more confused than ever, and she blamed it on inexperience. What if she did something wrong? Lately, that seemed to be the trend she was following. So getting away from Cloverly for even one night was something she welcomed with open arms.

Dean seemed like a nice enough man even though he and her mother had become the newest butts of her jokes. He was older than her mother, by fourteen years, and probably suffering from midlife crisis. But if their relationship suddenly ended, Lori feared her mother would take the brunt of the fall.

"Oh, Lori, wait until you see his house. You'll love it," her mother said, disrupting the silence. "And Dean readied a room for you in the west wing, overlooking the swimming pool."

Lori glared to keep from rolling her eyes. It was mid-winter, so a swimming pool was useless. "The west wing? Meaning you and Dean will be in the east wing?" She grunted.

"Just give him a chance, will you?" The imploring look in her mother's eyes filled her with guilt. Had she given her mother the impression that she didn't like Dean? She didn't mean to do that, but then again, she wasn't sleeping well since their relationship went public, so anything was possible.

"I don't have anything against him. I just think you need to slow down. Everything between you two is moving too fast. What's the hurry? Are you pregnant?"

"Lori! You know better than that. Of course, we're practicing safe sex." Her mother smiled, and Lori groaned.

"Did you really have to share that last part?" This time, Lori did roll her eyes, making her mother laugh.

"You're not a child anymore. I'm sure you know all about it."

Lori's eyes widened and her mouth dropped open. If only her mom knew how far from the truth that statement actually was. Deciding it would be best to avoid anymore of her mother's enlightening conversations, she clamped her mouth shut and closed her eyes.

"We're here," her mother chirped thirty-five minutes later, and Lori rubbed the sleep from her eyes. Pulling up in front of a large, brick house, Lori was stunned. She always thought Megan lived in a big house, but Dean's house dwarfed hers in comparison. As they walked up the concrete steps that led to a pair of wooden double doors, she glanced up at the twin chandeliers that were supported by heavy chains. Seeing what the porch looked like, she could only imagine what she would find on the inside.

"Wipe your feet." Her mother stomped to remove the snow from her shoes and motioned for Lori to do the same.

Following her mother through the door, Lori instantly felt small inside the room. The foyer alone was probably the size of their whole house, the upstairs included. It was nothing like their modest dwelling, and so unlike her mother. The walls were starkly white, matching the fancy, trimmed ceilings, and their footsteps echoed, suggesting there wasn't enough furniture to buffer the sound. "Is Dean here?" Lori asked as she walked into what she thought was a formal living room.

"He'll be here later. He wanted to give us a chance to talk, and for you to have some time to get familiar with the house." Her mother offered a nervous smile, and Lori wondered if she expected something to jump out at her. It was a beautiful house, costing a fortune, no doubt, but Lori couldn't shake the sense of unease that settled around her. *It's not home.*

"So this is where you've been spending all your time? It's huge; aren't you afraid you'll get lost?" Her mother laughed and Lori frowned.

"The floor plan is simple enough. This is the main part of the house, and the extensions run on either side. Relax, you'll love it here, and we'll have more time to spend together."

Lori took a seat across from her mother, on a matching sofa that looked brand new. And despite her mother's assurance, she would never love it there. It wasn't home, nothing like the small, three-bedroom house she grew up in. "I would think by living in a larger house, we would become more isolated. Is there an intercom system?"

"Actually, there is, but only in certain rooms. So what

do you think? I went through a lot of trouble so we could have the house to ourselves tonight. I wanted to talk and have a quiet dinner." Her mother looked around the room. "So, are you and Steve still dating?"

Are you truly that clueless? Lori wanted to say but didn't. Clearly, when she told her mother several months ago that Steve was attending college in another state, the conversation never registered in her head. "No, Mom, I'm not dating Steve. He moved to Oklahoma," Lori said in the smartass tone she knew her mother despised.

"Well, he wasn't the right guy for you anyway. He seemed nice enough, but a little too clingy, in my opinion. But hey, look at the bright side. More time for us girls! We can go shopping and buy you some decent clothes. Maybe even do something about that hair."

"Unlike you, I'm not trying to impress anyone so I think my hair is just fine the way it is." She crossed her arms over her chest, directing her scowl at her mother. Lori loved her hair. A deep chestnut brown with red highlights that hung halfway down her back. Granted, she didn't go to the trouble of styling it, but it had plenty of body and soft waves so there wasn't a reason.

"It's beautiful, but everyone needs a change from time to time." Her mother brushed her snarky comment away and smiled again. "Did you have a good New Year's Eve?"

Lori pushed up off the couch and started pacing the room. "No, I celebrated the new year alone." *Watching movies locked in my room, trying to forget about the most handsome man I ever met.*

"I'm surprised. I figured you were partying with your friends. I saw the note they left on the door."

Lori bit back the curse words that bellowed through

her head. "My friends were both celebrating New Year's Eve with their new husbands. I didn't want to be the third wheel." She turned to the window and pressed her forehead against the glass. It was useless to try to have a decent conversation with her mother, especially when her mind was so distracted.

"I'm sorry, sweetie. I wasn't trying to make you feel bad, but you'll find another guy to date, especially living here." Her mother's optimism was borderline irritating, and Lori snarled at her reflection on the glass.

"I don't want to find another guy. I have Hayden." *Even if things are complicated.* Trying to explain that to her mother would be dangerous for the pack, since she knew nothing about the wolves.

"Who's Hayden?" her mother asked, and Lori was surprised she was actually paying attention.

"You don't know him. He's Jesse's brother-in-law."

"Oh? Well, you really should browse more and not settle for the first guy that comes along just because he's good looking. I mean, we all want to wake up with a good looking man beside us, but you're still young, and you have plenty of time for that. Maybe Dean knows someone he could introduce you to." Her mother thought for a moment, but Lori stopped her before she could speak another word.

"I don't need you or Dean fixing me up! I want a guy that chooses me for who I am, and not because your boyfriend has money."

"That's not what I meant."

It never is. Lori sighed dramatically as her mother dropped back against the sofa with her hand pressed to her head as if she were checking for a fever.

"There are things going on that I can't talk about right now. If I did, it would just confuse you. But I will say this..." her mother flicked her hands in the air, "even if what I do seems sudden, you have to trust me and believe that I know what I'm doing."

"I do trust you, but... I've been so confused trying to figure out where I fit in ever since you started dating again. Every one of my friends has moved on and here I still sit. It's time I do what's right for me and live my life." Lori turned and walked over to the large, brick fireplace where she looked down and smirked. *Fake logs. Nothing but the best.* Her attitude verged on the spiteful side, which was so unlike her.

She trailed her fingers across the mantel where a large vase sat on one end, and a small photo framed in silver sat beside it. Even the picture of a waterfall that hung over the mantel lacked the magic to stir the imagination. She picked up the photo and studied it.

Her mom looked stunning, wearing a short, cream-colored dress. Her golden blonde hair, pinned up on her head, was beautiful with curls framing her face. Dean was standing beside her, holding her hand in his. The suit he wore was probably custom-tailored just for him. His red tie matched the red roses her mother held. She looked over at her mother, and then at the picture and her eyes widened. "What the hell is this?" she demanded through gritted teeth.

"Calm down, Lori. At my age, I don't think I need your permission to get married."

"No, but don't you think you should have at least notified me?" A sour taste filled her mouth, and she fought the urge to spit.

"It was a spur-of-the-moment wedding. We eloped."

"A spur-of-the-moment wedding doesn't include a cake and guests." Lori flipped the picture around to face her mother. "Was I not good enough to attend your wedding? Were you afraid I'd make you look bad in front of all your wealthy friends?" Anger pumped through her veins, and she bit her tongue to stop herself from cursing.

"It had nothing to do with that. You were busy, and we didn't want to wait. We decided to start the new year as a married couple."

"Mom, that was two weeks ago. Did you not hear what I said? I told you: I spent New Year's Eve alone. I could have been at your wedding, whether I wanted to be there or not. You never told me." She replaced the frame on the mantel and shook her head.

"I don't think so. We couldn't even get you to join us for Christmas," her mother shot back.

"That's because I didn't realize your relationship was so serious. I thought you were just reliving your teen years, humping around, but another marriage?"

"See? This is exactly why I didn't tell you. You are not mature enough to understand how a loving relationship works."

"Oh, do not preach to me about relationships. I've heard the rumors. You have a pretty impressive track record! But don't worry! I have no intentions of following in *your* footsteps." Lori marched across the room and stopped in front of her mother. "Give me the keys. I'm going home."

There was no mistaken the frustration on her mother's face, but as she stood, her face went blank. "Fine, but the house has been listed for auction; so by the end of

February, you'll have to find somewhere else to live if you don't take Dean up on his offer."

What the hell!? "You're kicking me out? How could you? Dad bought that house for us! And you're going to sell it just like that? Where's your loyalty?" Lori was beyond furious. If she didn't get out of there quickly, she would more than likely say something she would live to regret. She held out her hand, waiting.

"That was years ago, and as much as I loved your dad, my life isn't there anymore. The day he died, the house lost its spirit. I don't want to live in that house any longer, knowing I can never get back what I lost. I've moved on, and so should you. I'm tired of being lonely, Lori."

"You're tired of being lonely? How do you think I felt all those nights you spent away from home with yet another boyfriend? I even tried to tell you that, but we can't talk about me because everything has to always be about you!"

"That's a lie!" her mother yelled while looking around as if she were afraid someone would overhear.

"Mom, I wanted to attend college. I wanted to make something of my life. I gave that up to stay with you. Were you even listening? Did you even care?"

"Yes, I did. And Dean will pay for your college. Any school you choose. He's not a bad person."

"I didn't say he was," Lori said with an exasperated breath. "You know, I remember a time when we used to talk about everything and now..." Her words trailed off as she squeezed her eyes shut. The pounding in her head felt like it could explode from her ears. "I love you, but it's just too much right now." The headaches were getting worse, it seemed, and had been increasing for the past six months. Pain shot behind her eyes when she opened them, blurring her vision. “Can I just have the damn keys?”

“Sweetie, I understand this all seems very sudden to you, but Dean offered me this life. You can live here, too. I’ve already told you he has a room all set up for you.” Her mother was pleading, but Lori wouldn’t stay. She couldn’t walk away from her life in Cloverly. Lori’s Lingerie was doing well enough that she could quit her job at the library if she wanted to, and what about her friends? What would they think?

“You still don’t get it. I have obligations. I have a business. I can’t just walk away and leave my friends high and dry. I’m not like you. Just give me the keys.” Lori pushed her hand out further. “I don’t need Dean to take care of me. I can take care of myself.” When her mother finally handed her the keys, she stomped through the house, her footsteps echoing in the empty hall. She hated that house.

“If you change your mind, your room will be waiting,” her mother called out without bothering to follow her to the door.

Fifteen

Lori

That was it. Her life was over. Everything she'd done until now, everything she'd given up... Was it all for nothing? *What the hell was I thinking?* Lori knew the moment she walked in the door that talking to her mother was impossible. Still, Linda was her mother, so Lori had to at least try. She never planned to start World War III, but there she found herself, in the middle of what ended up being a damn pissing match. She wanted someone to confide in, someone that wasn't a wolf, or even connected to them. Her mother was the logical choice, but lately, any time they were together they butted heads.

Her lip trembled when she opened the door and walked out into the cold. The house she grew up in, the only thing she still had that belonged to her dad, was about to be auctioned away. The icing on the cake, however, was her mother's confession that she eloped on New Year's Eve. Even her mother managed to move on without worrying about her.

Lori shoved her hands into her pockets, tugging her coat tighter to ward off the chill. The acres of ground, now covered in a light layer of snow, looked like a frosty, winter wonderland. It was beautiful, a place she would have normally loved, but her heart said, "Hell no!" She looked to the left, hearing something in the distance. The tree line hid the house from the road, and feeling isolated, she shivered and hurried over to the car. *It's probably Dean*, she guessed as she pulled open the driver's door.

In her mind, she was officially homeless now, and after avoiding her friends for so long, she was too ashamed to confide in them.

Over the years, Steve was the only person Lori could rely on when she needed to talk. He was her best friend, and although most people considered them a couple, there was never any sexual connection between them. She once thought that in time, things would change, and they would always be together, but she was wrong. Their friendship grew stronger, and she loved him dearly, but it would never become anything more than that. She frowned and started the car. *What would Steve do?* She asked herself that question several times over the past month. She pulled her phone from her bra and dialed his number, but before it rang, she hung up. Steve had already done more than he should have, so she couldn't worry him with the disaster that had become her life. This time, she would have to figure it out on her own.

Shoving the phone back into her bra, she looked out through the windshield as snowflakes drifted to the ground. It was late, but the looming gray clouds made it seem not so dark outside.

Tears filled her eyes as she put the car into drive and fishtailed onto the highway. Like her mother, she hated driving in the snow, but it couldn't be more than an inch deep so she wasn't too intimidated.

She looked down at the speedometer and slowed the car. She wasn't speeding, but with the treacherous road conditions, it was better to drive slower than risk having a wreck. She clicked on the high beams and glanced over at a mile-marker, barely visible in the wildly blowing snow. She wasn't familiar with the road, only twenty-three miles down a straight stretch, but she felt confident in her abilities. Plus, Dean put new tires on the car just before winter. *How sweet of him.* Taking her frustration out on him wasn't fair when her mother was the one who pissed her off.

Turning on the stereo to block out her thoughts, she tapped her fingers on the steering wheel. Eighties rock was her go-to music, and anytime she was depressed, she would tune it in. Bobbing her head to the beat when the gas station sign came into view, she exhaled a long breath. Through the snow, she could see the stoplight flashing yellow, and all the tension that previously settled in her shoulders seeped away. *You're almost home.* But before she could relax, the windshield shattered, and she shrieked.

Lori slammed on the brakes as her heart raced an Indy five inside her chest. Everything moved in slow motion until the car fishtailed and slid sideways off the road. Glancing to the rearview mirror, her fists tightened around the steering wheel and she pressed back against the seat praying the car wouldn't flip. *Crap! Crap! Crap!* Her eyes widened and for a brief instant the image of Hayden flashed in her mind. *I'm sorry!* She pinched her eyes shut as her head slammed against the driver's window and the car came to an abrupt stop next to a culvert.

Leaning against the seatbelt strap, blood streamed down the side of her face as she reached for the door handle. The gut-retching pain behind her eyes, blurred her vision greatly, and she lay over on the seat, praying she wouldn't black out.

Her body shivered from the cold that seeped through the busted windshield. How long had she been there? She wasn't sure, but if the stiffness in her fingers were any indicator, it had been awhile. Pulling her phone out of her bra, she held it against her chest and closed her eyes as another sharp pain shot through her head.

Reacting out of anger, she stormed out of Dean's house without so much as a goodbye. Now she regretted that decision. *Karma.* Jesse's word taunted her again and if she died right there in that ditch, she certainly deserved it. She opened her eyes and lifted the phone. Calling the one person she knew would be there no matter the time, she waited for Jesse to answer.

"Jesse, can you hear me?" Lori yelled into the phone. "Are you there?" She looked down to see if the call got dropped, but Jesse's name was still on the screen. "Jesse, if you can hear me, I need your help!" As the phone slipped out of her hand, she finally passed out.

Sixteen

Jesse

It was well after dark when Jesse answered Lori's call. With no way of knowing where she was, since the phone went silent, the only person that could possibly find her was Hayden. The bond they shared, although still not sealed, could be used as a tracking device. At least it worked for Jack.

Standing back as Hayden struggled to connect with Lori, Jesse found it heart-wrenching to witness. Determination set Hayden's jaw as he closed his eyes, desperately seeking the one person that owned his heart. His hands trembled and Jesse squeezed his shoulder when he leaned his head back against the sofa. With Jack coaching him on how to track his mate using the bond and Tucker at his side, the worry that contorted his otherwise flawless face never vanished.

"Block out everything except for Lori," Jack instructed, but Jesse doubted it would do much good.

"I can't find the bond," Hayden hissed as he opened his eyes wearily.

"You have to find it! She's depending on you," Tucker growled. *No pressure there.* Jesse rolled her eyes.

"There has to be another way." Hayden stood up, his eyes searching, but unseeing. No one knew what he planned to do, and they definitely didn't expect him to bolt for the door, but when he did, they all followed.

It was blustery cold, and standing outside the boutique with nothing but her flannel sleep clothes to keep her warm, Jesse naturally shivered. The snow-covered sidewalk was slick, and she leaned into Tucker as he steadied her against his side. Her nerves were on edge, and the more time that passed, the edgier she became. She sniffed the air, trying to lock onto Lori's scent, but it was useless. *Lori, where are you?* Her mind questioned as Hayden looked up to the sky, the deep concentration visible on his face. Then her eyes widened when his clothes blew up around him, leaving a beautiful, mahogany wolf in his place—and renewing her hope.

She glanced over at Megan and Jack, who seemed captivated by the large beast that was now scenting the air. "Can he do that?" she whispered and the wolf froze, as if he were in a trance. Even Tucker had no idea what Hayden was about to do, but he fully trusted his brother so he gave him all the space he needed and backed up against the building. Then without warning, the wolf shot down the sidewalk like a rocket blazing across the sky. He was fast, determined, and without any doubt, homing in on his mate.

"Let's go," Tucker said, grabbing hold of Jesse's hand and helping her to the truck. By the time they backed out onto Main Street, Hayden was a mere speck in the night. And had it not been for the snow, he would have been totally undetectable in the dark.

Following Hayden's tracks, he ran alongside the highway towards the outskirts of town.

"There." Jack pointed off the road. The dim headlights shone like a beacon in the waning moonlight. "What was she doing out in this weather?"

"I don't know," Jesse said, chewing her nails. As soon as Tucker parked the truck, he grabbed a stash of clothes from beneath his seat and they took off down the hill. Jesse wasn't sure what they would find, but if Hayden could actually track her, she must be alive. At least, that was what Jack told them.

The top of the car was caved in and the windshield was shattered. The stench of gasoline drifted through the air and Jesse prayed the car wouldn't catch fire. "Hayden, where are you?" Jesse yelled as she rounded the scene, stopping abruptly.

A single tear rolled down Hayden's cheek as silent sobs shook his body. Sitting on the ground, holding Lori against his chest, he rocked her back and forth.

Jesse had never seen anything so devastating in her life, and tears filled her eyes. "An ambulance is on the way," she said, placing her hand on his shoulder. But when his eyes flashed a warning, Tucker yanked her out of harm's way.

Hayden was on the verge of phasing, his wolf raging just beneath the surface and causing his eyes to flare a constant, golden flame—then a harsh growl rent the night.

He was dangerous.

"Whoa, Hayden! It's me! Tucker. You have to calm down or we can't help you. Lori's going to be fine. You found her." He motioned behind his back and Jesse moved around to where Megan was standing next to the car with Jack at her side.

"No! The bond is gone," Hayden wailed as he buried his head against Lori's shoulder, unable to stifle his emotions.

Jesse's heart broke at hearing his pitiful cries, and she latched onto Megan.

"Help is on the way," Jack said, and then looked over at Tucker, then at Jesse and Megan. But he was thinking the same thing they all were. *Lori was dead.*

Hayden growled. His eyes were wild with rage as Jack hesitantly moved around the car with his hands in the air.

"Control the wolf!" It was a direct order, and when Jack's eyes flared, Hayden squeezed his eyes shut. "Lori will be fine as soon as we get her to the hospital. Here, let me show you."

Hayden reluctantly opened his arms far enough that Jack could kneel down in front of him and push the hair off Lori's blood-smeared face. Using two fingers, he placed them on the side of Lori's neck, pressing gently. Time ticked by and he closed his eyes, focusing on her pulse while Hayden restrained a growl. "Her heartbeat is very faint, but she's alive," Jack said, the visible relief glowing on his face.

"She can't be." Hayden looked down at Lori, his skeptical eyes rimmed with tears. "But she's so cold. I can't see her breath. I can't feel the bond anymore."

Hayden's body quivered and he looked up at Tucker.

"It's okay. She's still alive," Tucker repeated as he put his hand on Hayden's shoulder. "An ambulance is on the way. Dr. Williams will take good care of her, but you have to get dressed if you plan to go to the hospital." Tucker held out the clothes. "Let Jack take Lori."

Hayden pressed his ear to Lori's chest, listening for her heartbeat before handing her over to Jack. Once she left his arms, he fell back against the car and Tucker moved in. "Here, help me. You have to get dressed," Tucker said as Hayden slowly moved his legs and pulled on the sweatpants.

"Hayden, it's me, Jesse. I'm here to help." She slowly walked around the car and Jack stepped back with Lori's limp body in his arms. If he hadn't confirmed she was alive, Jesse could have been convinced she was dead. Swallowing down the lump in her throat, Jesse kneeled in front of Hayden. When he looked up, everything she was holding back erupted and tears began streaming down her face. She grabbed the sweatshirt from Tucker and pushed it over his head as Jack walked up the hill to meet the ambulance. Hayden was an emotional wreck, utterly lost without Lori, and Jesse prayed she would never have to go through that. "She's going to be fine; my dad will take care of her, but are you okay to go to the hospital?"

Hayden shoved his fingers through his hair, looking a mess. "I can't feel the bond anymore, but my wolf insists I protect her."

"I'll go with you," Jesse said and looked up at Tucker. Nothing Hayden said made any sense. If the bond were truly gone, his wolf couldn't acknowledge Lori, yet it insisted on protecting her. Jesse's mind raced with everything she knew about the bond, which was more than most people since she experienced it from both sides. Tucker's wolf moved on when he denied their first bond, but Tucker couldn't let Jesse go. In Hayden's case, he couldn't feel the bond, but his wolf still felt something for Lori. Again, it didn't make any sense. She stepped back as Tucker pulled Hayden off the ground.

Tracking up the snow-covered hill, Jesse watched while Lori was put in the ambulance before looking over at Tucker. "I'll talk to Officer Riley while you help Hayden to the truck."

Three hours later, Hayden was slumped in his chair, his eyes locked onto the white tile floor. The waiting period was brutal. Not knowing what was going on between Hayden and Lori was more than a little troubling.

Jesse leaned her head against Tucker's shoulder, staring across the waiting area. It was late, so there weren't too many people there, but enough that Lori's accident would surely make the morning headlines at the café.

"She's going to be all right," Tucker said and Jesse nodded, but until she could see for herself, she wasn't very optimistic. Lori was unresponsive and her face was covered in blood, a grotesque image that Jesse didn't think she could ever get out of her head. Noticing her dad, she stood up as he walked over to join them in the small waiting area.

"How is she?" Jesse asked.

"She has a broken wrist and a minor laceration on her forehead," Dr. Williams said.

"And..." Jesse looked over as Hayden held his breath.

"She's currently in a coma."

"Are you sure?" Jesse wanted to slap herself for asking such a stupid question. Of course, he was sure. He was a doctor.

"Yes, but we don't know why. The cut on her head wasn't enough to cause damage to her brain, and there's no swelling. I'll have to run more tests, but at this point, I have no idea why she is not awake."

"Can we see her?" Jesse asked hopefully, squeezing Hayden's hand.

"For a few minutes and only two people at a time."

"Jack and Hayden can go in first," Jesse said. Hayden needed proof Lori was alive; and being the alpha in Cloverly, Jack could control Hayden's wolf if necessary. She looked up at Tucker as he watched Hayden walk down the hall. "Could the coma be blocking their bond?"

"I don't know," Tucker said as they sat down beside Megan.

It would be a long night, Jesse knew, but until she saw Lori with her own eyes, she wasn't budging. Her dad said Lori was fine, but being in a coma wasn't fine in Jesse's opinion. Then her thoughts turned to Hayden. She'd never in her life seen a man break down like he did, which was why she sent Jack in with him. He wanted to believe Lori was all right, but the grief in his eyes indicated he wasn't convinced.

Jesse didn't expect Hayden to leave Lori's side once he entered the room, and she couldn't blame him. She stood up and stumbled over Tucker's feet, but he caught her just in time and prevented her from falling.

"Slow down or I'll be visiting you in the next room!" Tucker said as Jack walked over and took a seat next to

Megan.

Jesse waved him off and continued down the hall to Lori's room. Before entering, she lightly tapped on the door while peeking through the crack. Hayden was sitting in a chair beside the bed, with Lori's hand caged between his. He was oblivious to everything around him, and his mind was focused exclusively on Lori. When a tap landed on Jesse's shoulder, she looked back.

Dr. Williams motioned her down the hallway, and without question, she followed. He was being secretive, which, in itself, set her on edge, but when he pushed open the stairwell door, her eyes glazed over.

"What is it?" she asked after he shut the door behind them.

"Can you tell me what happened?"

"All I know is Lori called me and said she needed help before the phone went silent."

"That's it? If you know anything else, please tell me. I'm drawing straws here."

"She has a bond with Hayden, which is how we found her, but now he says the bond is gone. He was convinced she was dead. It was horrible." Jesse wrung her hands, remembering his grief. "I thought she was dead too."

"Well, after what you and Megan went through, I don't want any surprises."

"I don't think that's the case. Officer Riley and Nigel checked the area, but all they found were tracks leading off the road. Do you have reason to believe something other than her sliding off the road might have occurred?"

"Between me and you, I don't think it was an accident." He leaned against the wall, his hands tucked into his lab coat.

"Why?" Chills covered her arms, and Jesse tried to rub them away.

"Well, for one, I don't believe in coincidence. That was the exact location where Lori's father died in a car accident."

Jesse's knees buckled and she sunk down to the floor to keep from falling. "Who would want Lori dead?" She looked up with questioning eyes.

"I don't know. And I'm not saying that's the case. Just be careful until we know otherwise."

"But if someone is trying to hurt her, we need to stop them," Jesse said as Tucker shoved open the door and saw where she was sitting.

"Is it true?" Tucker asked as he lifted her to her feet.

"It's a gut feeling, and I could be wrong, so until the police report comes out, let's keep it quiet," Dr. Williams said.

"Fine, but we have a bigger problem." Jesse looked up at Tucker. "You saw how Hayden responded to us when we tried to help Lori. If he even gets wind that someone deliberately tried to hurt her, he'll go ballistic! I don't want to be around if and when that happens."

Tucker rubbed his jaw, and his face revealed his fear. "She's right! He won't settle for anything but blood."

Seventeen

Hayden

The sun broke over the horizon as Hayden gazed out the window, lost in thought. After a long night, during which he refused to leave the hospital, he also refused to sleep. His heart ached as his mind constantly struggled to find the bond. He wondered if that was how Tucker felt after denying the first bond he and Jesse shared. Glancing over his shoulder at the only female he ever loved, he always thought of himself as a strong male, but seeing Lori's face covered in blood, and not feeling the bond, his mind snapped and he instantly thought the worst.

Ashamed at his failure to keep Lori safe, he doubted his ability to control a pack. Lori was his bond mate, even without her acceptance of their bond, and he was destined to protect her. One person to protect, Lori, and he failed.

He thought about his mother and worried that she,

too, would be disappointed in him. When his father eventually stepped down as the alpha of the Smoky Pack, could Hayden move up and keep all of them safe like his father did? Granted, it wasn't the largest pack in the world, only three hundred strong, and most of them lived on the mountain, but they all depended on their alpha.

He glanced back out the window, the sun now much higher in the sky. It looked deceivingly warm, but with the six-inch blanket of snow, the day was anything but. He stretched his arms overhead and turned back to Lori.

She'd lost weight since her days on the mountain, and Hayden guessed it was a good ten pounds. He rubbed his hand up her arm. The hollowness of her cheeks was not appealing; hell! She was practically a skeleton. He would make sure the doctor knew about that.

"Lori, can you hear me?" he asked as he sat down on the side of the bed, but she didn't bat an eyelash. "I'm sorry I failed you. I got there as soon as I could." When he dropped his head to his hands, his fingers fisted his hair and he gently tugged. "I wish you would wake up." He sighed before getting up to pace the room.

He once heard that a comatose person could hear the conversations around them and he hoped Lori would hear them as well. When a knock sounded on the door, he turned to see Tucker entering the room and he gave a tight nod when another male walked in behind him.

"How's she doing?" Tucker asked and Hayden narrowed his eyes. Tucker's expression changed and he was smiling nervously until he introduced the unknown male. "This is Steve. He's a friend of Lori's."

"Boyfriend," Steve corrected, prompting Tucker to move over in front of Hayden.

"We'll see about that," Hayden said, glaring daggers at the back of Steve's head.

"Lori, baby, can you hear me?" Steve asked and lifted her hand, ignoring the commotion behind him.

"He better get the hell away from my mate." Hayden's vision went red and golden flames danced in his eyes, causing Tucker to grab his upper arm.

"Don't make me sit on you," Tucker hissed between his clenched teeth as he steered Hayden across the room. "This is not the time or place. She will never forgive you." Hayden knew he was right, but controlling his wolf was a big problem. "He's just a friend."

Hayden swallowed down another growl and bit his lip until he tasted blood. His wolf wanted to tear into Steve for even suggesting he was Lori's boyfriend, and if Tucker hadn't been standing in the way, he could've tackled the asshole and tossed him out the third story window. His wolf raged below the surface as he struggled to keep it under control. If he were back on the mountain, he would have destroyed Steve for even daring to touch her. "My wolf is for protection and you know it," Hayden said, the alpha in him emerging despite all his efforts to restrain it.

"He's no threat to you," Tucker grumbled, but Hayden didn't agree.

"He is a threat to our bond. If he thinks I'll just stand back while he steals something that belongs entirely to me, he's deadly mistaken."

The menace in his voice was enough to cause concern and Tucker leaned in to whisper, "Look, he doesn't know about us. He's completely clueless." Tucker arched an eyebrow, and Hayden looked back at Steve.

That was news to him because he thought all their friends knew about the wolves. Then he remembered Brian as he glanced down at Lori. Apparently, Brian didn't know about them either. And it was Lori who stopped him from exposing the pack.

A low growl rumbled up his throat when Steve leaned down and kissed Lori's cheek. "Then I suggest you get him away from her before he meets my wolf." His eyes flared with one final warning, but before Tucker could respond, the door swung open.

"Perfect timing, I see." Hayden jerked around as an elderly female walked into the room, carrying a huge floral arrangement. "How are you holding up, Hayden?"

"You know me?" he asked, glaring at the yellow and white flowers when she walked to the far side of the bed and placed the vase on the windowsill. If the flowers were from Steve, they would find a permanent home outside the window!

"Yes, my name is Brid. We met years ago." Hayden smirked as Brid moved over and gently nudged Steve out of the way. "Excuse me. I need to change the bandage."

Hayden couldn't remember meeting Brid, but as Steve said his goodbyes and he and Tucker walked out of the room, he sneered, "Puss!" There was no way he would ever let a woman nudge him away from Lori. Tucker was right, Steve was no threat. "I don't know you," he said, turning back to Brid.

"I imagine not, but I know you came here to protect her." She motioned towards Lori.

"Yeah, well, look how that turned out." He sat down on the foot of the bed. His day sucked, and the last thing he needed right then was some old woman reminding him of his biggest failure. He studied the tile floor to avoid eye contact with her.

"Despite what you believe, you haven't failed her; it was meant to be. She just brought you into the picture earlier than expected." Brid placed her hand on his arm and he shrugged it away.

"Really? She was meant to lie here in a coma without the doctor knowing why? That's the most callous thing I've ever heard! I'll warn you not to speak like that in her presence again." His wolf growled, instantly disliking Brid.

"It might seem callous to you, but that is not my intent. I'm here to support Lori and everything that has happened since you arrived in Cloverly has altered the vision. You are a member of the mountain pack. You and Lori were destined to share a bond many years ago. That was the reason you saw her in that window, and why you never returned to Cloverly until now."

"How do you know about that night? I never told anyone." He scowled at Brid's smile.

"Like I said, it was destiny. Fate will always lead you, if you're brave enough to follow," Brid said. "However, there are a select few that have a curious habit of altering the visions simply to suit their mood."

"Old woman, you are crazy!" Hayden got up and walked over to the window, more than done with their talk.

"Indeed, it would seem so, but let me explain." He turned to meet her gaze. "I am a fifth generation seer. I can see things that are meant to be. The visions aren't always complete, and I admit most of the time, a mere glimpse is all that's necessary to warrant a change, but the more in tune I am with a person, the clearer my vision becomes."

"So what you're saying *is* you saw Lori's wreck, and you failed to warn her?" Hayden scowled as he leaned against the windowsill.

"I have no power to alter the future, or destiny. So, yes, I saw the wreck and I knew the outcome. Something changed the vision, however, because Lori wasn't supposed to get hurt."

Hayden threw his hands in the air, his wolf grumbling low in his gut. "Then why didn't you warn her? She could have been killed."

"The wreck is the single factor that will bring Lori out of her shell. She has suppressed her ability for long enough and now it's time for it to emerge."

"And what ability would that be? Dying on the side of a highway?" Hayden scoffed and turned to the window, his eyes glowing.

"Lori is a seventh generation seer. Her father was the sixth."

Hayden glimpsed her form moving around to the side of the bed and frowned. "Okay, let's say I believe you. Why are you telling me this? Why does it even matter?"

"Because Lori will wake up from the coma on Sunday. She must first address her own problems before she can accept your bond. That's the way it has to happen or the vision will be altered."

He turned as Brid pulled the blanket up to Lori's chin, gently tucking it against her body. "What do you know about the bond? Hell, I'm not even sure there is one anymore."

"I know all about it. Which is why you need to listen

to my words. You are her intended mate, and because of that, you have to leave Cloverly. You were never meant to connect with Lori until she dealt with all the things she has been avoiding in her own life. Like I said before, there are a select few who possess the power to alter visions to suit their moods. Lori attended the bonding ceremony and then she ventured into the woods alone, but neither of those events was in her future, which is why it altered the vision."

"And if I don't believe you?" Hayden crossed his arms over his chest. He was already closing his mind to any thoughts of him leaving Lori.

"It will be the end of your bond. Lori must move forward, but in order to do so, she will have to revisit her past. Your wolf is extremely jealous, and it will never give her the space she needs. Because of that, she will ultimately deny the bond."

"Then we *do* still have a bond?"

"Of course you do! As soon as she comes out of the coma, she'll remember, but everything that happens from here forward has to be Lori's doing; any interference could..."

"...Change the vision? I get it." Hayden walked around the bed and sat down in the chair. "She's irreplaceable. You can't ask me to let her go. I can't let her go." Desperation filled his tone, and he nearly broke down right there in the damn chair.

"Letting her go and leaving Cloverly are two different things. You'll still share the bond between you! Despite how hard this is for you, it has to be this way," Brid said as she replaced the bandage over the cut on Lori's head.

Thinking it over, Hayden wasn't sure he fully

believed Brid. She looked rational enough, but her words made absolutely no sense. Then the door opened and Jack entered the room.

"How're you doing today?" Jack asked, directing his question to the old woman.

"I'm fine, and so are you." Brid smiled.

"You know her?" Hayden asked, looking between the two. "How?"

"She's the reason Megan managed to avoid Travis for as long as she did," Jack replied. "So what brings you here?" He turned back to Brid.

"Delivering flowers. It's my specialty," Brid replied and Hayden smirked.

"Those are pretty; she must have a secret admirer." Jack grinned at Hayden who was rubbing his bloodshot eyes. "Megan said if you need a break, she'd be happy to come here after work and sit with Lori."

"That won't be necessary. Apparently, my days here are already numbered." Hayden turned away, not wanting to engage in anymore conversation.

"Well, if you change your mind, just let her know," Jack said before leaving the room.

Hayden glanced over at Brid as the door shut behind Jack. She was playing him, she had to be. Why else would she lie? "If Lori is a seer, why didn't you tell Jack? Or is that just something you save for shits and giggles?"

Brid furrowed her brows, her wrinkled eyes glaring his way. "Don't get testy with me, young man. All things will be revealed at their appointed time, but for now, no one outside Lori's family, and you, needs to know what she is." Brid glanced back at Lori and Hayden thought she was ready to walk away. Then she turned and leaned against the foot of the bed, her eyes softening. “Years ago, most packs relied on seers until the risk of errant wolves became too much of a threat. Most nowadays keep to themselves, and far away from any pack. You see, back then, it was their job to assist the alphas and provide warnings of any trouble looming. This worked out great until the seers realized their visions were clearer when they shared them with another seer. Of course, in order to do so, the seers had to be from the same family and live in the same town, which meant, they would both encounter the same pack.”

Hayden’s brow scrunched in confusion. “I don’t understand why that would matter,” he said as she walked over and stared out the window.

“I knew Megan would be attacked from a sketchy vision. But when Lori’s father, my nephew, also had a vision of Megan, we put them together, which was how we knew a pack member would attack her and why.”

“Is that what happened to Lori’s dad? Did the wolf that was after Megan kill him?”

Brid moved the flowers from the windowsill to the bedside table. “I can only assume. I was in Arkansas visiting another pack when he had his accident. Since he had a family here, I agreed to go there. After the accident, I left town to protect Lori, and only returned a couple years ago. The alpha is well aware that I’m back. He suggested I become the official seer for the Cloverly Pack. It’s smaller, and most of the wolves in it were too young at the time to remember any connection I had with Lori’s dad. Even Lori is unaware that I’m her aunt.”

“And you think that’s enough to keep her safe? What if you’re wrong? You can’t tell me something like that and then expect me to leave. My wolf will take down anyone that threatens her."

"Which is another reason why you must go. Your wolf will become overly protective and Lori will push you away. She's confused with all the changes happening in her life, but she's also headstrong and determined to set her own path." Brid's pinched glare set him on edge.

Hayden scowled and leaned back in the chair, pissed that she was still insisting he leave Cloverly. His jaw clenched and he closed his eyes. *She's a seer; she'll know you're not asleep.* He couldn't hold back the smirk. Looking through his lashes, he watched Brid move over to the opposite side of the bed. She placed her hand on Lori's arm and it took everything he had to resist the urge to push it away. Suddenly, she started chanting words he couldn't understand. For all he knew, she could have been brainwashing Lori to turn against him. He opened his eyes and snarled. "What are you saying to her?"

"I'm passing down family secrets. If her father had not been killed so early, he would have done so himself. Now, if you don't mind, I liked you better when you pretended to sleep." She looked down at Lori and chuckled.

The next words that came out of her mouth, Hayden assumed, were about him. He frowned and closed his eyes. *Crazy, old bat.* Trying to tune out her family secrets, as if he could understand the words, he thought back to the wreck. Officer Riley logged it in as *weather-related*, but recalling the surge of emotion that passed through the bond, something must have frightened her. He peeked out one eye. *She probably knows what.*

Still not one hundred percent onboard with the seer,

he continued trying to piece together the events of the night. He could not connect with Lori, despite doing what Jack instructed, which not only frustrated his wolf but his human as well. Not knowing what danger Lori faced, his stomach roiled, and he scolded himself for failing her when she needed him most. That was when he realized the bond was gone. "There has to be another way." Then he turned to his wolf. Racing across the warehouse and out the side door, he knew what needed to be done. Standing on the sidewalk, he looked to the sky and instantly, his wolf came forward. He began listening as he carefully scented the air.

Still as night, his wolf zoned in on a mere ripple that carried on the wind. He didn't understand what the ripple meant, but trusting his wolf, he allowed it to lead. Running down Main Street as the snow continued to fall, he could hear Tucker's truck following him in the distance. He had no idea where his wolf was going, but he prayed Lori was safe. A mile out on the highway, just past the Welcome to Cloverly sign, his wolf veered off the road. As he approached the car, he phased and pulled open the passenger-side door. Not wanting to relive the rest of the memory, his eyes shot open to find Brid gone.

Every day, Brid continued her visits with Lori and by the middle of the week, Hayden's feelings towards her had changed. Instead of glaring when she walked into the room, he now greeted her with a smile. Apparently, the badass wolf had a soft spot for the seer, and on occasion, he even assisted her. Nothing big, mind you, just a low whisper in Lori's ear, urging her to move forward so she could take her place at his side. Planting little seeds in the back of her mind, insisting they were meant to be together and promising she would always be in his heart, he hoped with all his soul that she would know that before he walked away.

He was dreading the weekend, and when visiting hours ended on Saturday night, he turned down the lights and actually got down on his knees to pray that Lori wouldn't forget him. He wanted to see Lori's beautiful, blue eyes, but having to say goodbye tore his heart in two.

When Jesse and Brid walked into the room early Sunday morning, Brid pulled him over to the side. "It's time for you to go now, but you can stop by her house on your way out of town."

Hayden squeezed his eyes shut and ran his fingers through his hair. It was the hardest day of his life and he wasn't sure he would live to see the moon rise. He wanted to say, "Hell no! I'm not going anywhere," but so far, everything Brid said would happen did happen, and he couldn't risk the chance of Lori denying the bond. He swallowed down his emotions and walked over to the bed where he lightly kissed Lori on the cheek. "I love you," he whispered. Sadly, he turned and left the room, not daring to look back.

Eighteen

Lori

Staring out the front window with the world's largest frown on her face, Lori huffed her annoyance as Jesse and Brid brought in vases of flowers and placed them about the room. Apparently, her friends were eager to shower her with well wishes, but what she really needed most right now was to play in the snow. After being released from the hospital, she rode home in that horrid flower shop van. Then Jesse insisted she stay inside, out of the cold, but how taxing could one snow angel be?

She turned from the window, and instantly, the room darkened. Waiting for her eyes to adjust, she remembered the accident that landed her in the hospital—and her mind went blank. Officer Riley was certain she slid off the road, but Lori didn't believe that. She had an excellent memory and rarely forgot anything, but now, she couldn't remember to save her soul. And Brid called her a seer. If that were true, wouldn't she have seen her accident and swiftly avoided it altogether? Of course, Brid said no. It was weird to think of herself as a seer, and she was more than a little ticked that her mother didn't warn her beforehand. It was quite a lump to swallow if you dared to believe such nonsense. Then again, there were real werewolves living in Cloverly, and who in their right mind would believe that load of malarkey? A quiet chuckle shook her belly. But Brid's excuse was that she could not know about her ability until the appropriate time. As it happened, her five-day coma was just the beginning of that appropriate time.

"Lori, you have two options: stay here or go to Gramma's," Jesse said, interrupting her musings.

"I'll stay here." Lori looked out the window. She would be out of the house soon enough, so until then, she intended to stay put. Growing up in that house, she recalled the great memories she had, and everything she was today revolved around that solid foundation. What a sad day it would be when she had to pack her things and move out so that total strangers could take her place. "I'm perfectly fine taking care of myself."

"Don't start sassing me. My bedside manner will be wholly determined by your attitude," Jesse said causing Brid to chuckle as she pulled open the door. That woman was grating on her last nerve, what with all her rules and secrets. Lori fluttered her lashes when Jesse reached for her arm. With Jesse's help, she moved over to the couch but even from there, she could still see the auction sign planted in the front yard. One month was all the time she had left. She had to make peace with the idea of no longer living in the house, but she wondered if she could.

"I have to go to work now, but I'll stop by later and check on you. Get some rest, or better still, watch a soap opera." Jesse handed her the TV remote.

"Mom will be here later, so you really don't have to babysit me," Lori replied. She stuck out her tongue when Jesse smirked over her shoulder.

"Oh, I'm not. I'm just bringing you lunch." Jesse waved and followed Brid out the door.

Lori clicked on the TV and listened to the weather report, which was rarely accurate and often overhyped. She loved the snow, and it was just her luck that her broken wrist and the bandage on her head were more than enough to make her stay indoors. Six wasted inches of powder white, fluffy flakes. Yeah, it might have been childish, but the chance to make a snowman in her front yard didn't come around that often and she never missed an opportunity.

She looked over at the homemade paper snowman dangling on a wire hook. The small Christmas tree that occupied the corner of the room was nothing compared to the twelve-foot tree Megan decorated at the boutique, but bigger wasn't always better. A soft smile spread over Lori's face and her eyes drifted from ornament to ornament, each one holding a special memory of her childhood. The little stuffed bear came from a gas station when her dad stopped in for a fill-up—she was barely five at the time. And the star made out of Popsicle sticks hung from a red piece of yarn. She made it in first grade and could never forget the task of pasting the sprinkles of glitter onto the sticks. After a whole week of baths, traces of green glitter still shone in her hair. She gazed at the tiny nutcrackers that she liked to lift the levers of and pretend they were talking to each other—those were her favorites. Her heart was heavy with emotion as her eyes swept over the festive tree. Her last Christmas in the house would be forever remembered as the second worst one of her life. The very worst was her first Christmas without her dad. *Thanks, Mom...* A knock pounded on the door and she wiped her eyes and yelled, "Come in."

"Just the person I was looking for. You okay?" Steve's silhouette filled the doorway, and she lifted her hand to block out the glaring light. After almost three months since she last saw Steve, she honestly never expected to see him standing there.

"Oh, you know me... barely surviving." She grinned, her mood instantly lifting. "What are you doing in town? Aren't you supposed to be studying at school?"

"Yeah, but Brian called and told me about your accident. So here I am." Steve closed the door and joined her on the sofa.

"You didn't have to make a special trip home, but I'm glad you did. I missed you," Lori said, when he pulled her into a hug, bumping her cast.

"I've missed you too. It seems like forever since I've been back here." He glanced around the room and gasped at all the flowers, saying, "Looks like you have a special admirer."

She rolled her eyes. "Did you hear about Mom? She eloped on New Year's Eve!" Her eyes widened with his and she chuckled. "Crazy, right?"

"Yeah, never saw that coming. Guess it explains all the nights she spent away from the house." His eyebrow flicked but she ignored it, choosing not to venture there. "Is she happy? Are you happy?"

"She's in heaven! He's rich." Lori laughed. "He's not a bad guy, I guess, a bit older, but he treats her good."

"But..."

"She put our house up for auction. I'm sure you saw the sign." She frowned and glanced toward the window. "I'm still adjusting."

"So you're moving?" The scowl on his face told her he didn't like the idea, but there was nothing she could do about that.

"It would seem so, unless the new owners are willing to let me stay in the attic." She tried to play it off like it wasn't a big deal, but Steve knew her better than anyone. "Dean, Mom's new husband, offered me my very own wing at his house. By the way, he lives in a gigantic mansion. But I can't very well take Lori's Lingerie with me, can I? So I plan to move into Jesse's old apartment for a while."

"Miss Independent. At least now when I crash at your place, I won't have to sleep on the couch." Again, he flicked his brows, and she nudged him with her elbow.

"Good luck with that. It's only a one-bedroom apartment and I'm not sharing my bed with anyone." She glanced up at the grin she saw spreading across his face. "It's the couch or nothing." His grin widened even more, and she laughed. "Jesse and Megan would string you up by the balls if they caught you sleeping in my bed."

"Who said we had to sleep?" Her face flamed, and he chuckled. "You're an adult now. You don't need anyone dictating how you conduct your life. I doubt either of them is sleeping on a couch." His grin faltered when she narrowed her eyes.

"Don't tell me, you've been talking to the all-knowing Brian."

"Sorta. He's pretty ticked that Jesse married Tucker."

"Yeah, and his macho bullshit wears pretty thin after a while. He needs to get over it or get laid." The smirk on her face made him laugh.

"Funny, I suggested the exact same thing, but you know Brian."

"Unfortunately, I do, but he should stop strutting around like the cock-of-the-walk if the rooster ain't crowin'."

"How else can he gain any attention?" Steve laughed. "He also said something about you and Tucker's brother." His eyes bore into hers and she almost squirmed beneath his gaze.

"It's complicated, but I'm sure Brian must have filled you in on all the details."

"You know, I'll have to approve of the relationship. I will approve, won't I?"

"Probably not. He's an alpha male." Lori chuckled and picked up a small vase of flowers that Jesse placed on the coffee table. She sniffed the winter jasmine and lilies, and the scent promptly returned her thoughts to the mountains. She could almost picture herself there.

"You admit that and still think he may be the man of your dreams? How hard did you hit your head?"

Lori ignored the question and set the flowers back on the table. "Hayden is the opposite of Tucker. They might look alike, but they're as different as night and day."

"In other words, don't piss off the big guy." Steve flashed a forced smile.

"Ask Brian," Lori said, growing somewhat uncomfortable. "So, what about you? Do you have a girlfriend?" She had to change the subject, refusing to discuss Hayden with Steve.

"I'm currently working on that, so please, don't jinx me." This time, Steve flashed a genuine smile that reached his eyes and she smiled back. Just knowing he was interested in someone made her feel better about Hayden.

"I'm glad you came by," she said and she meant it.

"Well, I know you love the snow, and I thought you might want to head outside for a bit. It doesn't stick around forever." He stood and pulled her off the couch, against her better judgment.

Nineteen

Lori

Venturing outside would most likely earn her a tedious lecture from Jesse, but she wasn't willing to succumb to cabin fever. Standing on the front porch, she gazed across the yard, her eyes stopping, as usual, at the auction sign. She wasn't sure when the realtor planted the sign, but based on the number of vehicles that she noticed slowly driving by, she assumed it had been posted for at least a few days.

"What are you waiting for?" Steve jumped off the porch, causing Lori to laugh as she toddled down the steps. Distracted by his antics, her foot slipped, throwing her off balance, and he caught her mid-fall. "Careful, we don't want to damage the goods." His silliness made her giggle, but when she looked up and saw his smoldering eyes, for a brief second, she thought he would kiss her.

"I'm fine," she whispered, suddenly glimpsing him in a totally different light. He hadn't really changed since moving to Oklahoma. His brown hair seemed a bit darker, now that it was without the natural highlights. The spikes were still there though, and when he smiled, his eyes twinkled in the bright sunlight. He was adorable, and quite good looking—more so than she remembered. "We should probably go inside." Uncomfortable when his hands rested lower on her back, she regained her footing and quickly stepped away.

"But we just got out here." The disappointment on his face made her glance down to the pink sleep pants she wore. Feeling more exposed than she would have preferred, she shivered with the cold that brazenly ignored the thin material.

"I know, but that was a little jarring, and now my head is starting to hurt." She shivered again, but the icy chill that spread goosebumps up her arms wasn't due to the cold.

The hissing growl she heard was very real in her head and everything seemed to move in slow motion. Looking back over her shoulder, her eyes went wide when she spotted Hayden's black truck sliding to a stop. He shoved open the driver's door. Knowing instantly what was about to happen, she cringed when Hayden's eyes locked onto Steve, and he, in return, glared back.

Lori rushed across the yard, only slipping once, and regaining her balance as soon as Hayden grabbed her around the waist. She looked up dreamily while trying to silence the thumping in her ears. Inhaling slowly through her nose to calm her racing heart, her body tingled when she caught his intoxicating scent. The hold he had on her shook her to the core, and suddenly, with Steve right there, she felt as if she had crossed an invisible line.

"So is this what I can expect you to do when I'm gone?" There was no mistaking the hard edge of Hayden's voice, but unlike his precious pack, she wasn't intimidated. She didn't actually cross the line… but who said she couldn't toe it a bit? *Bossy ass men!*

"You can expect anything you want, but what I do is exclusively my own business." His stewing expression and the way his jaw clicked suggested she was crossing uncharted territory, but she wasn't used to a guy telling her what to do. And he was playing hell if he thought he would be the first. "Look, he's my best friend," Lori said, furrowing her brows.

"Yeah, and apparently he's hoping you're a really good friend with benefits." Hayden spat.

As far as Lori knew, Steve didn't know Hayden, but Hayden's reaction suggested otherwise. "Don't be ridiculous. There has never been anything between me and Steve! Now, would you stop growling?" She nudged him to his truck, sloshing through the slushy snow as the ice melted and soaked her socks. "Just trust me. Can you give me that?"

"Yeah, I'll show you the same courtesy you gave me," Hayden said as he turned and pulled opened the driver's door.

"It's not the same. He's my best friend," she insisted.

"Of course he is. You've been together for years and I should just accept him with open arms. Yet Katherine is a member of my pack. Not even a friend of mine. And because you read more into it than there was, you stormed out of my life. You've been avoiding me ever since. I came to Cloverly just for you. To apologize for something I didn't actually do. I stayed, hoping you would listen, and I actually thought you had, but here we are, and nothing's changed. I love you, Lori, but like you, I also have my pride and the one thing I will never do, not even for you, is beg." Hayden shrugged her hand away and got into the truck, mumbling something about having to leave.

"Well, I wouldn't expect you to. He's just a friend."

"Yeah, I know what he thinks about your precious friendship. He's just biding his time until he can change your heart. And trust me, he will try if he hasn't already." When he narrowed his eyes, Lori expected him to confront Steve, and she saw herself trying but failing to prevent an all-out brawl. His jaw ticked with the clenching of his hands, and she silently prayed he would stay in the truck. She loved the idea that he would fight for her, but it was Steve, a guy she was perfectly capable of handling.

"Why do you always have to be so damn hardheaded?" She honestly hoped he and Steve would be friends, but seeing how the two glared at each other, hell would have to freeze over before that happened.

"We're two sides of the same coin. You figure it out." He slammed the door shut.

"So you're just going to leave?" Fresh tears welled in her eyes and she angrily wiped them away. She refused to cry in front of him.

"If I stay, I will have to take out your boyfriend. My wolf already has his scent, and it will hunt him down. And because I'm out of my own territory, anything I do here will reflect on Alpha Cooper. So, yes, Lori, I'm just going to leave before I do something that is guaranteed to ruin my future."

"Hayden, he's just visiting. He was worried about me." She glanced up through her damp lashes as he shot another glare at Steve.

"You can make all the excuses for him you want, but I'm not my brother. I will never stand by and watch you cavort with another male. Never!"

"I'm not asking you to do that. I'm asking you to trust me."

"My leaving is me trusting you. What you do with that trust remains to be seen." Hayden put the truck in drive and without another word, drove away.

Lori closed her eyes for just a second to staunch the rising heat that climbed up her neck before facing Steve. He had been the center of her life for so long. She loved him and trusted him. He knew her demons. Despite how often she thought they would eventually be together, after meeting Hayden, her feelings for Steve didn't compare.

Steve smiled as she turned back to the house, but it didn't conceal the concern on his face. He was soft-spoken, friendly, and fun to hang out with. Hayden was committed, strong-minded, and in short, a man's man. That quality had grown on her and she learned to love it since meeting him a month ago.

"I take it he was pissed I was here," Steve said as he and Lori walked up onto the porch.

"He has his reasons." Lori dismissed the issue and pushed open the door. Now dreading her decision to go outside, she walked over to the couch and kicked off her snow-soaked house shoes as Steve sat down beside her and pulled off her socks.

"Well, whatever his reasons are, he needs to get over it," Steve said and she instantly wanted to put more distance between them. *Why?* She wasn't sure, but his comment seemed so irrelevant and out of place, she frowned.

"Just because I'm not here on a daily basis doesn't mean I'm going to let him walk in and assume my place in your life. You mean the world to me. I just didn't realize how much until..." he took hold of Lori's hand.

"Until you thought I moved on with Hayden," she finished for him.

"Yeah. I don't want to lose you."

"You're not," Lori replied. Caught between her past and what could possibly be an amazing future, she could have used some motherly advice. "It's hard when you need to talk but no one is listening." Her heart ached when she thought about Hayden. *What you do with that trust remains to be seen.*

"Lori, I know my going to college out of state hasn't been easy on you, but all you have to do is call me and leave a message. I need to know you'll be here when it's all over."

"I'm not the one that left! I've always been here. You're my best friend. That hasn't changed."

"*Boyfriend,*" Steve emphasized as he tapped her nose.

Lori slumped back against the couch, feeling like a heel. "Best friend. It's always been best friend. The boyfriend was just an act. There has never been anything between us."

"But that doesn't mean there can't be," he said. When she looked up, he leaned down, causing her breath to hitch.

Oh shit! The kiss felt wrong on all levels, and her toes failed to curl, unlike what she experienced with Hayden. Steve was like a brother, not a lover, and she pressed her lips together tightly, not allowing him to go there again. Her stomach churned and she pulled back, afraid she would throw up in his lap.

"I'm not trying to pressure you." Steve sounded sincere, but his eyes lacked the spark she saw in Hayden's eyes when he looked at her. Steve was safe, and even comforting, but she wanted more. Like the anticipation of knowing when he kissed her, her body would burn with passion at his touch, longing to meld with his and become one. Steve's kiss didn't make her head spin and her heart zing—or take her breath away. No, it simply wasn't there. "Just think about it. That's all I ask."

Twenty

Jesse

"Knock, knock," Jesse said when she pushed open the front door, carrying a bag from the local burger joint. Following Megan into the house, she noticed Lori wasn't in a good mood so she made an excuse to get napkins before she continued to the kitchen. No one else was in the house from what she could see, but clearly, someone *had been* there. Lori's mother wasn't due there until later that afternoon, which left only one other person that she knew of. "Aren't you hungry?" she asked as she placed a stack of napkins on the table next to the overloaded cheeseburger and fries—Lori's favorite.

"Not really." Lori grabbed a napkin, tightly twisting it in her hands while staring out the front window.

Pursing her lips, Jesse glanced at Megan. After

clashing with Hayden earlier in the day, his foul mood and infectious sneer had Jesse snapping at Tucker for no apparent reason. Even she had to wonder why. Hayden's constant rants, saying things like, "I shouldn't have to leave" and "she is my mate" were physically grating on her. Jesse didn't think Hayden leaving town was a good idea and apparently, she was right. "What happened between you and Hayden today?"

"Oh, you know... just the usual." Lori tossed the napkin onto the table and picked up a fry.

"I call bull. He was pretty damn pissy at the store, and I doubt very much it was because of the weather."

"He doesn't get pissy," Lori smartly reminded her, nibbling on the fry, and deliberately avoiding eye contact.

"You know what I mean," Jesse hissed, her anger spiking. "Fine, but if I call Hayden and discover he said something..."

"Just back off! I have a lot on my mind if it's any of your business." Lori dropped the fry on the tray and sat back on the sofa. "You wouldn't understand."

"Then explain and make me understand." Jesse was growing tired of Lori's attitude. If she didn't start talking soon, Jesse would have to take matters into her own hands. She really didn't want to have harsh words with Hayden, but she was growing desperate for answers, and would have done just about anything. "I'm waiting." Lori glanced her way and Jesse knew she was pondering what she wanted to say.

"I was supposed to spend the night with Mom that night." Lori drew in a hesitant breath and Jesse frowned. "I always said I'd never leave Cloverly... and that was because I didn't want to leave Mom alone. She eloped on

New Year's Eve! The house goes up for auction at the end of this month." Lori wiped her eyes. "Do you know the plans I could've made if I'd known she wasn't planning to stick around? I wanted to go to college! I wanted to earn a degree! I gave all that up, and for what? So she could run off with her boss and get married?" Tears streamed down her cheeks, and she angrily wiped them away. "I know you think I've been acting this way because of Steve leaving, and you're partially right. I depended on him to keep me sane for a while. He knew what was going on with my mom, and he delayed his college career for a whole year because he was that worried about me. I didn't want him to leave, but I couldn't ask him to stay any longer."

"Why didn't you tell us? We're your best friends. You should have told us." Jesse was feeling guilty when she sat down beside Lori and handed her a napkin to wipe her eyes.

"Because I was so ashamed. You all have perfect families. I only had Steve and my mom, and she was only part-time. You were always so happy to be here. I couldn't wait to escape."

"Lori, you have to know you're part of our family, and we need you," Megan chimed in, blinking the moisture from her eyes.

"Well, before you make that decision, you may want to hear me out. I was mad at you." She looked over at Jesse and then at Megan. "Both of you actually. I wanted what you had. A guy that would look at me like I was his whole world. Don't get me wrong, I'm grateful for Steve. I'll always love him, and he knows that."

"But..." Jesse said as Megan moved over to the couch.

"He was safe, being my best friend. He knew me better than anyone. My dad died when I was too little to remember much about him and Steve is the only guy I've ever opened up to. Then along comes Hayden. Just being with him makes me want so much more. Things I have no right to ask for, much less, deserve."

"You have every right to a life of happiness, the same as everyone else. Can't you see that?" Jesse exhaled a heavy breath.

"Hayden said we shared a bond. I know you both have bonds with your men, but I'm not a wolf. What happens if he decides he was wrong about me and walks away? I don't think I could handle that right now." She lowered her eyes.

"No, Lori, a bond is forever. When a wolf finds its true mate, it's a lifetime commitment. There is no other. Please give him a chance. You've seen him with his family. He's a good man," Jesse pleaded, which did nothing to stop Lori's tears.

"I know he is. He could have taken advantage of me, but he didn't." Lori squeezed her eyes shut with the memory.

"Did you know he left today, heading home? Did you really want him to leave?" Megan asked as Lori opened her eyes.

"I didn't want him to go, but he was upset with me. I know I haven't been the nicest towards him, but dammit! I don't know what he expects or wants from me. Look at how I've treated him. I couldn't tell him about my feelings because I was hurt and I used that against him. At the time, I just wanted proof that what we had was real, but he acted like he wasn't interested," Lori said, inhaling and hiccupping.

"The bond is your proof! It only brings you together if your hearts are aligned. Think about when you first met him, how did you feel? That feeling never goes away. Even when you're upset or pissy. Nothing ever changes. The feelings only grow deeper for your bond mate," Megan said.

"Don't push him away. You don't know what it's like to lose that kind of connection. You saw me, and that's just a shred of what I went through," Jesse added.

"But I'm not a wolf! I have nothing to offer that part of him. I didn't want him to leave, but he deserves someone like Katherine."

"That's bullshit and you know it," Jesse grumbled as she slipped off the couch. When her knee landed on the sopping wet slippers, she scowled. *Pick your battles.* She didn't say a word as she leaned in on her elbows and reached out to Lori. "Dr. Stevens' wife is human. They have a new baby. You don't have to be a wolf to complete him. You just have to accept him for what *he* is."

"It's too late; he left because of me." Lori looked away. "He thinks I'm serious about Steve."

"What in the world would make him think something like that?" Jesse began to worry that maybe Hayden's angry remarks that day were justified, and a sinking feeling settled in her stomach.

"An hour or so after you left this morning, Steve came by. I didn't even realize he was in town, and I was pretty shocked to see him." Lori grabbed another napkin and wiped her nose.

"What did he want?" Megan asked, but Jesse didn't miss the hint of irritation that flared in her eyes. Clearly, they were both thinking the same thing when it came to Steve. She glanced up at Lori and frowned.

"He wants me to wait for him, and expects us to live together. He said he was wrong to leave me and only realized that when I told him about Hayden."

"He actually blamed it on Hayden? That's the reason he now wants you in his life?" Jesse was totally blown away and looked over when Megan got up and walked to the front window.

"So basically, he just wants to steal your happiness. That's what I took from that," Megan said. Jesse couldn't see her face, but when she kept tapping her lip, Jesse knew she was upset. "He left for college, and I knew you weren't with him on New Year's Eve because his mother stopped by the store and said he didn't come home for the holidays this year. Which means: you haven't seen him since Halloween—over three months ago." Megan turned back to face Lori. "He only came back because Brian called him and told him about the accident. He was worried. We were all worried. But when you talked to Steve, did he pour his heart out to you? Did he tell you he was so afraid you might have died, that he would have died also?"

Jesse looked between Megan and Lori, slightly astonished at the tone of Megan's voice. She'd seen her get mad plenty of times, but this? She was furious. "Megan, I..."

"No, Jesse. She needs to know."

"Know what?"

"I was afraid for Hayden the night of your accident. He thought you died. Did he tell you that? When we caught up to him, he'd already gotten you out of the car. He was holding you, and rocking your body, looking utterly devastated. Hayden thought he lost you and I thought we lost him. He wasn't in a good place. Lori, he broke down. Jack and Tucker finally managed to bring him out of it. He was so upset, he couldn't even dress himself. Tucker and Jesse had to do it for him." Megan turned back to the window and rubbed her forehead.

"Is that true?"

"Of course it is. It was horrible. I hope I never have to endure what he went through that night. He said he couldn't feel the bond with you, and it scared him. I know he's a rough mountain wolf, but when it comes to you, he would never, ever do anything to hurt you."

"But if he couldn't feel the bond, how did he manage to find me?" Lori asked as fresh tears welled in her eyes.

"Oh, he first tried to connect with you the way Jack did with Megan. But when that didn't work, he turned to his wolf. *His wolf found you.* He phased right there on the sidewalk outside the store."

"In town?" Lori frowned. "Why would he do that? He could have been seen."

"He did that for you. The chances of finding you outweighed the odds of anyone seeing him," Megan said as she walked back over to the chair. "Steve came home out of concern for your health and safety, but he took it one step further strictly because of Hayden. He's such an ass! How dare he try to put that on you after everything you've already been through! Hayden would have never done that."

Jesse bit her lip to stop it from trembling. She didn't want to relive that night, especially Hayden's breakdown. She blinked the tears from her eyes and nodded to Megan. Megan basically said exactly what Jesse was thinking, which Lori wasn't expecting. "Lori, Steve cares about you, and there's no doubt he's experiencing what you went through when he first left for college. Because of Hayden, he now wants what he can't have. How selfish of him to even suggest you wait for him! You need to think long and hard before you make any decision regarding him. Once Hayden walks away, there's no getting him back."

Twenty-One

Lori

No words could ease the piercing pain that carved big chunks from Lori's heart. After what Hayden went through because of her, she puked her guts out before she mentally shut down. She didn't want to hear any comforting words from Jesse. Nor did she deserve them. If only she hadn't bolted out of the apartment. If only she had told Hayden how she truly felt. If only she hadn't allowed Katherine to make her feel like shit. *If only you had half a brain.* She flopped over on the couch, irritated that she lacked faith in her true gut feeling.

Granted, her feelings were hurt that day, which was why she ran out of the apartment. She feared Hayden found her repulsive. She was skin and bones, but lately, she just didn't have any appetite. Blame it on nerves, or depression, or seeing her life crumble before her eyes. Then, on the mountain, when she watched Hayden take off with Katherine that sealed his fate. Ignoring him for the entire ride home, even when he unloaded her bags at the side door of the boutique, she just looked away. His faded jeans fit his butt so nicely and holy shit! She wanted to tackle him to the ground right there on the sidewalk. Instead, he grabbed her arm, and she yanked it away like a total idiot. Having made more than a gazillion mistakes in her eighteen years, Lori knew that walking away from Hayden was by far her worst blunder. Seriously, though, who was she kidding? His family had money out the hoo-hah, and he had Katherine; how could she compete with that? A blubbering idiot, she was living proof he deserved better.

She wiped her eyes with the blanket and looked around the darkened room. She must have slept some five hours or more, since the porch light was shining through the front window. Lifting herself off the sofa, she listened to the hushed voices; Jesse's stood out and then Brid's.

If Brid were there, her mother had to be close by, so she prepared herself for another battle. How many more would she have to fight before her life would finally level out and allow her to be happy? *After how you treated Hayden, you don't deserve to be happy.* Although she hadn't actually done anything to hurt him, her conscience said otherwise. *He was right about Steve.* She must have officially lost her mind; arguing with herself was visible proof of that. *Well, you are your mother's daughter.* That's it! She was doomed to a tedious life of more misery. She yanked the quilt up over her head. *Nothing but the best for you!*

A few minutes past six that evening, her mother and Dean walked into the house followed by a large bouquet of flowers. Why Brid insisted on bringing flowers over every time she visited was beyond Lori's comprehension. Lori used to laugh at flowers and called them a *girly thing*, acting as if they were something she would never display or buy, but deep down, she loved them. Laying there on the couch, the winter jasmine soothed her cabin fever, filling her mind instead with the cool crispness of the mountains. She sat up when Brid placed the vase on the end table and switched on the light.

"For you," Brid said, patting Lori's arm.

"How are you feeling? Jesse told us you were sick earlier," her mother said as she walked over to where Lori was sitting.

"Mom, I'm not helpless," Lori hastily retorted, but her mother ignored her and tucked the blanket around her legs.

"It's pretty drafty in this old house, so keep under the blanket until I get back. I'm going to run to the grocery. Is there anything you might want while I'm out?"

Lori nodded and closed her eyes. "Strawberries." Seeing how her mother kept hovering, Lori sensed she must've thought Lori could die at some point during her hospital stay. If her eyes had been open, Lori would have rolled them. Waiting until her mother and Dean walked out the door, Brid took a seat across from her and Lori peeked out through her lashes.

"I know this has been a lot to take in but I hope you remember what I told you at the hospital. You are a seventh generation seer and I am your great aunt, and also a seer. The coma was simply due to a seizure you had, which also caused your accident."

"Yeah, I know, but if you think Jesse will fall for that, you're even crazier than I originally thought." Lori opened her eyes.

"Dr. Williams was informed of the situation and he provided the diagnosis. So as long as you hold onto that story, no one will be the wiser."

"I know... it's dangerous to have two seers in the same family, especially living in the same town," Lori said. She'd always suspected she was different, but to be bordering on the freaky side? Only she could get that lucky.

"Being a seer is a sanctified privilege," Brid scolded her and Lori scowled.

"So now you can read my mind?"

"No, but I can read you. And being a seer isn't about us, it's about helping the people we encounter. Our visions are sketchy at best and we never see the same ones, but together, we can get glimpses of the bigger picture. Your father and I used to share our visions, which is how we knew Megan would be attacked. But instead of warning her, we prevented her from being found until the time arrived for the vision to play out. That is all we're allowed to do; anything more than that invariably alters the future."

"Fortuity."

"No, that was part of the vision as well," Brid said as she leaned back in the chair.

"Then what?"

"Chlorine. It basically made her invisible, with or without the perfume."

Lori pondered the answer for a moment as she

studied Brid. Who was she really? To Lori, she would always be the flower shop lady, but now she knew they were kin. Jesse would be thrilled at the news. "So if you knew Megan was a wolf, did you also know about Jesse?" Lori finally asked.

"Of course. Who do you think put the newspaper articles in those books?" Brid smiled cunningly.

"Because you wanted me to find them?"

"You crave knowledge' and being a seer, you had to know about the pack."

"So you've had multiple visions of me."

"Let's just say I've had a few."

"Then riddle me this… 'You are the voice he protects.' Was that from a vision?" Lori asked, enjoying her role as interrogator.

"It was just a snippet. I can't say with any certainty who actually protects you. One would assume it's Hayden, and that was his reason for being here in Cloverly. It was probably based on an altered vision of you going into the woods. 'He watches from a distance, and it will be you who reveals his identity.' That also came from a vision but the location seemed out of season; so once again, I'm not certain whom the *he* refers to."

"I doubt that's as ominous as you make it sound. *He* was Nigel, who just happened to be passing by Sallee's Rock the same day I was there. He was concerned at the late hour and said he worried I wouldn't get out of the woods before dark. He even offered to walk me home and gave me his business card."

"That's assuming the vision was about you. Again, it was just a snippet and I have no idea who he is or whom he watches.

"Well, if it is Nigel, he's been nothing but supportive. He's one of my best friends, actually, if a girl can call an older guy a friend. He's been pretty helpful at dispensing good advice."

"I see." Brid thought for a moment and Lori stretched out on the sofa and unfolded her legs. "I guess it fits, him watching you. But you have to ask yourself, what's in it for him?"

"Friendship, maybe? I don't know. He knew Dad."

"Yes, I guess he would. He's from the Kinsley Pack and they would have been close to the same age. Still, you need to stay alert. Things aren't always as they seem."

"I know. The visions." She would have rolled her eyes, but what was the point?

"Lori, having visions is not a bad thing, especially when they keep you safe."

"Seatbelts keep you safe. Smoke detectors keep you safe. But visions can't prevent someone from breaking into your house."

"No, but they can prepare you for the intrusion," Brid replied. "He that destroys the family steals the future."

Lori chewed her lip. That made no sense at all. "And if I choose to avoid it altogether?"

"Then you've altered the vision; the next one may not provide the outcome you want, which is why we are here. You changed the long-term vision when you went to the mountains. The altered consequence was the wreck you had."

"Oh, right, pin it on the clueless one!" Lori scowled. "I had no idea there was a vision for me. Hell, I didn't even know I had an aunt! And how am I supposed to explain you being at the hospital every day?"

"I delivered your flowers. It is my job." Brid winked and Lori snarled.

"Right, which is something else I'll have to explain. I've never in my life received a bouquet of flowers."

"Surely you don't think they were from me! Had you not been in a coma, perhaps you would have read the little cards that came with them."

Lori scanned the flowers in the room. "I didn't see any cards."

"Of course you didn't. If you had, it would have altered the vision again."

"But they were mine," Lori insisted.

"And they still are but only when it's safe to read them, will you receive them."

"That's not fair! Can't you at least tell me who they were from?"

"In good time."

Lori huffed, feeling as if she were missing something extremely important. "So then, tell me this, have you seen my future?"

"The future is not what I see, only a glimpse of what is to be," Brid said. "Forgiveness is the key to acceptance. Everything you have been, done, and seen, has prepared you for this day. Now you must be brave enough to accept your personal destiny and move forward with your life. It may not always be easy, but it will be very rewarding."

"That doesn't sound rewarding."

"Dear, you don't have a clue what's waiting for you," Brid said as she walked over to the front door.

"Then why don't you tell me?" Lori retorted with a smirk.

"I already did. Forgiveness is the key to acceptance.

Try it out; you might be amazed at how liberating it is. Now, if you don't mind, your mother has returned and I must leave for a while. If you have any more questions, just call me up and order some flowers." Brid chuckled as she pulled opened the door.

Lori didn't say anything else as she watched Brid leave. Five minutes later, when her van drove away, her mother walked in, carrying three bags of groceries.

"Get some rest and I'll get dinner ready," her mother said passing through the living room.

Lori lay back on the couch, her mind running a mile a minute as she recalled everything that happened in the past two weeks. Her mother pissed her off; what more could be said about that? *Hayden.* She had a vague memory of seeing him at the hospital, and she recalled he wasn't happy with Brid. That she actually understood.

Brid was too persistent, and Lori was aggravated to learn she hid her identity for so many years. Her inability to move on with her life wasn't because she was afraid, but because she thought her mother had no other family members. Yup, she was wrong.

Steve thoroughly confused her. She loved him dearly, and their relationship was always one of friendship, not romance, so why was he so determined now to make them a couple? How could that work?

She closed her eyes and listened to her mom moving around the kitchen. She felt like a kid again, lapping up the carefree days she often longed for.

The next time Lori opened her eyes, it was because the smell of pepperoni made her stomach rumble. She loved pizza and sensitive stomach or not, she fully intended to eat.

"I know you missed lunch today, so I'm hoping you're hungry," her mother said, turning on a small table lamp next to the sofa. "I made your favorite."

"I'm starved." Pulling the blanket off her legs, Lori dropped her feet to the floor and pushed her damp house shoes under the coffee table. Her mother didn't need to know she went outside with Steve, or got into a pissing match with Hayden.

"Here, let me help you."

"You've done enough, Mom. Now let me grow up." Two weeks ago, Lori would have killed for the chance to relive her childhood days, but since the accident, she was changed. It was time she stopped expecting others to do things she was capable of doing herself. Of course Brid's little revelation boosted her confidence, and she intended to ride it for as long as she could. She wasn't a loser, but as for her mom? Well, that was yet to be determined. She smiled and slowly walked into the kitchen where two large, homemade pepperoni pizzas awaited her. "Those smell delicious."

"Good, I hope you brought your appetite." Her mother pulled a chair out for her before slicing the pizzas. "I think it's time we had a long talk." She glanced over at Lori.

"As if we could actually do that!" Lori snapped, expecting the worst, but her mother ignored her. *Nothing new there.*

"I'm sure Brid explained why things happen the way they did. I wanted to tell you many times, but she warned me against it. She said altering the visions could lead to a different outcome, and at the time, the outcome wasn't supposed to be a bad one. I'm not sure why the vision changed, but it scared me when I found out you were actually hurt in the accident. You were never supposed to get hurt."

"Yeah? Well, being in a coma for five days with Brid talking in my head didn't feel so great either," Lori grumbled.

"Don't be too hard on her. She's been looking out for you since you were just a little girl."

"Well, I guess I should be thankful for that," Lori said, but again, her mother ignored her snarky remark.

"You know, I never wanted to leave you alone, but you had to stop depending on me in order to take your place as a seer. All those nights, I was a lot closer to you than you thought," her mother said.

"Really? How close is close?" Lori shot back.

"Flower shop." Her mother grinned and Lori's jaw dropped. "And I know all about Steve being here."

"So he was part of the vision too?"

"No, but he didn't alter it either. And if Dean and I hadn't eloped, you would have been the first person invited to the wedding."

"Why didn't you say so? I thought you didn't care anymore."

"Sweetie, I will love you until the day I die. You are the greatest thing that ever happened in my life, and the only extension of your father that I still have. I loved him so much, but our future wasn't destined to be. He knew it, and so did Brid."

"But you married him!" Lori looked up as her mother wiped a stray tear from her eye.

"Of course I did. I loved him, even knowing I would lose him."

"I miss him so much, but at times, I wonder if he even existed."

"Oh, believe me, he did, and you are his daughter. I see him in everything you do. You look like he did when I first met him. You have his hair, his beautiful, blue eyes, and that silly, little smile. Sometimes when I look at you, I actually think I'm looking at him."

Tears welled in Lori's eyes as she reached for a slice of pizza. Her stomach was empty, and she could actually attribute it to starving, judging by the fit of her clothes. "I'm sorry for all the hurtful things I said to you. I feel like such a fool. There were rumors going around... and Dean, and everything between you happened so fast. Heck, I don't even know what your last name is now."

Her mother chuckled and moved her chair closer to Lori's. "Those were just rumors. I've been seeing Dean for the past four years. He isn't actually divorced because his wife died seven years ago. It wasn't something he found easy to talk about, and as rumors go..."

"So... is he really rich? Or was that also..."

"He's rich, all right. We got married at the home of the Justice-of-the-Peace and the people in the picture weren't the guests, but the staff. As for the cake? It was a spur-of-the-moment luxury, and we got it from the bakery next door. If you actually look closer at the picture, you'll see another couple's name on it. You know I don't care about petty things like that, and it seemed fitting." Her mother smiled.

"What about the house? Are you really selling it?"

"Yes. Keeping the house would tie you to Cloverly, and your future isn't here. And, Lori, Dean's last name is Anderson."

"That's a nice name." she said as she looked down at the pizza that was cooling.

"Yeah, I thought so too, but I kept my own name. I've always been proud to be a Mayfield."

Lori reached over and hugged her mother as tears streamed down her face. "So where do we go from here?" she asked as she pulled out of the hug. Wiping her eyes, Lori couldn't help but smile.

"Well, if you don't mind, Dean would like to join us. That would be a start."

"I don't mind, and I still have your Christmas gift under the tree," Lori said. She pushed back her chair at hearing a knock on the door.

The rest of the evening, was spent with Lori snuggled against her mother's side while she and Dean talked and made silly jokes. That was the reason they were always laughing when he came over. He was pretty entertaining, to be honest, and seeing her mother's happy smile gave Lori renewed hope that someday she would also be happy.

Twenty-Two

Hayden

Three days of running, pacing, and running some more didn't settle Hayden's wolf. He intended to pour his heart out to Lori before making an excuse for why he was returning to Tennessee, while hoping that she wouldn't forget him. His wolf was totally against leaving her behind, but if he didn't, he feared she would break the bond. That's what he was told, but now, trusting the old bat sounded pretty damn ridiculous.

He should've been relieved to at last be home, a place where he could show his ass and ease the frustration that consumed him—a place where no one would interfere. Blazing a trail along the mountainside was their first choice when mountain wolves had to deal with stress, and it wasn't unusual to find him doing that. He clenched his jaw as a growl worked its way up his throat, his wolf infuriated by the turn of events. Just five minutes was all he needed. He longed to take Steve down a notch, but being out of territory, he knew the law would not be on his side. Having mulled the idea for so long in his head, if there were the slightest possibility that he could have gotten away with it, he would have definitely tried.

A sneer spread across his face when he glanced up at the night sky. "Thank you, Brid," he said, flipping her off. He was hoping it would appear in one of her life-altering visions. He knew it was immature and not the kind of behavior an alpha-to-be should ever engage in, but Steve crossed the line when he suddenly jumped back into Lori's life. And after what Brid said, he couldn't even fight for what belonged to him. His wolf balked at the idea and threatened to force a phase, but Hayden kept calm in order to retain his bond. Now that he was back there on the mountain with only his thoughts for company, he couldn't help wondering, *what if Brid was wrong?*

Taking a seat on an old, log bench, he stared out over the mountainside. The air was fresh with the newly fallen snow and it instantly reminded him of the night Lori called Jesse. Just knowing she was outside in the cold, hurt and all alone, scared the hell out of him. She needed help. He was bound and determined to be her help. Finding her unconscious after losing the bond devastated him and he kept thinking he'd lost the most important person in his life. It was the single worst night of his existence, and whenever he thought about it, a sharp pang of sorrow and regret swept through his body. His wolf knew better, however, and the coma was what really disengaged the bond; something Brid said was necessary to the vision.

In the end, the extra-large shit sandwich was made to order, and like it or not, he would be dining alone. His wolf growled. Anytime he thought about that day, his wolf grew more irritated.

Since day one in Cloverly, nothing went right no matter how hard he tried to connect with Lori. She masked her scent and attempted to hide from him, but there was no need for that. He promised he would give her all the time she needed, even if it meant restraining his wolf. He didn't understand how their bond could be so strong, considering she hadn't accepted it yet, but he didn't question why. His concern was solely with Lori, and even though she kept pushing him away, he could feel the bond growing stronger.

Unable to concentrate on a single coherent thought, he searched his memories for a clue, any sign of evidence. He had to prove Lori was actually interested in him. Did he mistake her friendly nature for more than it truly was? If so, did Steve have the advantage when it came to Lori's heart? She knew him longer, and clearly, there was a relationship between them, but Hayden trusted Lori, so he had to believe it was nothing more than friendship. He could live with that, even if he didn't like it. He could also resist the urge to beat the shit out of Steve as long as Steve didn't try to stake any claim on Lori. His hands fisted and he stood up, stifling another growl. Unfortunately, Brid said Lori had to revisit her past, but Hayden didn't realize by *past,* she meant her ex.

"Hayden," his mother called out from the door as his shadow stretched across the snow-covered yard. "Come inside now and get out of the weather. You ran long enough." The lines creasing her forehead told him she was worried, and he already worried enough for both of them.

"I'm fine. She hasn't denied the bond," he said, following her through the door. It was early morning, and the rest of the family were still tucked away in bed, a place where he would have been too if he thought he could actually sleep.

"Your dad's worried about you." She poured out her cold coffee and walked over to the bar. "You look exhausted. Are you hungry?"

"No, just tired," he said, pulling off his coat and hanging it by the door.

"I can fix you something hot to eat that'll warm you up before you head off to bed."

"Thanks, but I'm not really hungry. I'll eat when everyone else does." Hayden pulled Lucia into a hug and inhaled her familiar scent. He instantly remembered a time when motherly advice was easy to ask for and screwing up was just another of life's lessons. He sighed, a slight smile lighting up his face. His family saw past his faults, and would always be there to comfort and support him, no matter how messed up his world could become. "Everything will work out in time." He had to believe that; if only to retain his sanity. "I'll see you in the morning." He kissed the top of her head and she squeezed him tighter.

Hayden walked out of the room, hoping Lucia wouldn't follow him. He loved his mother, but his wolf wasn't settled enough to sit down and discuss what happened in Cloverly. He knew she was only looking out for him, but all he wanted was some time alone and three days weren't enough. He sat down on the side of the bed and kicked off his boots. Getting undressed was painful to his aching muscles as he lay back on the pillow. His thoughts, once again, drifted to Lori. Having a bond mate sounded wonderful in the beginning. After seeing Tucker and Jesse together, he wanted what they had. In hindsight though, Hayden discovered that bond mates should come with a serious warning—hazardous to your heart.

Sunlight filtered into the bedroom and Hayden pried his eyes open as the smell of sausage and biscuits wafted up, making his stomach rumble. The thought of eating caused his mouth to water, and he rolled over on the bed and pushed himself into a sitting position. His energy was zapped, but once he got up and began moving around, he felt okay. He looked down, getting disgusted. The clothes he wore reeked of sweat, dirt, and dare he think it? *Wet dog smell.*

He swiftly rid himself of the stinking clothes before he even got to the bathroom. A quick shower would be enough to wake him up and definitely make him smell better. He turned to face the mirror, and was shocked by what he saw. Rubbing the facial hair shadowing his jaw, he wondered if he trimmed it up, would it look so bad? Would Lori like the bristly stubble? It did make him look more daring, maybe dangerous even; he made a mental note to remember to ask his sisters.

After adjusting the spray, he stepped into the shower. The hot water gently massaged the tension from his shoulders as his chin rested on his chest. *"Give her time, she'll come around,"* Tucker said. For his brother to believe he was doing just that, he couldn't very well tell him he was leaving Cloverly because of the bond! That was the very thing that brought him there to begin with.

He quickly washed himself clean and shut off the water before wrapping a towel around his waist.

Being around his big family was a nice distraction for his mind, which was why he quickly dressed and hurried down the stairs. But as his breathing grew rapid, his wolf became irritated. *Deep inhale*, he told himself as he walked into the kitchen. It had been a matter of days since he last saw Lori, and he could only imagine what his wolf would be like in a month. Thankfully, his dad could control his wolf, and he expected to spend many nights running the mountainside. *In time, buddy. In time.*

The emptiness he felt as he sat at the table with his family could only be filled by one person and she wasn't there. He turned to his dad, trying to push Lori out of his mind. "Where are we today?" His plan was to stay busy and pass the time; the only thing that could stop him from heading back to Cloverly and risking the chance that Lori could break their bond.

"We need to check the southern border. There's been a lot of activity going on down there this past week. It's probably nothing; shiners, maybe, or Bear, but it needs to be monitored," Alpha Wilson said.

Hayden nodded. "It's probably just Bear. Word's going around there's been a disturbance at Stony Falls. I'll contact him later and see what's up." Hayden finished his breakfast and looked over at Sawyer. "It's not over yet."

"I know, and don't worry; I can handle it here. When you need to leave, I've got your back. Just bring Lori home." Sawyer got up from the table and as he passed Hayden, he squeezed his shoulder.

Hayden pinched the bridge of his nose, a subtle attempt to clear his misting eyes, before anyone noticed he was on the verge of falling apart. As the pack's future alpha, showing weakness was not something he did very often. He cleared his throat. "Thanks. I know I can depend on you. You're going to make a great beta." Hayden stood up and Sawyer grabbed him in a bear hug.

"I won't let you down." Sawyer's excitement made Hayden laugh. And for a fleeting second, he forgot about his own troubles.

"You've earned the right, and I look forward to working with you," Hayden said as the two walked out the door. Over the years, the plan was for Tucker and him to run the pack, but things had changed. At last, he was seeing what destiny had in store for him. Tucker was an alpha, who deserved to have his own pack, but he would be sorely missed on the mountain. Sawyer, on the other hand, was still young, but just as determined and had earned his place in the ranks. *As thick as thieves,* Hayden thought as the sun shone down on them. He knew the order of change was exactly as it should be.

Twenty-Three

Hayden

After a long, hard day on the ridge, Hayden sent Sawyer home and decided to take a walk through town. The cold wind chilled his ears and if he listened hard enough, he would have sworn he heard Lori's voice taunting him. *Go back to the mountains, wolf-boy.* He grunted. "I'll show you a boy." The smile on his face when he recalled that day… the sway of Lori's hips before she flipped him off—she had no idea of the racy thoughts she provoked in his mind.

"Hey, Hayden, what has you all smiles today?" Katherine asked, walking out to meet him at the edge of the street.

He shook his head. "Nothing you'd be interested in knowing." He continued down the road, unable to remove the grin from his face.

"So how's the little mate?"

Hayden stopped and turned when Katherine batted her lashes but her smile faded and he scowled. "She's fine." His wolf bristled, distrusting the snarky blonde. "Thanks for asking."

"Oh, Hayden, I really wish you could see her for what she truly is. You know, there's a reason why we don't have many humans in our pack. Not only can they not be trusted, but most of the females would never settle for just one mate." Katherine looked up through her lashes. She was a pretty female, and he liked the way the sun shone on her hair and danced in her eyes. Wearing the latest winter fashion, she looked like she just stepped off the cover of a clothing magazine. Her fleecy suede coat, the rich color of burnt umber, and the black designer jeans that she tucked into a pair of brown hiking boots, complemented the red scarf and mittens she wore. "She's a spindly, weak human! She can't offer you the things I can. You really should think about the pack for once, and not just yourself. Your man brain may like the thrill of having something different, but your wolf could never be satisfied with the likes of her."

Hayden's growl sliced through the air, and he grabbed her wrist before her hand landed on his chest. "That's enough! I will not allow you to disrespect my mate. You've been warned once. This is the last time." Anger flashed in his eyes.

"I'm sorry. I wasn't trying to disrespect anyone. I just thought that..." Katherine lowered her eyes, but Hayden could see her fear and he dropped her hand.

"Walk with me, Katherine," he said, and she looked

up, surprised. He was tired of all the hate she spewed, but his gut feeling knew she wasn't a bad person. "I know you always thought you and Tucker would be mated. To be honest, I did also, but we can't control the people we are destined to bond with, and Jesse is his true mate. You need to move on. You're a beautiful female; you'll find your mate when it's right for you. Right now is not your time." He didn't intend to upset her, but she blinked back tears. She came from a good family and he hated the idea of banishing her from the pack, but if it came down to Lori or her, she would have to go.

"You think I'm beautiful?" Her face flushed with the question and she looked away. He chuckled, and that made her smile.

"Yeah. You're a very beautiful female, and someday, you will find your true bond mate, and he will think he's the luckiest male alive." At least that was how he felt about Lori. "The bond is not something that can be rushed. We don't know when or why it happens, but when it does... you'll become happier than you've ever been. The connection alone makes your bond worth fighting for," Hayden said, his own words mocking him. He would fight for Lori until the end of time if that's what it took to bring her home.

"But you're not bonded. What if she doesn't want to bond with you?" It was an innocent question, but he knew where it would lead. "What if it doesn't work out?"

"It doesn't matter. My heart belongs to Lori and no one can ever take her place."

Katherine nodded and stared down the road before finally asking, "Do you believe in karma?"

Hayden took hold of her arm, pulling her to a stop.

"Not really. I think we get what we deserve in life. Some give more, some give less. Why?"

"I don't know. I guess I'm more afraid that the reason I haven't bonded..." She paused and looked away.

"Karma has nothing to do with bonding. If your heart's in the right place, you'll find your mate. You have to believe that. I know what you're going through. I thought the very same thing until I met Lori."

"So you really think a male will be lucky to have me as a mate?" She looked up, her rosy blush deepening.

"I do, and you'll feel lucky to have him." Hayden shoved his hands in his pockets as they continued down the road.

"Do you miss her?" she asked when he glanced her way.

"Every minute of every day." They walked in silence until they came to a small cabin at the end of the road. Hayden looked up to gauge the time and hoped he could make it home before dinner.

"Then why haven't you gone after her?" she asked, meeting his eyes. "The Hayden I know may be patient, but he's also demanding and determined. Shoot from the hip? Take no prisoners? That's the Hayden I adore, and I bet it's the Hayden Lori is looking for. You've changed just to win her heart, but why? Especially when you already owned it?"

As her words hit home, Hayden pondered the possibility. Had he changed? Was he so determined to bond with Lori that he lost himself in the process? He looked back at Katherine who studied him closely. "What would you do?" He felt strange asking for her advice but she seemed to know more about him than he knew himself.

"I would go after her," Katherine said, coming to a stop in front of her house. She lifted up on her toes and planted a kiss on his cheek. "Unless, of course, you'd rather have me." Her tinkling laughter filled the air and she skipped up the sidewalk, making him grin.

Of all the things that could have happened that day, an enlightening conversation with Katherine wasn't anything he ever expected. Waiting until she waved from the door, he nodded before heading for home. Who would ever believe Katherine, as bad as she was, could turn out to actually be quite helpful? Running his fingers through his hair, he thought, *maybe it's a sign of things to come.* He glanced up when the alpha house came into view.

One day, Lori would be waiting inside that very house for him to come home to her. He smiled as his younger siblings raced across the yard and into the house, eager for the evening meal. One day, he would have his own family, and they would gather around that same dinner table to share the activities of their day. His smile turned to a grin and he took off in a jog as his stomach rumbled with hunger.

After enjoying another rowdy family meal, Hayden went outside to sit in the swing.

"Can I join you?" Lucia asked, following him out the door.

"Sure." He moved over in the swing.

"Did you have a good day?" she asked when she sat down beside him.

He nodded. "I talked to Katherine."

"Please tell me she didn't start her crap again."

"Actually, she didn't. We had a nice conversation for

once. I think it went well."

"I'm glad. I really like her family, and I can't blame her for trying to better herself."

"Yeah, I don't blame her either, and as much as I would like to, I also can't blame her for Lori leaving." He shrugged.

"I don't think she meant to cause trouble. She got caught up in the petty politics of daily life. What female in her right mind would pass up the chance to snag an alpha male?" Lucia looked over as Hayden lifted a brow. "You know what I mean." She laughed.

"I'm going back," he said, cutting her laugh short.

"When?"

"Soon. There were some complications with Lori's accident and my wolf is insisting on keeping her safe."

"What do you mean by *complications?* That doesn't sound good."

Hayden paused, debating whether or not to reveal Lori's secret; but knowing his mother wouldn't approve of him returning to Cloverly without a good reason, he decided he could confide in her. "Please keep this between us at least until I can get Lori home. She's a seer." He took hold of his mother's hand when she gasped. "It's complicated, but before she can accept the bond, she has to revisit her past." He lifted his mother's hand and kissed her knuckles. "There's nothing you can say that I haven't already thought about. Our connection is so strong, that sometimes, I think I can feel her emotions. I hear her voice. It drives me crazy not having her with me and knowing she's in danger..." He swallowed hard. "Like me, she's confused, so I thought I'd pay her a quick visit. In and out before anyone noticed my presence. I need to make sure she doesn't forget about me."

"Do you think that's wise?"

"I think if fate put us together, then it shouldn't mind if I fight for what's mine. She doesn't think she has anything to offer my wolf, but my wolf already connects with her. The night of the accident, I couldn't find her using the bond, but my wolf located her without a problem. That has to mean something, which is what I intend to prove to Lori."

Twenty-Four

Lori

Sitting in the middle of the living room floor, Lori sorted through yet another box that Dean brought down from the attic. Preparing for the big move, she had her choice of the apartment or Dean's place, but she still hadn't decided.

"What is this?" she asked and her mother smiled at the box full of folders.

"It's souvenirs from your childhood. I kept almost everything you brought home from school."

"Talk about a fire hazard! Between this old house and the paper for kindling, it would go up in a flash!" Lori pulled out a folder that was ripped down the spine. Homework pages from her elementary years were sorted by date and she chuckled. "Well, now I know how you spent most of your leisure time." Picking up another folder, her breath hitched when she saw the drawing of her parents and her. She couldn't have been older than six at the time, based on the stick figures. But even so, her dad's eyes drew her in. She pulled the picture out of the folder and placed it on the coffee table. "I'm keeping this one." Lori's eyes misted and she continued to sort through the boxes. As hard as it was to throw her memories away, it was time.

Opening a picture album, she grinned and ran her finger over a photo of Steve. It was right before her freshman year of high school, and he and his friends were playing ball at the park. He was a grade ahead of her, but he never failed to walk her to school every morning. That was how their friendship started, and as time went on, they spent more and more of it together. She was a tomboy, spending many after school hours hanging out with him and his friends playing basketball. She sucked at it because of her height, but every time they teamed up, Steve chose her.

How was she supposed to walk away and forget him when her world had been revolving around him for so many years? Five to be exact. Could she be his girlfriend? Two years ago, she would have given anything for him to call her that, but when he left for college, things changed.

Hayden occupied her heart now, which sounded totally off the wall. She hadn't known him long, but with each passing day she slipped deeper beneath his spell. He brought excitement to her life if she dared admit it. He was everything she fantasized the man in her life would be, yet for some reason, she continually pushed him away. She wanted someone that loved her for herself, not because of jealousy or a stupid bond.

What the hell was a bond, anyway? It may have mattered to a wolf that his mate and he share a bond, but Lori only wanted honesty, loyalty, respect, and a love so deep, it could move mountains. She swallowed hard, refusing to revisit the concept even in her head.

"Break time," her mother said, helping Lori off the floor when Brid walked through the door.

"How do you feel today?" Brid asked before setting a small vase of flowers on the coffee table.

"My sinuses are driving me crazy from those musty boxes. Are you sure I have to go through all of them? It's getting pretty damn depressing." That wasn't a lie, and the more boxes Lori sorted through, the sadder she became. *Even Hayden moved on without you.*

"You have to revisit your past. What that means exactly, I don't know, but you have to start somewhere, and this is about as deep into the past as you can get," Brid said.

"I guess so, but it sucks." Lori took a seat at the table and Dean handed out the food trays he had brought in. How could she have been so wrong about him? She grinned as he flirted with her mother. They were cute together, and seeing her mother happy, again, was nice.

"Have you decided what you're going to do?" he asked and Lori looked back.

"What do you mean?"

"Are you planning to stay here? Or are you coming home with us?" His smile was reassuring, and she sensed he really did have her best interest at heart.

"I can't very well just up and leave all my responsibilities here. So until I can figure out what to do with Lori's Lingerie, I'll probably take Jesse up on her offer of staying at the apartment. Long term, I don't know yet because everything is happening so fast that I can't wrap my mind around it all."

"I understand that, but in the event you do change your mind, the room is yours, or if ever you need it."

After a quick meal of fried chicken and homemade biscuits, Lori stretched out on the sofa, rubbing her belly. It had been weeks since she actually had an appetite and the chicken and rolls were nothing less than delicious. "I'm so stuffed, I don't think I'll be of much use sorting through the rest of those boxes," she said and Dean chuckled when her mother turned and glared. "Geesh, woman, take a joke." She pushed up into a sitting position and groaned at the box that appeared before her. "Thanks, Mom."

That night, when Lori went up to bed, she was exhausted, but her mind wouldn't shut down. She eventually had to face Steve and give him an answer; he would be heading back to Oklahoma soon. *It's what you wanted for so long.* Her thoughts clashed; although it was true, it meant giving up Hayden. *Loyalty, your whole world revolves around that.* Another concern that pushed her closer to Steve and further from Hayden. Her heart grew heavy at the thought of never seeing the sexy mountain man again. Not a day went by that she didn't think about him, and she often found herself daydreaming of what it would be like back on the mountain.

Lori tossed and turned for the better part of the night, which she blamed on the stifling heat of the house. If it weren't for incurring an outrageous gas bill, she would have cracked open the window, but instead, she just kicked off the blanket. Unable to sleep, she turned on the small bedside lamp and walked over to her closet. Not wanting to wake anyone, she pulled the boxes out again, and began to sort through them to pass the time until morning.

The large shoebox belonged to her dad so that's where she decided to start. Pulling off the blue construction paper that was taped to the sides, she ran her fingers over the image of a steel-toed boot. She could picture her dad wearing those boots. She smiled as the happy memory replayed in her mind.

Waiting by the window as he pulled into the driveway, she ran across the room when he walked in the door and threw herself against his legs. She reached up until he took her hands as she stepped onto the toes of his boots. Moon-walking her through the house to where her mother was busy cooking in the kitchen, she giggled and tried to push them apart when they greeted each other with a kiss.

A tear rolled down her cheek. If only she could slip back in time. She blew out a breath before opening the box.

The large pink valentine she made for her dad rested on top of a red and white teddy bear she stashed away the same day her mother gave it to her. It was painful to see, being the last gift her dad bought for her. It was also the reason she hated Valentine's Day. She pulled the bear out of the box and held it tightly against her chest. "Dad, I love you," she whispered as she squeezed her eyes shut.

The image of her dad stuffing a piece of paper into the heart-shaped pouch before he placed the teddy bear on the dashboard, flashed in her mind. Then the truck veered off the road and her eyes shot open, ending the vision.

Her heart shattered, knowing that moment ended in her father's death and she shivered. Then she remembered how she veered off the road.

Pushing herself off the floor, she carried the bear over to her bed where the light shone the brightest. She dug her fingers into the small pouch, and her heart thumped with anticipation when she found the folded piece of paper. With a calming breath, she read, *Take my heart, for it has always been yours.* Lying back on the bed, fresh tears filled her eyes. A message from the grave, one she needed to read no matter how hard it suddenly became to breathe. If only she had known at the time that the message was there, would it have changed her future? She always felt like she never mattered and was somehow out of place. Those simple, heart-felt words stirred her emotions. Now, more than ever, she longed to feel as loved as she did right then. She fell into a peaceful sleep as she held tightly onto the teddy bear.

Twenty-Five

Hayden

Lost in thought, Hayden turned off the highway just before the *Welcome to Cloverly* sign. The narrow, gravel road was dark and based on its rough appearance, rarely traveled. He slowed his speed to make the sharp S-curve as adrenaline pumped through his veins, causing his wolf to stir. Worry creased his brow, but his need to see Lori outweighed all the consequences of being caught.

Alpha Cooper wouldn't care if he were there unless he was causing trouble and that wasn't his intention. Brid, however, would more than likely drag her broom out of the closet and chase him back to Tennessee before he had a chance to see Lori. *The old hag.* He couldn't help harboring some bad feelings for the seer, who dared to keep him and Lori apart. And if he got caught, he would plead insanity. Why else would he go against the seer's advice? *Because you're an alpha male and no female controls you!* Well, there was that, but since meeting Lori… dammit! The stupid shit he did.

He didn't think it was too late to turn back, but believing his wolf could actually connect with Lori, he plodded on. All the while, he kept hoping the late night trip wouldn't be for nothing. When the gravel road turned to asphalt and the cemetery came into view, he sent up a quick prayer. "Don't let this be a mistake."

Turning onto the service road that ran alongside the cemetery, he headed to the rear into the furthest corner of the parking lot. Hidden from view, his black truck blended in with the shadows of the tree line and he cracked the window open, listening. Confident he wouldn't be seen, he climbed out of the truck and scanned the area. The waxing moon shone in the sky, but it wasn't bright enough to light the night. He pulled his shirt over his head and shoved it through the open window. His body shivered from the cold air when he kicked off his boots and pushed them beneath the truck. Then he took off his jeans, and that was when his plan registered in his mind. *Fate*, he told himself, *was the reason he was there*. Lori was the bonus. Lifting his head back, he willed his wolf forward.

In a flash, his wolf raced up the hill towards Hunter's Ridge, a dangerous place for wolves during the daylight hours. With hunting season winding down, he didn't expect to see too many hunters, but if he did, he would have to phase to protect his wolf. It wouldn't be the first time he had to hike up a trail buck-naked, and he expected it wouldn't be his last either. He paused long enough to detect the sound of small rodents burrowing nearby before continuing down the hill towards Sallee's Rock.

The run didn't take long and before he knew it, he was standing in the tree line, staring up at the boulders. He sniffed the air. Sallee's was a favorite place for wolves to hang out and although he wasn't worried about the pack, his primary intent was to get in and out without being seen. Satisfied he was the only one there, he cut across the clearing and headed down the trail to the oak tree. Sneaking around the small wire fence and leaping through the backyards like he did that night—so many years ago—his heart pounded in his chest. Would she recognize him as the wolf from her childhood? Did she know he was a wolf that night? Was she too young to remember? Too many questions remained unanswered and he was beginning to think the odds were stacked against him.

He paced back and forth at the edge of her backyard, and paused to listen. A few vehicles traveled down Main Street, but none turned or drove past her house. Even if they did, he was fairly sure he wouldn't be seen. Most of the snow had already melted and his wolf blended well with the shadows.

Taking a seat on the damp, cold ground, his wolf stared up at her bedroom window. *Lori, it's me, Hayden.* He cocked his head to the side. *Can you hear me?* His wolf shifted, and hunkered down as footsteps traveled up the sidewalk, but thankfully, they turned at the corner. He sniffed the air. It was a wolf, of that he was sure, so he lay motionless, grateful he was downwind. Once the coast was clear, he sat up. *Lori, it's me, Hayden*, he repeated. He was positive his wolf could connect with her through the bond, unless she already forgot about him. A low growl vibrated in his chest. It was stupid to think he held that kind of connection with her, but his wolf adamantly refused to leave.

Hayden silenced his mind and focused only on the memory of the blue eyes that stared between the blades of a window fan. *Wake up!* As a dim light clicked on, his wolf stiffened. Was it too soon to think his wolf might have succeeded? *Lori, come to the window.* When the curtain pushed to the side, his wolf ran a tight circle and then stopped as it looked up. Staring at the blue eyes that captured his heart seven years ago, he waited for her to acknowledge him. Could she see him in the dark? His eyes flared, and she smiled. *Do you remember me?* His wolf bayed and rolled over onto its back, his eyes never leaving hers.

"Hayden?" Lori called out as she eased open the window.

Hearing his name, his heart soared with the possibility that she did recognize his wolf. *It's me! Do you remember?* He phased and stood there in the shadows as she lifted the window higher.

"I remember your eyes." Fascination laced her voice, and her nervous chuckle was music to his ears.

"I've always known you were the one," he said and he honestly believed that. His heart searched out blue-eyed females, which was why he never gave Katherine the time of day. "I can't stay. I just needed to know you remembered me. Remember my wolf." That was the last thing he said before he phased.

His wolf bristled as the footsteps from earlier sounded in the opposite direction. He hoped whoever it was hadn't picked up his scent yet, but he suspected they had. Were they circling around to sneak up on him? *Fat chance!* His wolf growled its annoyance, and with a quick glance towards the window, he tore through the yards, frustration fueling his stride. It was just his luck the neighborhood watch would be out roaming the streets tonight, and because it happened to be a wolf, he had no choice but to leave.

Breaking every tree branch that got into its way, his wolf blazed through the woods. He was irritated that he connected with Lori, only to cut their visit short… He would be a brooding mess by the time he got back to the mountain.

Once he returned to the truck, Hayden phased and grabbed his shoes off the ground as he jumped into the driver's seat. Without looking back, he started the truck and tore out of the parking lot, expecting he would be followed.

It was a close call, and once he turned onto the highway, he blew out a breath that lifted the hair from his eyes. He glanced in the rearview mirror as the adrenaline dissipated, and his body calmed. A grin spread across his face when he realized Lori connected with his wolf, something unheard of in the wolf world. He attributed that to her being a seer. Reaching over, he grabbed his shirt off the seat and slipped it over his head before turning the heater on to warm his body. After he passed the county line, he pulled to the side of the road and quickly slipped on his jeans.

Hayden didn't remember the drive home, and if he didn't know the road's curves and turns by heart, he would have probably driven to the moon. Lori was his soul mate, and he would do everything in his power to make sure she stayed that way. When he turned into the drive, his mother rushed out the back door with a serious frown on her face. Seeing his grin, she ran down the steps, meeting him in the yard.

"Hayden, please tell me you didn't…" But before she could finish the sentence, he grabbed her in a hug and spun around.

"Mom, she knows my wolf! She has a connection with my wolf!" Unable to rein in his excitement, he laughed and blinked happy tears from his eyes. "She knows my wolf!" He carefully placed Lucia on her feet and dropped to his knees, offering a prayer to the moon.

"Sweetie, I know you believe that but please don't get your hopes up. I don't want you to get hurt." His mother leaned over and hugged him around his neck.

"But it's true! My wolf called her through our bond. It called her and she answered."

"I'm happy for you, Hayden, but I'm also afraid of what will happen if she doesn't accept the bond. Your heart is fully vested, and you saw what it did to Tucker."

"My heart has belonged to Lori since I was sixteen. That was the first time we crossed paths, and it wasn't me then either, but my wolf," he explained. "Do you remember the night when we were visiting Cloverly, and Ben caught us running through the neighborhood? I didn't say anything at the time, because I knew we were already in trouble, but we were seen."

"Lori saw you?"

"Yeah. We were in her backyard and she was looking out the window. I saw her, but the others didn't. I never told anyone but I can remember it like it was yesterday.

She was young, so I didn't think too much of it at the time. Brid said our meeting was fate pulling us together. I know that sounds crazy, but she is a seer and so far, everything she told me has come true."

"It would seem that way, but you have to remember she also said you had to leave Cloverly or Lori would deny the bond."

"I know, but the way Lori responded to my wolf... She needs to know that when she's ready, I'll be waiting."

"For your sake, I truly hope everything works out for both of you. We've never had a seer in the pack, and she would be a great asset to you as an alpha. She has more power than you realize. A wolf mating with a seer? Your young could possibly share that trait, which, in itself, is unheard of."

"I know it worries you, but I promise I won't do anything that could interfere with our bond." Hayden stood up and wrapped his arm around his mother's waist as they headed into the house.

"So does that mean you're going back?"

"As soon as I can, yes!"

Twenty-Six

Lori

Lori couldn't contain her excitement when she saw the wolf outside her window. After so many years, she went back in time for a brief moment, a moment she'd never forget. She found it hard to believe she saw a wolf that night because the eyes that stared back at her were soothing, and something she had often dreamed of. She pretended they belonged to her guardian angel who was sent by her dad to protect the house.

Growing up without her dad, she missed the security she had when he was alive, and seeing those amazing eyes reassured her. It was silly girl stuff, just a fairy tale, but on nights when she was alone and felt afraid, those golden eyes were the most comforting factor she always pictured in her mind.

Her heart strummed in her chest at the sight of

Hayden, but when he bolted across the yards, she scowled at the shadow that she noticed on the sidewalk. It was still quite a distance away, but from the second story window, she could tell it clearly belonged to a man. She stooped out of sight and allowed the curtain to fall back into place, then peeked out to see who could have caused Hayden to run. As the man continued up the sidewalk, she would have sworn his steps slowed, if she weren't being overly dramatic.

Shivering from the cold night air, she grabbed the teddy bear off the pillow and held it to her chest. At times like these, she wished her dad were alive to protect her from the boogeyman. Then the man turned and looked up at her window, and she recognized him, which instantly settled her mind. She glanced down at the cast on her arm and imagined if she were outside right that minute, she would have knocked Nigel over the head with it! She squeezed her eyes shut as a ripple rattled through her brain and she blinked a few times to clear the haze.

Slightly pissed, she slid the window completely open and leaned into the screen. "Hey!" she yelled, startling him, and Nigel jerked around. "Easy there, I'm not going to hurt you." She rolled her bottom lip to keep from laughing. "Do you often make a habit of skulking around people's backyards?"

He paused and for a minute, she thought he, too, would run. But he soon composed himself and looked up at the window as if he knew she was there the entire time. "I thought I saw someone in your yard. It's me, Nigel."

"Oh, hey, Nigel." She played along, her voice light and cheerful, but there was no way he could have seen Hayden coming from the direction he traveled. She glanced over at the small block building that used to be a carwash but now was no more than a lot of overgrown weeds and a peeling paint job. "Well, we *are* in wolf country, so I'd assume it was one of those mangy mutts." Normally, she wasn't good under pressure, but this time, she had to admit, winging it seemed to be her forte. She chuckled silently when he shifted his feet and looked back towards the woods. "I don't know why they're always lurking in the darkest places. Heck, I wouldn't be surprised if they weren't standing back somewhere right now watching you." That got his attention and his head whipped around so fast, she thought it would snap off his neck.

"What do you mean, *watching me?*" He took a step closer towards the house, as if he were trying to keep their conversation quiet.

"Dude, it was a joke. Funny, ha ha."

"Oh, yeah, hilarious." His grin lit his face up as he shoved his hands into his pockets. "I've been wanting to talk to you about your accident. Maybe we could get some lunch?" His voice sounded a lot calmer, and he glanced over his shoulder before returning his gaze to her.

"I might be able to shake my shadow next week, but for now, my mother's not wholly convinced I'm not dying." She laughed nervously, hoping she wouldn't wake her mother. "So will this be a business lunch or a shoulder to cry on?"

"I'll leave that up to you. I'm good for either." He ran his hand over his jaw and she pictured the scruff there. Then he pulled out what looked like a pocket watch and held it up to the light as if he couldn't see the time. "I need to be going now, but we'll talk soon."

When Nigel walked away, she stayed in the window, intentionally watching him. He only looked back once. *Yeah, I'm still here.* She wasn't sure where he was going, but when he headed back in the same direction from which he'd come, she instantly frowned. Had he walked over to her house simply to run Hayden off? *He watches from a distance; it is you who will reveal his identity.* But hadn't she already done that? She lowered the window halfway and climbed into bed, but she couldn't settle her mind. Something felt off with Nigel, but she was unable to see his face clearly, so she couldn't detect his emotions. She pulled the covers over her head and eventually fell asleep.

That morning, Lori awoke to the delicious aroma of breakfast drifting up the stairs. Her stomach growled and she sat up in bed as a light breeze lifted the curtain. She forgot about leaving the window open the night before, so she leaned over and pushed it closed. Glancing down to where Hayden was standing the night before, she saw no sign that he had ever been there now. Had it not been for her conversation with Nigel, she would have sworn she was dreaming. She'd been doing a lot of that lately, ever since Hayden left. Then her eyes widened in a moment of understanding. *He's back.*

"Lori, are you awake?" her mother asked, peeking into the room.

"Yeah."

"We have to run over to Dean's house; do you want to come with us?"

"Maybe next time. I have a lot of work to catch up on and I asked Jesse to meet me at the store today." It wasn't a total lie, but she knew Steve would be stopping by and she didn't want to get into that conversation with her mother.

"Well, at least eat something before you go. Dean left you a plate on the stove."

"Wait." Lori picked up the teddy bear off the pillow as her mother pushed open the door and entered the room. "I was sorting through a few boxes in my closet last night and I came across this bear." She held out the teddy bear as her mother sat down beside her on the bed.

"I remember it well. You were so upset, you threw it across the room, saying, "I don't want no stupid bear, I just want my daddy." You cried so hard that night." A sad smile appeared on her mother's face as she rubbed her hand over the bear's head.

"I had a vision last night, or at least, I think that's what it was." Lori expected her mother to say she was crazy, but instead, she waited attentively to hear more. "Dad was driving down the highway, and he placed the teddy bear on the dash of the truck. He was smiling and happy, just like he always was when he was at home. Then a loud thud sounded and the truck swerved."

"He was coming home from work when the accident happened." Tears filled her mother's eyes when she looked down at the teddy bear. "To this day, no one knows what caused the wreck. Did you see anything else?" her mother inquired.

"No, just Dad putting a piece of paper into the heart pocket." Lori nodded and her mother looked down. "Go ahead," she urged.

Her mother was a bit hesitant, but she pulled the paper out and unfolded it. Lori wasn't sure how her mother would respond, but when the smile lit up her face, she smiled with her.

"That sounds like something he would write. I have so many letters from him; he was a romantic at heart." Her mother sighed, remembering. "He loved you so much. I'm glad you found the note." She wrapped her arm around Lori and pulled her into a hug.

"Me too."

Twenty-Seven

Lori

Lori waited until her mother and Dean pulled out of the drive, then she got dressed and headed down the stairs. Swiping a piece of bacon off the plate when she passed through the kitchen, she decided she would eat later. She draped her coat around her shoulders as she hurried toward the door. The house seemed empty since her mother and Dean left, and for the first time in her life, she understood what her mother meant when she said the house had *lost its spirit.*

After locking the front door, Lori pulled her phone from her bra and dialed Jesse's number as she ambled over to the swing. "How's it hanging?" she snickered, knowing Jesse would probably roll her eyes at the greeting. "You want to meet up at the store today? I thought I might go in for a few hours."

"Sure, what time?" Jesse asked. Lately, Jesse had been keeping regular tabs on her, and although it wasn't necessary, her intentions were good.

"Thirty minutes. Steve just pulled up and I'll have him give me a ride." Lori looked up as Steve put the truck in park and silence stretched over the phone. Jesse didn't think being there with Steve all alone was a good idea, but that was because she was on Team Hayden, ever since hooking up with Tucker. "It's not what you think, so loosen the reins and I'll see you shortly," Lori said as she hung up the phone, but not before wolfy-girl growled her disapproval.

"Why are you outside? Are you trying to freeze to death?" Steve asked as he rounded the truck with a huge grin on his face. Lori grinned back.

"Nah, freezing to death would be an unexcused absence, and Jesse would never let me live it down." Lori laughed when Steve's brows knitted in confusion. "I have to work today."

"Oh. I thought the boutique was closed on Saturdays. I was hoping we could spend some time together," Steve muttered, and his disappointment didn't go unnoticed. He wasn't angry, or even the type of guy to show anger... although she did remember one time in her junior year when he practically shoved Rafe Michaels through the gymnasium wall. Lori swore she was fine and never mentioned the headache she received from the well-aimed football. Or the wink Rafe gave her once Steve turned away.

"Well, I still have an twenty-five minutes before I have to be there, so you can give me a ride." The awkwardness that arose between them the last time he visited was back and she swallowed the dread as Steve took a seat next to her on the swing.

"So, did your mother kick you out?" Steve chuckled, but Lori saw the quick glance he shot at the front door.

"No! I needed to clear my mind and being trapped inside isn't working." He reached over and pinched her snarled lip, leaning back in the swing, his jean-clad legs stretching in front of him.

"You know, I have to leave today." He placed his arm behind her head and twirled a strand of her hair between his fingers. It was a friendly gesture and one she was usually comfortable with, until now.

"Yeah, I figured you would be heading back soon. I'm sorry we didn't get to hang out, but with the packing and all." She fidgeted, and he smiled.

"So it's really happening? You're moving?"

"Yeah, how crazy is that?"

"You know, it's going to be weird, you not being here. I always thought you would live here," Steve said as Lori tucked her hands between her knees so he wouldn't see how nervous she felt.

"I did too, but eventually, everybody grows up and moves on. And it's for the best." Lori stiffened when he put his hand on her chin and turned her to face him.

"I love you," he said, his eyes searching hers before he pulled her into a hug. It felt desperate and unsure, not like Steve at all.

"I love you too." It wasn't the first time she told him she loved him, but it was the first time he ever looked at her as if there could be something more going on between them.

"But..." He pulled back as she gazed at his boots.

"You mean more to me than you realize. You've always been here when I needed you, but you never needed me." He started to object and she lifted her hand. "I don't blame you for leaving Cloverly. And I was only upset because everyone I loved was moving on with their lives, and here I sat." She gave a side glance as he looked over at his truck, probably planning his next escape.

"There's nothing wrong with you being here. I liked knowing you were here. It gave me something to look forward to whenever I came home," he said, studying her.

"But you don't come home that often anymore. You weren't here for Christmas, or New Year's, and if it hadn't been for my wreck, you probably wouldn't be here now. I'm not blaming you, or mad, but I'm ready to proceed with my life and in order to do so, I have to leave Cloverly."

"Can't you wait until after I graduate? Then you can move in with me! We can be together, just like old times. Hang out, and go anywhere you want." He took her hand and she pulled it away to cover her mouth, pretending to cough.

"I know you mean well, and it sounds wonderful, but I don't want to be here anymore; my heart is in the mountains." She tucked her phone back into her bra, causing Steve to chuckle, and she rolled her eyes.

"Then *we'll* move to the mountains. It's not my ideal place, but I'll adjust as long as we're together."

"That's easy to say now, but eventually, you'd hate me for making you live there. You would go crazy. It's not where you want to be. I remember all the times you talked about moving west." She looked down at his hand that was now resting on her thigh. “You’re the best friend a girl could ask for. There’s a special girl out there for you, just waiting to fall in love with you. You deserve to be happy with a woman who adores you.” She looked up and met his eyes.

“I’m here with you though, asking you to fall in love with me.” He leaned in and kissed her, but she didn’t return the kiss.

“You don’t understand,” she said when he pulled back. She didn’t miss his brooding expression, and she sensed he knew what was coming. “I’ve already given my heart to Hayden.” She picked at the rip in her jeans, unable to face what she knew she’d see in his eyes. “I’m sorry. You’ve always had my love, but you just never managed to capture my heart.”

Steve drew in a deep breath as he stood and walked across the porch. His shoulders slumped with her rejection and she wanted to take everything back, if only to make him happy. “Steve,” she said and he held up his hand.

“Don’t. I shouldn’t have come here expecting you would want to be with me after the way I left you... when I knew you needed me. I could have waited another year, and we could have gotten an apartment together, somewhere off campus. I was selfish then and I failed to consider your feelings.”

“But you’re doing what makes you happy. You’re living your life, which is exactly what I want to do. I want to go to college and pursue new experiences for the rest of my life. I want to spend it doing what I want, not what others expect me to do. We don’t have to give up what we have even if we do run in different circles. You’re my best friend, and you always will be until the day I die. You've always been like a brother to me, watching over me, but I'm not that little girl anymore. I love you with all my heart, so don't walk away thinking I don't give a shit about you… because that's not true. I need you as my best friend, now more than ever. I mean, who else is brave enough to keep me in line?" She stood up and walked across the porch, placing her hand on his shoulder.

"You know, I never wanted to cause a problem between you and him... I just saw you slipping away and I tried to prevent it." Steve looked down, blinking the moisture from his eyes, which made her feel like a total ass. He was so sweet. Why he put up with her even now, was a complete mystery. There were plenty of girls in high school that he could have dated, and on occasion, he did go out, but mostly, he just hung out wherever Lori was. "Life is hard, and it's so much harder when you see the one person that has always been there, waiting in the wings, suddenly start moving on. I don't fault you for wanting to leave. I just didn't want you to leave me."

"I'm not leaving you! I'm just branching out to see what life has to offer." She bit her lip; her own eyes tearing as her heart crumbled into a million pieces. *Would it be bad to give in, and try to be with him?* Best friends who become lovers was a dream she often had, but no longer did her dreams revolve around Steve.

Steve smiled and lifted her chin, his eyes staring into hers. "Promise me you'll always be my best friend. And that I can call you anytime." That was already a given. He didn't have to ask.

"Of course you can. Nothing's changed. That's what best friends are for," she said and he leaned down and kissed her forehead. Tears threatened to spill from her eyes again, but she wrapped her arm around his waist, so he wouldn't notice.

"When did you grow up and become so smart?" he asked, rocking her from side to side, his cheek resting on top of her head.

"When you pushed me out of my comfort zone," she mumbled into his coat and he laughed.

"I don't like this, but I understand it, unfortunately." Steve released his hold. "Tell your boyfriend for me that he won, but I will always be waiting. One screw-up from him and I'll be back with a vengeance."

"I'll be sure to pass on the message but I'm not sure he'll ever come back. He's in Tennessee now. He thinks I chose you over him."

"That's my fault, not yours. I was angry when I saw him at the hospital with you lying there in that bed. I lied and told him I was your boyfriend. My world crashed that day. I knew I lost you to someone I couldn't compete with. And you don't have to make any excuses. I saw the way he looked at you. I knew then I didn't have a snowball's chance in hell, but you can't blame me for trying. He's a lucky man. He'll be back."

"I hope you're right," she said as a tear slipped down her cheek. Steve was the only person that had ever seen her cry, until she met Hayden. Now it seemed that was all she ever did, and she wasn't a wimp-ass, timid girl. She wiped the tears away. "Could you give me a ride to the store?"

"As if you had to ask." Steve took her arm and helped her down the steps. *You could give him a chance... what could it hurt?* But if it meant she would have to give up

Hayden, the thought alone made her stomach churn.

Once Steve had her belted in the truck, he closed the door and hurried around to the driver's side. *Damn that grin.* She smiled and said, "If you don't have anything to do, you can hang out with us at the store. I have a lot of boxes to move, and it's kind of hard to do with only one hand." She chuckled as he started the truck and backed out of the drive.

"Oh, I see how it is. You don't want my heart, but you'll keep me around for my brawn." He flexed his arm but through his heavy coat, she couldn't see his muscles. She snorted. "I can live with that, but how do you think your boyfriend will feel about me spending the night at your apartment?" Steve flicked his brows suggestively and grinned.

"He'll be pissed beyond reason, but he'll just have to deal with it." Lori snickered.

By the time they arrived at the boutique, Lori's ribs hurt from so much laughter, and Steve returned to being her best friend. The morning was spent with Steve moving boxes out to the floor as Lori and Jesse sorted through the newest shipment that arrived on Friday.

"I'm glad to see you and Steve are working things out," Jesse said when he disappeared into the warehouse.

"Yeah, too bad he has to leave." Lori smiled and glanced over her shoulder, finally able to breathe again.

"So does that mean you're going to give Hayden a chance?"

"I'm still not sure how I fit into his life. It's not like I live on the mountain, and I don't think any long distance relationship will last." Lori looked back but didn't miss the frown that Jesse quickly hid.

"Well, ladies, this is the last box," Steve announced, cutting their conversation short. "And as much as I love hanging out with you, I must now leave." Lori snorted when he bowed and Jesse chuckled and rolled her eyes.

"Care for an escort?" Lori asked, and his grin widened.

"But of course, milady." He held out his arm and Lori latched onto it and walked with him to the door. "Love you," he said, pulling her into a tight hug.

"Love you, back. Be careful and call me when you get home," Lori reminded him as he kissed her forehead and waved goodbye to Jesse.

"Keep it real." He smiled before walking out the door, and Lori's heart dropped to her stomach as she ran out after him.

"Don't forget me."

Steve grabbed her around the waist and lifted her off the ground. "Tell your boyfriend I'll be checking in, and often. I can be his worst nightmare if he does anything to hurt you." Hearing the serious tone of his voice, Lori expected he would hold true to his threat. She sniffled when he placed her on her feet and rubbed his hand through her hair. It was a reassuring gesture she always loved over the years, but now, she was beginning to think she missed something that could have been. She glanced up, not expecting to see the emotion she glimpsed in his brown eyes. "Stay out of trouble."

"That's easier said than done," she said and he winked. Lori stood on the sidewalk until Steve drove out of sight, her heart trailing after him. He'd been like a brother to her for so many years that it hurt like hell to watch him go. She drew in a deep breath as she turned to the door.

"I'm sorry. I know that was hard for you, but it's Steve, and he'll be back," Jesse said before pulling her into a hug.

"No, I think too much has changed. He never needed me, and as soon as he gets back to school, I'm sure he'll realize that," she said as she wiped her eyes. "I'm going to miss him. So much." Lori sighed as they walked back into the store.

"Are you okay?"

She nodded yes, but there was no mistaking the sadness in her eyes. She feared she would never see Steve again, on top of the possibility she would never see Hayden again either, and those two thoughts soon had her holding back more tears.

"He's your best friend, right? Best friends last forever; no matter what, they will never desert you. Ask me how I know." Jesse smiled, leading Lori further into the store. "Now, would you mind telling me why you insisted on working on Saturday?"

"It was the best excuse I could come up with to avoid going back with Mom and Dean. I want to pack my things. I'm taking the apartment."

Twenty-Eight

Lori

Who said living on your own was exciting? It sure as heck wasn't Lori. She licked the spoon she was holding as she glanced across the small living room. It was Wednesday night, and she wondered if she could survive the boredom until the weekend. She hoped it would change once she was settled into the apartment, but nope, four days later and still nothing. She was alone most of the time, which she didn't totally mind. But she missed her neighbors if only to wave at them from the front porch.

And what the hell was up with Steve? Waiting two full days before calling to tell her he arrived safely and was back at college. Was she that easy to forget? It pretty much confirmed that she made the right decision by not surrendering to his requests.

Lori glanced over at the flannel shirt lying on the back of the sofa. Apparently, Hayden was in such a hurry to get away from her that he didn't bother to check the laundry basket beneath the bathroom sink. But if he were so hell-bent on putting more distance between them, why did his wolf return? She mulled that over as she shut off the television.

Watching Monkey-Man playing baseball on T.V. usually lifted her spirits, but now she was even more depressed. She chalked that up to Hayden, *the big baboon*, and made him the reason why she ate so much strawberry ice cream that she thought she would puke.

Dragging herself off the sofa, she grabbed Hayden's flannel shirt and held it up to her nose. A deep inhale had her gliding into the bedroom, her mind traveling back to the morning she awoke in his bed. His musky scent filled the air and she could almost imagine him wearing the exact same shirt, unbuttoned and hanging open. He was so magnificent to look at and nothing about his body screamed snakes, snails, or puppy-dog tails. No way! He was rugged, ripped, and sexy as hell. She tittered as she pulled the shirt on over her t-shirt, allowing his scent to soothe her soul.

It had been four days since she saw Hayden's wolf outside her bedroom window, and she wondered if it had returned to the neighborhood. Would it sense she moved out of the house? If so, would it come looking for her? Secretly, she hoped Hayden would return to plead his undying love. She rolled her eyes, knowing she would never admit that. What the hell was it, anyway? Bond mates for life? It sounded too good to be true, and well, everyone knows how that ends up.

Her mother and Dean finished moving everything out of the house and it now sat empty, a symbol of what Lori's life had become. Why did she think that moving into the apartment was a good idea? Now, she felt more isolated than ever. She could only thank her rebellious nature for that. She was offered the west wing of a beautiful mansion, but her pride insisted she didn't need her mother's boyfriend to take care of her.

Unfortunately, being in the apartment just made her think of Hayden. Everything she saw reminded her of him and she wasn't sure her heart could take anymore rejection. *You didn't stop him from leaving. It's your fault he's gone!* Her inner voice would have been screaming at that moment if it could actually have been heard. She pulled the shirt tighter before crawling into bed. She had lost another three pounds, making her look more like a stick figure than the young lady she was. Squeezing her eyes shut tightly, she waited until her body warmed up before drifting off to sleep.

Restless dreams kept her mind strumming and she tossed and turned on the mattress. Mumbling out loud, and even swatting back, her fist began hitting the pillow and her breath caught as she struggled against the unseen attacker. "No!" she screamed when she shot upright in the bed. The dream was so real, she could still feel the knife slicing through her ribs. She glanced around the room and listened when the heating unit kicked on. "It was a dream," she whispered to comfort herself but that didn't stop her body from quivering, or block the image of red blood dripping off the blade. She reached overhead and parted the window blinds, allowing the streetlight to brighten the room. *You just had to watch the vampires, didn't you?* She couldn't stop the grin on her lips, knowing Hayden would have been frowning if he knew she was on Team Edward. How funny was that? Then her eyes widened. *Are vampires real?*

Mentally rolling her eyes, she crawled out of bed, trying to forget her shitty life. Since when did she take life so seriously anyhow? *After meeting Katherine and her snotty friends on the mountain.* That was just another reason why Hayden would have been better off without her. She shouldn't have tried to be something she wasn't to gain his favor. It sucked.

Wide awake, she slipped on her shoes and walked out of the room. Her nerves were strung tight and she longed to hear an encouraging word, someone who could tell her everything would be all right... but those words never came. She sighed and put on her coat as she glimpsed the DVDs lying on the coffee table. *Oh yeah, Hayden would be pissed!*

The metal steps creaked beneath her weight as she descended the stairs, causing the security lights to click on. The overhead pipes clanged randomly in a sinister tune—a cacophony only a horror fan could fully appreciate. She shivered and zipped up her coat.

She glanced over at the stack of pallets that were completely hidden in the darkest corner of the warehouse and her heart grew heavy. Remembering the kiss she shared with Hayden, she wished he would return. She longed to confess everything she held in her heart, and expose her soul. If that didn't work, she was ready to get down on her knees and beg. She loved him.

Reaching inside the small, zippered pocket, she was searching for the house key, and sighed when she felt it safely tucked away in there. Homesick for her bedroom, she pulled open the side door and glanced down the road. Two blocks further and she would be home, back in the house where she grew up, the vault of all her childhood memories. Just one more night was all she needed. At least that was what she told herself as she exited the building. She tucked her hands into her pockets and lowered her head against the whispering breeze as she hurried toward Main Street.

Stopping at the corner, she blew into her hands, warming her nose and looking across the street to the park. It was two in the morning and most everyone was asleep. Her thoughts drifted. She liked having fun and laughing. It was better than dwelling on shit she couldn't change, or unleashing her suppressed sailor whenever anyone ticked her off. *Yeah, too bad you didn't introduce that dormant beast to Katherine!* She snarled and looked both ways down the street, weighing her options. *The park or an empty house?*

When the signal turned green, she took it as an omen and ran across the street to the park swings that were swaying in the breeze. With half a glance at the rusted chain clinking against the flagpole, she sat down in the nearest swing. She sucked in a deep breath and turned to her left, picturing Hayden in the swing beside her. Being with him that day, her heart felt light and free, and she was so happy. Another reason why Hayden was better off without her. She was too foolish to see what was right in front of her eyes. *You made your choice, and it wasn't Hayden.* She jumped out of the swing and ran over to the tornado slide to escape her toxic thoughts. If she thought it could help, she would have beaten some sense into herself, right there in the dark.

As the winds rustled the barren branches, she rested her head against the metal cage of the slide. Hidden in the shadows of a large oak tree, it was the perfect place to hide out, unseen from any passersby. Her version of the porch swing, a favorite place she could visit on nights when sleep eluded her. Then she remembered Hayden's arms, and how much she loved having them around her as they slid down the slide.

How could a person be so wrong about everyone in their life? Hayden, her mother, even her father, when she thought about it now... Nobody was what they seemed. Including Megan and Brid. Steve might as well be lumped in there somewhere too. The one person who remained the same, despite being changed, was Jesse. She held no secrets and had no ulterior motives, and she would never do anything that could result in heartache. *So why aren't you listening to her advice?*

Lori pulled her knees to her chest and closed her eyes as her mind quieted until the only sound was the low ringing in her ears. Then the winds picked up, and her eyes opened as she peeked out of her hidey-hole. Hearing the sound of rustling leaves, she tilted her head as if that would magnify it. She was being ridiculous if she thought Hayden would come back for her now, but that didn't stop her from inching out of the metal box and scanning the park below. When she was positive she was alone, she quietly climbed down the steps.

The dizzying scent of mountain air, smoke, and crisp, cold nights slammed into her stealing her breath. She staggered backwards and dropped to her knees, unable to control the dull ache that settled deep inside her core. It had been much too long since she last saw Hayden and her body was craving his touch like a junkie craves his next fix. She inhaled a deep breath and thought she had to be out-of-her-mind crazy to be alone in the dark. She was hoping to see… what? A werewolf?

Golden flames flashed in the night and she sucked in a quick breath, her suspicion confirmed—it was Hayden. *But what if you're wrong?* No, she couldn't be wrong about that. Only Hayden could make her heart flutter with his nearness. Her thoughts raced, and she expected to see him in wolf form. Funny but the flare of his eyes automatically eased her mind, and the idea of running her fingers through his wolf's fur seemed much more appealing.

With her head down and her chin tucked firmly against her chest, her body quivered as the wolf stalked closer. Praying her instincts weren't wrong, the steps slowed, and she froze, wondering if she had made a mistake. What if it wasn't Hayden? *It's a wolf!* Her inner voice screamed as she gasped so hard, it lifted her hair. *I know!* She mentally screamed back. She was at the point of no return and willing to risk everything to see him again. She peeked out through her lashes, seeing the large paw that rested on her knee. With the slightest movement, her fingers lightly rubbed its toes, and then its claws, while her eyes drifted up, meeting the wolf's gaze.

"Hayden?" she asked, uncertain, yet very sure. "You came back." She slowly offered her hand, and he sniffed and then licked her palm, making her smile. "I'm so glad you came back." Throwing her arms around his neck, she cried into his fur as he nuzzled against her. The warmth of his body chased away the cold. Lori wanted to stay right there on the ground until sunup. "I wasn't sure I'd ever see you again." Her heart felt lonely although being there with Hayden's wolf rekindled her hope that they could work things out. Then the wolf bristled and jerked out of her arms and she looked away, hoping it wouldn't see her as a threat. *Karma,* she thought, yelping when a pair of large hands grabbed her off the ground and pinned her against the oak tree.

His shushing voice whispered in her ear, warning her not to move. He inhaled through his nose, and his own body trembled. "I like when you touch my wolf." His breathing grew more rapid, and he looked down, meeting her eyes, his desire now becoming hers. "What are you doing out here alone? It's not safe."

"Why?" she mouthed, watching his eyes as they pierced the night, searching for something she couldn't see. He was fully alert, and she was on edge, together, their hearts drummed a symphony behind that damn tree. What on earth could have frightened him? A badass wolf? Then her dream flashed in her mind and being in the park suddenly scared the hell out of her. Resting her head against his chest, her pulse skipped when she realized he wasn't wearing any clothes.

"When I tell you to run, go, get back inside," he instructed while her heart thumped in her ears and she shuddered.

"What about you?" she said so low, she wasn't sure she actually uttered the words.

"Lock the door."

"But..."

Hayden lifted her against the tree, and she wrapped her legs around his waist, his warning instantly forgotten.

With her arms fastened tightly around his neck; she wanted to feel his body next to hers, their hearts beating as one. She pulled him into a kiss, needing him to want her the way she had wanted him since the first day on the mountain.

He licked over her bottom lip as he pulled out of the kiss, his panting breath lifting her hair. "I love you, Lori. Never forget that." He slowly placed her back on her feet, her heart skipping with his words.

Was that goodbye? Before she could ask him, a familiar voice sounded behind Hayden and he spun around, shielding her from Beth.

"How inappropriately appealing," Beth said, her eyes trailing down Hayden's naked body.

"What do you want?" The sneer in his voice sounded more like a growl and Lori scrunched her brows.

"Come on, Hayden, haven't we already established that?" A menacing grin spread across her face as she stepped forward, her hand landing on his chest. "You really should reconsider my offer."

"Get your nasty ass away from him!" Lori spat as she emerged from behind Hayden, her glare aiming daggers at Beth. Apparently, their conversation at the boutique was more complicated than it appeared, which explained why Beth was so pissed when she walked out of the store. Hayden never mentioned her offer, but Lori never really gave him the chance.

"What is she doing here?" Beth narrowed her now angry eyes. "You want to talk nasty? Did you tell Hayden how you were huddled up with Nigel at the gas station? How he was standoffish, protecting his little female fling? Yeah, you thought no one noticed, but I saw everything,"

Beth sneered, her words stealing Lori's breath. "You're like a pesky gnat that never goes away."

"It was not like that," Lori said defensively, but seeing Hayden's glance, she knew he wasn't so sure.

"Poor, little Lori couldn't keep Hayden's attention, so she ran off in the night, crying on Nigel's shoulder. I guess for his age, even you were better than nothing." Beth laughed when Hayden growled. "Don't act like you didn't notice. I can smell his scent on her from here."

"Do not insinuate things you know nothing about," Hayden warned. "She is my mate!"

Beth's eyes flared as she locked onto Lori, a low growl rumbling her chest.

"It was you, wasn't it?" Hayden asked, pushing Lori behind him.

"I was trying to do you a favor so you wouldn't look so pathetic mating with a human female." Beth squared her shoulders and looked down her nose.

"Those were your prints in the snow, and you were masking your scent." Hayden growled as his body stretched taller, towering over Beth.

"Yeah, but you can't prove that." Beth refused to back down.

"Are you sure?" Hayden shifted his body, his growl becoming much louder. But it was the next word out of his mouth that unleashed a bolt of fear that raced up Lori's spine. "Run!"

Everything happened so quick, it didn't even register that Beth was moving towards her until Hayden roared and grabbed Beth by the hair, slamming her against a tree.

"If you ever touch my mate again..." Hayden didn't have time to finish his threat, before a low growl cut through the night and he yelled back to Lori. "Get out of here!"

Lori jumped to her feet, long past tired of the she-wolves that thought they could bully her. "No!" she screamed. "If it's me she wants, here I am! Take your best shot!"

That was all it took to provoke Beth, and Lori froze when Beth's eyes flared right before she phased. Locking eyes with the large, gray wolf, Lori thought it looked like a rabid monster out for blood. Namely hers. Her thoughts turned to Jesse, and the seriousness of the situation coldcocked her back to reality.

"GO NOW!" Hayden demanded, but it was him phasing right before her eyes, that had her running for her life.

Twenty-Nine

Hayden

Sneaking back to Cloverly in the early dawn hours, Hayden was beyond pissed when he found Lori alone at the park. After receiving a call from Tucker the night before, he was excited to learn Steve was back in Oklahoma, and Lori hadn't fallen for his boyfriend routine. But finding out she was now living in Jesse's old apartment troubled his wolf. He wanted to pull her into his arms and shake some sense into her. She was reckless in her actions, and it was high time he put his foot down. He peered around the park, and waited until Lori came out of her hiding place, before exposing his wolf to her. He realized she immediately recognized him by the sudden gasp and the slight smile that followed. How could he be irritable about that?

Striding over to where Lori was kneeling on the ground, he took in her sweet scent. He wanted to lap her up, every inch of her, until she squealed with delight. That was wishful thinking, and now, not likely to happen.

Scenting another wolf in the neighborhood, he phased and grabbed her off the ground. Holding her against the tree was his means of concealing her scent while hoping the wolf would continue on its way.

But Beth appearing behind him wasn't something he foresaw, and Lori being there seemed to surprise Beth. Admitting she was at the accident site was the first of Beth's mistakes. The second was when he recognized her odor was unusual. Beth didn't understand the role Lori played in Hayden's life, until he foolishly made the mistake of calling her his mate. Beth had formerly believed Lori was nothing more than a nuisance, but now she knew better.

His hackles rose when the blonde shifted her attention to Lori, but what Hayden didn't perceive was Lori issuing her own threat and refusing to leave his side… it made him proud to be her mate.

Seeing the fire in Beth's eyes, and her wolf urging her to phase, he harshly yelled for Lori to go. It wasn't his intent to frighten Lori, but one nip from the demented, gray wolf was all it would take to change her into a new blood—if she lived through the transformation. If she died, it would devastate Hayden, and he wasn't willing to go about his life without Lori.

Unable to hold back his wolf, Hayden phased as Beth darted past, his mighty jaws catching her by the scruff. His wolf gave a firm shake as Lori pushed open the door and ducked into the dark building.

The growl that escaped Hayden was vicious, and outright deadly. But it was best to let Jack deal with Beth since he was the alpha in Cloverly. Had they been on the mountain, Beth would have faced her maker. He slammed the wolf to the ground and bared his teeth in warning.

Stepping away, Hayden didn't miss Beth's wolf searching for an escape. She would go into hiding, if she had the chance, especially now that he was onto her. She was the wolf at the accident sight, and he believed she was also the reason for the crash. He growled another warning when Beth rolled over onto her belly and then stood on wobbly legs. She was fighting off Hayden's alpha vibe, realizing he had no authority to hold her there. She was very clever, but he would be her downfall.

Hayden stepped back and allowed Beth space, expecting if she were wise she would phase. If not, she would encounter the wrath of his wolf, and his wolf was determined to take her down.

Glancing up at the apartment windows, to see if the lights had come on, Hayden suspected Lori was frightened, and he hoped it wasn't because of him. Then movement out the corner of his eyes had him jerking his head when he grasped there was another wolf in the vicinity. He sniffed the air, the scent vaguely familiar to his nose.

Taking his distraction as an opportunity to flee, Beth bolted toward Main Street. Without thinking, Hayden followed what he felt to be the immediate threat, and was hot on her heels. Trying to catch up with Beth, while maintaining a visual of the male rushing across the park, Hayden failed to notice the truck that swerved to avoid a collision with the gray wolf.

Rolled beneath the truck tires, he laid on the side of the road barely able to breathe. The impact was felt instantly, the burning pain crushing his chest. His wolf could heal the severe injury, but seeing the male wolf phase, and follow Beth, he was even more determined to get Lori help.

It took everything Hayden had to peel his battered body off the ground, but Lori needed protection and that would come in the form of Tucker. *If you can get to his cabin.* It was risky for him to move until the damage was healed, but this time it couldn't be about him. Hayden staggered until he gathered his bearing's and then bolted down Main Street.

Seeing the lights on at Tucker's cabin gave him hope that his brother would be able to protect Lori, since he had obviously failed her. Twice. Rushing up onto the porch, he quickly phased, putting his own life in danger. But without Lori, he didn't deserve to live.

Shouldering the door open, Hayden face planted onto the floor, his energy spent. He couldn't move. He couldn't open his eyes. He couldn't warn them that Lori was under attack. He could, though, hear, and Tucker's voice instantly comforted him.

"Hayden, what happened?" Tucker's footsteps bounded across the room, and he kneeled, the floorboards groaned beneath his weight. Still, Hayden was unable to communicate, and when Tucker rolled him over, Jesse gasped.

"Who did this?" Tucker roared as Jesse moved closer to the scene. Hayden's eyes briefly opened and then rolled to the back of his head. Tucker shook his shoulder. "Call an ambulance!"

"Get Lori!" Hayden wheezed, knowing if he survived to see daylight he would be lucky.

"We have to get you to the hospital," Tucker argued, and Jesse walked around them and out the front door. She was speaking swiftly, to someone on the phone, and realizing what Hayden already knew. He was a goner, but if they acted quickly, Lori still had a chance.

"Lori!" That was the last thing Hayden said as his body shut down, surrendering to the injury.

The next time Hayden opened his eyes, the glaring overhead light surged through his brain. He squinted, unable to bring his hand up to cover his eyes. "Where am I?"

"You're in an ambulance," Dr. Williams replied, before advising him to remain still.

Hayden fought to get off the gurney, but apparently, restraints were in place. "I can't stay here. He's after Lori!" He winced when the needle penetrated his skin and within seconds, his eyes became heavy and his mind muddled.

Everything around him relaxed as his body drifted on an easy breeze. *It was pleasant, and warm, the sunlight casting soft shadows over the mountainside. He could see the ridge, and the alpha house, and suddenly he was standing in the backyard. He was home, and as he turned, he smiled when Lori stepped out the backdoor to greet him.*

"What took you so long?" she asked, rushing across the yard to wrap her arms around his waist.

"I don't know." He was disoriented, and he chalked it up to being excited about the day. He led her over to a

small weathered bench that overlooked the mountains. He wasn't a romantic male, but he had every intention of winning Lori's heart. He dropped onto one knee and held out a small black box for her to see. "Lori, I know I'm far from perfect, but if you will do me the honor, I promise to cherish you forever." He flipped open the lid and her eyes widened. "Will you be my wife?"

"Hayden," Lori replied, shock registering on her face. "I know the plan was for us to live here on the mountain, but I would be misleading you if I said this was where I wanted to be."

Stunned by her confession, Hayden couldn't find the words to question why. He hurried to his feet, assuming he had heard wrong. She had yet to accept the bond, but the proposal was essentially the same concept. Right? He recognized the confusion in her eyes and heard the sudden intake of air as she reached to close the box. Her actions speaking loud and clear.

"This," she fluttered her hand in the air, "is beautiful, but my heart is in Oklahoma."

His heart stopped beating in that brief moment as he struggled to recall what Oklahoma meant to her. "Why? When? I thought..." He didn't know what he thought. Lori had turned his life upside down in a matter of seconds, but what she said next totally destroyed his world.

"I love you, but this isn't the life I want. I refuse the bond."

Hayden wanted to beg her to reconsider, but it was too late. She didn't want to be with him and he contributed that to him being a shifter. He couldn't change what he was, and he couldn't force her to stay. His wolf was distraught and should have walked away, but instead, it insisted on finding the male that stole Lori away from them.

Watching as she turned and sauntered away, Hayden fought hard, but ultimately his wolf forced a phase. Blazing a trail down the mountainside, not only had Hayden lost the one female that meant everything to him, he had also lost control of his wolf.

Hayden sucked in a pained breath and his eyes shot open. It was just a dream, but that didn't stop his heart from shattering.

Thirty

Jesse

Parked beside the boutique, Jesse could see the side door open, so she grabbed the clothes that were tucked beneath the seat and jumped out of the truck. Racing to find Tucker, she didn't care that she left the headlights on, or that the driver's door was open. She slid to a stop inside the warehouse where Tucker phased and took the clothes she held in her hand.

"Where's Lori?" she frantically asked, her eyes searching.

"I think she's upstairs."

"Lori!" Jesse yelled, taking the stairs two at a time. She had no clue who would be after Lori, but if anyone touched her best friend, they would soon deal with the wrath of her wolf. She turned as Tucker raced up behind her, his shoulder shoving open the door. "Lori!" she yelled again, moving toward the bedroom with Tucker one step behind.

Jesse pushed open the bathroom door and shoved the shower curtain to the side. "She's not in here." She looked over as Tucker reached for the closet door and held her breath. She expected if Lori were in there, she could be wielding a baseball bat and ready to target the first person that came into sight, but that wasn't the case.

"Lori, are you okay?" Tucker asked, stepping into the walk-in closet and stooping down to the floor.

"Don't touch me!" Lori screamed as she kicked out from the corner and hid her face on the floor.

"Shh, it's okay." Jesse stepped past Tucker and moved over to Lori who was fighting frantically against what she presumed to be a serious threat.

"Leave me alone!" Lori struggled to get away from Jesse, her fist hitting anything in her reach. "It's my fault!"

"No, it's okay. Hayden's okay." Jesse tried to play it down, but there was no mistaking the panic in Lori's voice. Hearing her hysterical screams, and seeing the fear in her eyes, her own body tensed up.

"She stabbed him. He's dead!" Lori hissed through gritted teeth.

"That's not true. The ambulance is taking him to the hospital. Dad is with him right now." Jesse tried to wrap her arms around Lori, but she couldn't be contained. She looked back as the emergency lights from the ambulance flashed through the blinds when they passed down Main Street.

"Liar! She was at the park. He told me to run."

"Who was at the park?" Tucker asked, his confusion echoing Jesse's.

"Beth! She was the reason I wrecked. He called her out. I should have never left him. She was after me."

"No, Lori, you're in shock. You need to calm down," Jesse said in a soothing voice.

"I know what I saw! The blood was dripping off the knife!" Lori glared and jerked away from Jesse.

"Lori, wait." Jesse pushed past Tucker but Lori wasted no time before she was heading out of the bedroom after emerging from the closet. "Where do you think you're going?" Jesse demanded. Tucker's face suggested he wasn't expecting her to nail her best friend with a red glare.

"I have a score to settle. It ends tonight!" The long drawn-out hiss and sneer of Lori's words as she turned, waving a long-handled butcher knife, was proof Lori wasn't thinking straight.

"Put the knife down." It was an order, but Lori wasn't listening as she moved across the room. "Put the knife down, now!" Jesse shot a glance at Tucker who was slowly making his way to the door.

"I will, right down her damn throat." Again, the sinister sneer in her words told Jesse to keep her distance. She always knew Lori was a hellcat, and now she was witnessing it firsthand.

"Stop it! You are not leaving this apartment," Jesse shot back, and when Lori turned, she slapped her across the face. "Get out of your head, dammit! Hayden is alive!" She didn't condone violence, but the slap caused Lori to drop the knife and Tucker swooped in and grabbed it off the floor.

Tears spilled over the red welt on Lori's face as she looked up at Tucker. "I never meant for Hayden to get hurt. I should have just walked away and none of this would have happened."

"No! You can't do that," Tucker pleaded. "It will destroy him."

"I've already destroyed him!" Lori yelled. Her body shook uncontrollably and when her knees buckled, Tucker caught her before she hit the floor.

"Call her mother," Tucker said as he laid her on the sofa before rushing over to the kitchen sink to get a damp towel.

Jesse's hands trembled as she searched her coat for her phone and her eyes glazed over. She'd never seen Lori so worked up, and witnessing the injury inflicted on Hayden, she had to wonder if Lori were the one who actually caused it.

"I know, I know. I'm right here!" Tucker grumbled and Jesse squeezed her eyes shut.

"Sorry." Jesse knew he was referring to her wolf sight, but when she was frightened, she couldn't control it. Her teeth chattered as she spoke into the phone, but Tucker placed a hand on her shoulder, and her body instantly calmed. The things that Lori said didn't make any sense to her, and she worried she was having a nervous breakdown.

"She's going to be fine," Tucker said while wiping over Lori's face.

Jesse shoved the phone back into her pocket as Brid called out from the warehouse. "Up here," she yelled and hurried down the steps to make sure Brid wouldn't fall coming up. "We don't know what happened, but Lori's talking out of her head. Can you stay with her? We have to get to the hospital."

"I'll tend to her, you go." Brid shooed them out the door as Seth walked into the warehouse.

"Can you stay?" Jesse asked, her eyes tearing up at the sight of her friend. "Please."

"That's why I'm here. Your dad is at the hospital with Hayden. Go."

"Thank you," Jesse called out as she and Tucker ran for the door. Since meeting Seth at the dance several months back, he had become one of her best friends.

"I know what you're thinking, but Seth is cocky and he can hold his own," Tucker assured as he helped Jesse into the truck.

Lori wielding a knife was the most frightening thing Jesse had ever seen, and the stiffness of her jaw was a further indication that Lori could land a punch. Lori had a smart mouth and could run a good bluff, but Jesse never saw her so enraged that she would actually threaten to kill someone. Whatever happened was very bad, based on Lori's actions alone, and she could only imagine what Hayden must have endured. Why was Hayden back in town anyway? "Can you make sense of this?" Jesse asked when Tucker started the truck and took off down the road.

"No, but if Beth were involved, there could only be one reason."

Thirty-One

Jesse

Jesse paced the waiting room while watching Jack shake his head and Alpha Cooper frown. It wasn't a heated conversation, but one she didn't dare interrupt. Her attention was drawn to the sliding glass doors when Tucker and Officer Riley entered the building.

"Anything?" Tucker asked as he hurried over to her side.

"No, but Alpha Cooper is here." She nodded and Tucker grabbed her hand, leading her in their direction.

"So he just showed up at your place?" The alpha asked when Tucker and Jesse joined them in the far corner of the room.

"Yeah, but it wasn't a social visit. He was trying to protect Lori," Jesse explained, and Tucker squeezed her hand—she frowned. She wasn't trying to be snippy with the Regional Alpha, but Tucker was in no shape to answer his questions. His main concern rested with his brother. "We found her hiding in the closet at the apartment..." Jesse's words trailed off when her dad and Dr. Stevens walked off the elevator. *That can't be good.*

"Something's wrong," Tucker whispered as Dr. Williams ran his hand over his jaw. He was stressing, that was the only way Jesse could describe his actions, and she expected they would all be before long.

"Alpha Cooper," Dr. Williams said as he and Dr. Stevens approached the group. "I'm not sure what Lori was talking about, but Hayden wasn't stabbed. His chest wound is deep, but that's not the worst of his injuries. The internal bleeding suggests he was run over, but why would he phase? The wolf heals faster than the human so it makes no sense why he would risk his life when the wolf could have healed the injury."

"He was protecting Lori. If he hadn't phased, she would most likely be dead now," Jesse said as her dad put his hand on Tucker's shoulder.

"Hayden is being transferred to the trauma unit in Tennessee. The life flight team is on the way. Alpha Wilson will be waiting for them there."

"When is he leaving?"

"They're flying in as we speak. If you would like to see him, now would be the time," Dr. Williams said, taking hold of Jesse's arm when she turned to follow Tucker. "Could I have a word with you?"

NO! She wanted to say, but if her dad wanted to speak to her, it suggested there was a problem so she prayed it had nothing to do with Hayden. She followed him down the hall and into an office where Sonya was waiting. "What's up?"

Dr. Williams stood by the door and closed it when Alpha Cooper and Nigel walked into the room.

"Nigel confirmed Beth was at the park, and that Hayden was hit. So if anyone asked, Hayden was on his way to my place when he ran out in front of a truck. Until we get all the details, including why Hayden was here, and why Lori accused Beth of attacking him, it needs to stay quiet," Alpha Cooper said as Nigel backed out of the room.

"Why would Beth attack Hayden? She didn't really know him." Jesse looked between her dad and Ben.

"That's not the rumor traveling through Kinsley. Supposedly, Hayden denied the bond with Lori after meeting Beth at the boutique," the alpha said and Jesse's heart dropped to her stomach.

"Oh, no! It's all my fault!" Jesse staggered over to the chair next to Sonya, not hearing her dad call her name. "I only wanted to make Lori jealous so she would value her attraction to Hayden more and know it was real. I never meant for this to happen. Lori thinks it was her fault that Hayden got hurt when really, it was mine."

"You didn't cause this." Dr. Williams was quick to defend her, but he didn't understand the ferocity of vindictive females.

"I did. I put the plan into motion. I told Tracy to brag about Tucker's brother and how he was going to become the alpha of the Mountain Pack. She said he was like royalty and she-wolves could smell it a mile away. I should have known better."

"Despite what you think, if Beth wanted to be with

Hayden, she wouldn't have attacked him. Something else must have happened and until we can talk to her, we can't jump to any unproven conclusions," Sonya said, reaching over and taking her hand.

"I agree. There's more going on and until we can speak to Beth, it's best we keep this quiet." Alpha Cooper rubbed his jaw, and she knew he was trying to play out different scenarios in his head.

"Except for one small detail we're not factoring in," Dr. Williams said. "Hayden said, *he's* after Lori, and I think he would know the difference between Beth and a male."

"I think Hayden was confused. Nigel chased after Beth, so he's probably the *he* that Hayden was referring too. We'll have to wait until we can talk to him again, so the story, if anyone asks, is that it was an accident. Is that perfectly clear?" Alpha Cooper looked over at Jesse. "Is there any way you can question Lori? And find out what she knows?"

"I'll do my best but I'm not sure she's in any condition to talk right now."

Jesse was exhausted by the time she left the hospital, but more worried about Lori. Hayden was in Tennessee undergoing surgery, and Tucker was out with Seth and Nigel, trying to piece together what happened. Everyone wanted to know why Beth responded the way she did.

Sitting at the small kitchen table, Jesse couldn't shake her guilt since she had a hand in Beth's attack. Not directly, but telling Tracy to flaunt Hayden to the unbonded females was her idea. She glanced toward the bedroom where Lori was still sleeping. It wasn't that long ago when she was living in the very same apartment. Boy!

How things had changed.

The smell of cut onions brought her attention back to the small kitchenette where Brid was busy fixing a large pot of vegetable soup—large enough to feed a small army. She looked up as Brid placed the lid on the pot.

"Can I ask you something?" Jesse took a sip of her cold coffee and then pushed it back on the table.

Brid turned and nodded.

"I called Lori's mother, but you showed up. How did you know?"

"Well, dear, I've known Linda for most of my life, since she moved here from Buffer County. And when she's out of town, I usually try to keep an eye on things."

"Oh, a friend of the family. It just seemed weird that you showed up so quickly after I talked to her. It makes sense now."

"Normally, it's quiet around here, so hearing the commotion, dare I say? I feared the worst," Brid explained. "I'm sure Linda tried to call me but since my apartment is right next door, she probably figured I was over here already."

Jesse jumped when the door opened and Tucker entered the room. He ditched the jogging pants for jeans, but still wore the black sweatshirt. She hurried over and greeted him with a kiss, pushing the hair out of his eyes. He was tired; she could see it on his face. He needed to sleep, but she hated him going home alone. "Any news?"

"Mom called and Hayden's out of surgery. Everything looks good." He sighed, blinking back tears. The positive news sent goosebumps up Jesse's arms as the strain exited from her body and she inhaled a deep breath.

"I'm so glad. I've been praying for him. I even called

Gramma to put him on the prayer list at church. Are you okay?" It was clear Tucker was still struggling to hold it together, but Jesse knew he would have to let it out or it would eat him alive.

He nodded and gently kissed the top of her head. She didn't miss the way he chewed his lower lip and sensed he was about to lose it. "You need to get out of those clothes," she said, leading him through the apartment to the bathroom. "There's nothing more you can do. Hayden will be okay. He's safe now, and where he needs to be."

Tucker waited until she shut the bathroom door, sealing them in the confined space. "I thought he was dying. I thought I lost my best friend." He shoved his fingers through his hair as tears welled in his eyes. There was no holding them back. She reached over and turned on the shower to drown out his sobs.

"I know you did. I was so worried about you." She pulled his shirt over his head and inhaled his scent. Just being there with him was calming and she kissed his chest where his heartbeat felt the strongest. "I love you so much. I can't stand to see you like this." A tear slipped down his cheek and she wiped it away. Her gentle giant seemed so sad, and her heart broke when he drew in a hesitant breath. His family was his world, and she was surprised he wasn't storming the town in a rage.

"You are not to leave my sight until this is straightened out. I won't lose you!" he said before drawing her into a kiss. The tender nip, followed by his warm tongue, heated her body and he placed her on the counter so she could wrap her legs around his waist.

What started out as a simple distraction ended up being the most passionate kiss Jesse had ever experienced.

Melting in his arms, she didn't even notice he had stepped into the shower until the warm water trickled down her face.

He placed her back on her feet and waited for her to remove her shirt and wiggle out of her jeans. She needed to be with him, more than she needed air to breathe. She closed her eyes as he trailed kisses along her shoulder and unfastened her bra, dropping it to her feet.

Thirty-Two

Jesse

Dressed in Tucker's shirt, Jesse sipped her coffee, while Tucker slept soundly on the sofa. Once Brid was gone, Jesse picked up the red rose she left on the small dinette table, and took a sniff, remembering her first date with Tucker.

He was caring and compassionate as he struggled to hide his emotions, thinking they made him look weak. But what Jesse experienced in the shower was living proof that a sensitive soul could be an amazing lover and she closed her eyes to envision it more vividly. *There was so much pain, passion, tenderness as he held onto her, his tears washing over her body.* A single tear rolled down her cheek. The love that bloomed in her heart burned deep in her soul and she knew if she ever lost him, her life would also be over.

She stared at the rose as Lori's raging image flashed in her mind. It was obvious she loved Hayden, and high time she did what was right for them both by accepting his bond.

Hearing a muffled sob, Jesse quietly got up and walked over to the bedroom door. The blanket shook with silent tears, and she slowly walked over to the bed and sat down on the floor. As she pulled the blanket back, Lori's blue eyes were red and puffy when they stared back at her. "It's okay, Lori." She gently pushed the hair off her face.

"No. Everything is my fault." Lori squeezed her eyes shut and hot tears streamed across her nose.

"Lori, listen to me. Just listen. Please." Jesse lifted Lori's hand and kissed her knuckles. "Hayden loves you more than life itself, and will stop at nothing to protect you. He would be lost without you; you have to know that." But Lori didn't respond. "Lucia called and Hayden is in recovery now. He's still alive." Lori's eyes snapped open as she stared through Jesse as if she were trying to picture Hayden.

"I know what I saw," her voice was tiny, as if she weren't convinced.

"What did you see? Tell me what happened."

"We were at the park, Hayden and I. Beth came up and... she got pissed I was there." Lori blinked rapidly as she squeezed Jesse's hand. "It was me she was after, not him." Her hiccupped breathing returned. "Hayden told me to get inside and lock the door. I hid in the closet because I was afraid."

"And you should have been. You were facing off

against a wolf that was twice your size. Hayden did the right thing by telling you to run. I'm just glad you were smart enough to listen." Jesse laced her fingers with Lori's. "There was no knife. Hayden ran out in front of a coal truck. It was a total accident."

Lori closed her eyes and her lip trembled. "That can't be. I swear, I saw a knife. It was large, a hunting knife, I think. It had a double-sided blade and wavelike hooks on one side. I felt it cut into my skin." She looked at Jesse. "It hurt like hell," she said as Jesse moved up on the bed. "The handle was camo with a small red R in a circle, and centered in a triangle. I've never seen that brand before." Jesse remained silent as Lori continued to recall her dream. "It was dark, and the breeze was warm. I could smell water."

But Jesse couldn't hide the incredulous look on her face, causing Lori to scowl. "I'm not saying you didn't see a knife, but it was a dream. It's not real."

"Do you swear Hayden is alive? That he's going to be okay?"

"I would never lie about something like that. He's recovering in Tennessee at a trauma unit. Alpha Wilson is there with him." Jesse draped her arm over Lori, but Lori pushed her away and sat up on the bed.

"If I tell you something, you promise you won't repeat it?" Lori was fidgety, nervous even, and Jesse crisscrossed her finger over her heart. "I'm not supposed to tell anyone. It's dangerous."

"I promise on my life, I will not breathe a word of what you tell me if you don't want me to. I love you like a sister, and when you hurt, I hurt." Jesse spoke from the heart, and although Lori was hesitant, they were best friends and Jesse would never in a million lifetimes betray her trust.

"Brid is my great aunt," Lori whispered and Jesse's brows knitted together. "She is a fifth generation seer. My dad was the sixth." Lori glanced up, meeting Jesse's stare. "I had no idea about it until the coma, but apparently, I'm the seventh."

Jesse was silent, and then her mouth gaped open. "You're a seer? Like Brid, a seer? That was the reason she was at the hospital. That explains the flowers, and why she gave you a ride home the day you were released. But why is it dangerous? We all know Brid is a seer."

"Because no two seers have the same vision, but when they are from the same family, they can put their visions together and get a bigger picture. My dad and Brid shared visions, and that's what kept Megan safe."

"And if anyone knew you were a seer, or related to Brid, you become a threat."

"Which is why Mom is selling the house to force me to leave Cloverly. It's not safe for me to stay here any longer."

Jesse pondered for a moment and then asked, "So you thought Hayden was stabbed because you saw a knife in a vision?"

Lori nodded, another tear slipping down the side of her face. "Yeah, but if he wasn't stabbed, and I wasn't, maybe it *was* just a dream. I've never had a vision while I was sleeping, and I'm not sure I would know the difference. Except, well, my head gets fuzzy and sometimes, it gives me a headache." Lori lifted her hand to her chest, her brow creasing. "It just felt so real, and the blood... I saw it dripping off the blade. I can still see it if I close my eyes." She sniffled and wiped her nose.

"So you can have visions about yourself? That sounds really messed up," Jesse said, her face creased with worry.

"I don't think so... No." Lori thought for a minute. "Brid said that wasn't possible." She flopped back on the bed and groaned. "Could I be anymore stupid? All this time, I thought it was a vision when it was only a damn dream."

"You don't know that for sure. Maybe you only thought it was you in the vision," Jesse reasoned.

"Maybe I only thought I felt the knife in my chest too. Either way, it makes me look like a deranged idiot, which probably isn't too far from the truth. Are you really a wolf? Or is that also a figment of my overactive imagination? I just don't know anymore."

Thirty-Three

Lori

The sliver of light at the bottom of the closed door dimly lit the bedroom and Lori stared at the ceiling. It had to be evening, and judging by the hushed conversation behind the door, almost everyone had already gone home for the night. Pretending to sleep, she was avoiding Brid, although she sensed her aunt knew better. Her talk with Jesse earlier in the day proved she wasn't ready to be a seer, especially if she couldn't even tell the difference between a dream and a vision. That conversation was not one she was ready to revisit at the moment.

She was relieved the alpha wasn't taking any chances by posting plenty of scouts outside the building. Faulting her own stupidity as the reason Hayden got attacked, even she questioned why she thought hanging out at the park in the early morning hours was a good idea.

Her brow creased as she replayed the events in her mind. Hayden was there, holding her against the tree. He kept whispering directions while looking across the park. Then Beth showed up, startling them. Lori pondered a moment longer… *If Beth were behind them, who was Hayden watching?* Her eyes went round, and she sat up in the bed as the door swung open.

"I hope I didn't wake you," Nigel said from the doorway and Lori sighed and shook her head no. "Everyone left for the night, but if you need anything, I'll be right outside here," Nigel informed her before pulling the door closed again.

After a quick shower and a change of clothes, Lori skittishly peeked out the bedroom door as if she expected Beth to be waiting for her. It was her apartment, but after all the foot traffic earlier that day, anything was possible.

"She emerges," Nigel teased, removing a pan from the stove.

"Yeah, cabin fever hit me pretty hard," she said as she walked into the room. "Something smells good."

"I thought you might be hungry. Jesse said you hadn't eaten today." He motioned her to the table and placed a bowl of soup and a sleeve of crackers in front of her.

Lori was never so glad to see anyone as she was to see Nigel. He had become one of her most trusted friends that only she knew about. The embrace he offered was familiar and suddenly, all she wanted to do was cry.

"Are you sure you're all right?" he asked, rubbing over her hair.

"I'm okay. I just wish I had someone I could…" She hugged him tighter.

"That's why I'm here! You can talk to me. I know who you are, and what you can do." She looked up, surprised, and he wiped the tears from her eyes. "Well, I didn't actually know who you were when we first met, but once you confirmed you were Jared Mayfield's daughter, I knew who you were then."

"Who told you?" She pulled out of the hug and took a seat at the table. Her guard rising as Brid's warning sounded in her head: *Things aren't always as they seem.*

"Your dad. I owed him a debt and keeping you safe is my way of paying him back for everything he did for me. He basically saved me from following a pack that no longer exists. He had a vision and warned me about it. At first, I thought he was crazy, but once I saw all the signs..." His words trailed off and she could tell he was reliving the moment. "Anyway, I owe him my life and I swore I'd repay him for his kindness, even if, at the time, I didn't deserve it."

"You should have told me you knew who I was when we were at Sallee's."

"I planned to, but it's not a subject that should be discussed; not when there's a chance others might overhear. Your dad knew that, but in order to help me..." Nigel set his bowl on the table before looking back at Lori. "Still, to this day, I think someone overheard our conversation. I was going to tell you after you mentioned getting involved with a pack member because I was afraid you exposed yourself. But when we arrived at the gas station and Beth showed up, I couldn't risk her overhearing." He took a seat across from Lori before continuing. "I don't like Beth. I can't really explain why, just something about her demeanor. She comes off as devious, and usually never leaves pack grounds. So when I saw her at the station, I knew something was up." Nigel ate a spoonful of soup and washed it down with a sip of water. "I tried to follow her that day, but she phased and took off through the woods. She knew I was parked at the library, and had it not been for me taking you to the station, she would have never picked up on me watching you. I'd been secretly guarding you since our meeting in the woods."

You are the voice he protects. Lori swallowed hard, suddenly understanding the vision and why Nigel was protecting her. Then she thought about how he always showed up at just the right time. A small smile lifted her lips. *Thanks, Dad.* She looked over at Nigel. "Did you see Hayden getting attacked?"

"Not exactly. I was napping in my truck. That's when I noticed you in the park. It was blue-cold outside, and I couldn't believe you wanted to go down the slide." He lifted a brow. "I had half a mind to boss your butt back across the street, until lover-boy showed up. I had no idea Tucker's brother was your bond mate. I also approve, by the way."

Lori blushed and looked down at her bowl, causing Nigel to laugh.

"Yeah, it got a little steamy there for a minute. Had I not turned away just then, I may have seen Beth when she approached you. I have no idea where she came from."

"So you saw..." Lori smiled sheepishly.

"Oh, no! I have sisters, remember? I learned really quick when to look away. Plus, Hayden was with you so I knew he would keep you safe."

"Did you see a knife?"

"No, but I heard Hayden yell and I saw you run. He kept Beth back long enough for you to get into the building, until he saw me getting out of the truck. That was when Beth darted past him. You were already inside by the time she ran out in front of the truck. The driver swerved to miss her, but hit Hayden instead. It was an accident, and Beth didn't look back. I honestly thought Hayden got killed until he took off down Main Street. I suspected he was going to Tucker's, so I went after Beth but her scent disappeared." Then Nigel frowned and placed his spoon in the bowl before changing the subject. "If I'd known at the time that your dad and Brid were related, maybe I could have prevented his accident. I'm not sure what happened that day, but I doubt he just ran off the road."

Lori crushed a cracker in her soup and glanced up at Nigel. "Do you think Beth could have caused my accident?" She blew on the spoon to cool down the soup before taking a bite.

"Yeah, I do. She's been looking for a mate and knows who Hayden is, so she would do just about anything to take you out of the picture. But you have to know this: I will protect you for as long as you are in Cloverly. I won't let anyone get as close as Beth did last night. I specifically asked the alpha to let me guard you until you left town. I know you're leaving and as much as I hate to see you go, your place isn't with this pack. You will do great things with Hayden, and in Tennessee no one can touch you."

"Have you heard anything about Hayden? Jesse said he came through surgery successfully." She swallowed her soup and hot tears stung her eyes. "How am I supposed to face him after everything I put him through?" Lori pushed her bowl back on the table and rested her head on her arm. She was hungry, but talking about Hayden made her feel very ill.

Nigel smiled and placed his hand on hers. "You are his mate. There is nothing you could do that would make him reject or deny you. He will be back when the time is right. Now eat. I don't want him to suspect I've been starving you. He's a mountain wolf, and I'm not the rowdy teenager I used to be."

Lori couldn't help but giggle as she lifted her head off the table. "Thank you for everything you've done for me. I owe you and Hayden my life. I'd hate to think what would have happened if you all hadn't been there."

"Think nothing of it. I expect you to have a long, happy life with Hayden. You deserve it."

Lori smirked, and he laughed. "So what about you? How will you spend your time once you are relieved of sitter duty?"

Nigel mused for a minute and then his eyes lit up. "I have a new gig in Buffer County. Seems Alpha Cooper saw something worthy in me and offered me an alpha position."

"It's about time! I've always known you were alpha material." She smiled and dipped her spoon into the soup. "Dean lives in Buffer County."

"I know," Nigel said as he glanced over at the door. "He and your mother should be here soon."

Lori was glad to know Nigel guarded her, and as much as she didn't want to leave Cloverly, she was long overdue to move on.

Thirty-Four

Lori

As the days turned into weeks, Lori's thoughts remained constantly on Hayden, although she abandoned the idea of them ever being together. He was in Tennessee and he contacted Tucker on a regular basis, but she still hadn't received any calls. At first, it made her angry, but after a few days, she admitted she wouldn't have called her either. Jesse kept her informed of his news, for the most part, and Lori hated knowing she couldn't go to him. But since she was the reason he was injured, she suspected his family might run her straight off the mountain.

To help pass the days, she did the chores and most of the cooking, and to her surprise, she soon gained several pounds. Her stick figure was transformed into *a young lady*, her mother happily reminded her. She glanced down at her chest and then in the mirror as she pulled her shirt over her head. Her bra size went from a B-cup to a C and that, in itself, was reason enough to celebrate. But why? What was the point?

Her mother insisted that she stay clear of the pack until Beth was found. So moving into her own wing at Dean's mansion gave her time to ponder her life. She could mull over the feelings she had for the one man who meant the world to her. Unfortunately, she still couldn't see how the relationship would work, and wasn't convinced it ever could... but now she at least considered the idea. *Too bad for you, that boat already sailed.* Her jaw clenched as she tried to swallow the lump of reality that always managed to choke her up. She blinked the tears from her eyes. Everything that happened between them was all on her. She couldn't even blame Katherine for her blindness or stupidity.

Her circle of friends grew smaller, and she felt more isolated, so she was glad Nigel kept his word. Now the alpha in Buffer County, every night, he made a special run past their house. Sometimes, she would see his wolf skirting the property line, and other nights, she could hear his howl in the distance. It didn't bother her knowing her best friend was a wolf, so why should having one for a boyfriend be any different?

Lori felt the loneliest when she sat outside by the pool late at night. *I love you, Lori. Never forget that.* Hayden's words echoed in her head and she hoped they were still true even if she didn't deserve to hear them.

Meeting Hayden was a turning point in her life, and she liked his family, so naturally, she wanted them as well. Aching to see him again, she often looked up at the stars and wished she could make it happen. In her mind, she saw him there in the swing, and it eased the longing that would have otherwise driven her mad. If only she could have flashed back in time, all the things she would have done differently... The most important change would have been choosing to stay on the mountain.

The longer she was away from Hayden, the more his memory taunted her. He was so perfect, and he loved her enough to fight for her, something Steve would never have done. He was the only guy she ever truly loved, but he got hurt because of her, so how could she bear to face him again? Her heart ached over her jealousy of Katherine; that was when she pushed him away. It was stupid, and Katherine never should have occupied her life or her mind.

She thought about the bond they shared, and wondered if that were the only reason she was attracted to him? He looked so much like his brother, and well, her ovaries seemed to swoon in his presence; so her attraction to Hayden would most likely have existed regardless of the bond.

Then a god-awful voice cut through her silence and she cringed as Brid walked into her room. "What are you doing here?" Lori sneered, but she knew she had no right to ask. Since her father's death, Brid was only looking out for her and ensuring their secret was safe.

"Nice to see you've made a full recovery." Brid smiled cunningly.

"Yeah, well, it's too bad my full recovery has to cost me my freedom."

"Lori, it isn't that bad." Brid's pinched glare didn't help her cause, and Lori scowled.

"This... all of this is your fault! I never wanted to be a seer. I never wanted Hayden to leave."

"Hayden didn't leave you. He knows what's going on and the only way he can keep you safe is by staying away right now."

"According to you! Right now, I'd rather scoop my eyeballs out than have another one of those damn visions!"

Brid chuckled and Lori glared. "The visions don't appear in your eyes, so unless you're willing to cut off your silly head, you'll continue to have them forever."

"You are the most insensitive person I've ever met. There is no way you could possibly be my aunt." Lori pulled on her nightgown and sat down at the two-chair table next to the window.

"Dear, I know it seems bad now, but I told you it wouldn't be easy."

"The way I remember it, you said it would be rewarding! When does it become rewarding? I've lost everyone I love! I have nothing to show for it!"

"And that's the whole point. Until you move on, things won't change. Your destiny isn't here, not in Kentucky."

"And exactly how would you suggest I move on? I currently have no job, no friends, and no way to escape. I'm stuck here whether I like it or not."

"Well, seeing how immobilized you currently are, maybe this will help you pass the time until you can figure out the rest of your life." Brid tossed an envelope onto the table. "Everything has to be your own decision." With that, she turned and walked out of the room just as Jesse entered.

"I was in the neighborhood and thought you might need some girl time." The grin on Jesse's face as she pulled Lori into a hug made Lori smile. "Are you doing okay? I miss you something awful."

"I'm frantically bored out of my mind, and going stir crazy, but other than that, I'm good. How's Hayden?" It was always the question she asked anytime she talked to Jesse or Megan. "Have you seen or talked to him lately?"

"Hayden's fine, but he's giving you more time, which is what you wanted all along." Jesse tried to keep the frown from distorting her face, but failed. "He's healing, but he's also angry. He fears you'll break the bond for Nigel. Care to explain?" She pinned Lori with a questioning stare.

"What does it matter? Everything that happened is all my fault and he will never forgive me."

"You're right! It is your fault," Jesse agreed as she knitted her brows to look more serious. "If Hayden weren't in love with you, he would have never risked his life by phasing. He could have died! But no-o-o-o! He had to rescue the one person that meant the world to him. The one person that seemed to despise him more than she despises her own pathetic life. Why he loves you… hell, at this point, I sure don't know. You are the most hateful, nasty, single person I've ever met. Grow the hell up, Lori! Life sucks balls!" She drew in a sharp breath, and her voice softened slightly.

"But that doesn't mean you should give up on it. Do you honestly think I wanted to be changed into a straggly, frickin' mutt? Hell no! I would never wish my life on anyone. But I accepted the cards I was dealt, and now I'm grateful for what I am. I've never been happier." Jesse turned and stared out the window—her rant finally over.

"By all means, don't spare my feelings." Lori glared at the grin on Jesse's face, which was reflected on the glass.

"Lori, it wasn't too long ago that I was in the same situation as you. My heart was so heavy with regret until the day I woke up and realized my world was sitting right in front of me. And when I did, it was great."

"But I'm not you! When I fall into a bucket of shit, I just smell like shit."

"I think you smell quite alluring," Jesse said. When she turned to look at Lori, her eyes flared.

"Shut up!" Lori hissed, but that didn't stop the inadvertent snort. "So, is this where you eat me up?" She giggled when Jesse licked her lips salaciously.

"Your scent reminds me of Gramma's fresh baked cinnamon rolls."

"Really? That's what I smell like to you?" Lori lifted her arm and sniffed. "I smell like baby powder."

"Yeah, that too, but a shower will solve that problem."

Lori sat down on the edge of the bed and Jesse sat next to her. She snickered and stuffed the envelope under her pillow, forgetting about Brid. "Why are you here so late? Where's Tucker?"

"He's outside in the truck, talking to Hayden. He's having a hard time dealing with everything."

"But you just said he was good."

"Health wise he is, but as for his mind? That's a different story. Tucker said he just sits and stares. He's waiting for you to deny the bond."

"Because of Nigel?" Lori asked and Jesse frowned. "It's not what you think. Brid had a vision—*you are the voice he protects*—Nigel knew what I was even before I did. That's because he was friends with my dad. When he found out my identity, he started secretly guarding me to repay a debt to my father."

Jesse laced her fingers with Lori's and leaned against her shoulder. "I didn't realize you and Nigel were so close. Seeing how old he is, I told Tucker there was nothing sexual between you two, although Hayden said Beth insinuated there was. So how did you and Nigel become such good friends?"

Lori turned on the bed and lifted Jesse's other hand, holding them both in her lap. "I met him in the woods that day when you found me at Sallee's. He told me I needed to head home soon because it was getting dark. He gave me his business card, and I was making fun of his last name. He asked me my name, and then he figured out who I was because he knew who Dad was. It had nothing to do with romance or flirting; it was just a friendly exchange of words."

"If you were just friends, why didn't you ever tell me about him?" Jesse worked her lip between her teeth while waiting for an answer.

"You had just bonded with a great guy who came from a great family. I wanted a family like that, and I wanted a life like yours. I've always wanted to feel like I mattered to someone. Nigel was practically a brother to me, or what I imagine a brother would be. It was nice having someone actually listen to all of my problems. I just wanted to keep him to myself for a while. I needed to have one person I could totally confide in, someone who didn't see all of my faults." The sympathetic look in Lori's eyes apparently wasn't enough to satisfy Jesse, so she cleared her throat and continued.

"The day Hayden told me we shared a bond, I wanted so badly to be with him. Then I got terrified. It meant—our relationship would have to change. He's intense, all in or all out, but never on the fence. I don't know what came over me. I wanted to be like Katherine, except I freaked out and that scared me. I left that day so he wouldn't see me cry. I hated trying to be like her and playing that stupid game, and I couldn't do it very well. I wasn't ready.

"Nigel practically ran over me when I raced out of the building. I jumped into the passenger seat of his car and ordered him to drive. I needed to escape, and he was my friend, so he did as I asked. We went to the gas station and Beth was there. She got angry when she saw me, but Nigel basically told her to mind her own business. Then I called Mom, and she came over and picked me up. I wasn't there longer than fifteen minutes." She drew in a deep breath and exhaled slowly as a kinder expression settled on Jesse's face.

"I wish you'd told me sooner. There were so many mixed signals between you and Hayden. Had I just stepped back and let things play out as fate intended..." Jesse paused and glanced down at her hands, still resting in Lori's lap. "I'm sorry for my part in all this, and I'll do whatever I can to help you straighten it out. I just want you to be happy, healthy, and my best friend. I miss our long chats on the phone and your smutty talk." Jesse grinned. "I could use some pointers."

Lori rolled her eyes and laughed. "I doubt I'm the best person to give you any pointers. I'm not even bonded."

"Yet." Jesse chuckled. "Maybe when things settle down, you and Hayden can work it out. I mean, it has to be your choice. And I'm not telling you this to influence your decision, but the night Hayden got hit by the truck, he thought he would die. That's why he came to our cabin. He only came there to get you help, and phasing actually made his injury worse. He loves you, Lori. You can see it in his actions, and in his eyes. Everything about him says it, and it's all about you."

"That's why you showed up at the apartment when you did. I should have known."

"Yeah, but I didn't come here to sway you into accepting Hayden. I wanted to let you know Beth's wolf was found dead on the side of the highway. Looks like karma turned around and bit her right in the ass."

"Let me guess... was it a coal truck?"

"Oh, yeah! It couldn't have happened to a better wolf. So now that you know Beth is no longer a threat, are you coming back to Cloverly?"

Lori shook her head no. "There's nothing left for me there. It's time to move forward with my life."

"I'm still there! You're my best friend."

"But even you are getting ready to move to Berkley! I don't want to be the last man standing. There are too many bad memories and not enough good ones."

Jesse pulled her into a hug. "I love you. I wish things had worked out differently for you," she said through her tears.

"Well, you know me. I'll just sulk for a while and have a pity party before I come back full force—and swinging."

After Jesse left that night, Lori stared out the window as a deep sadness split her heart. Every memory she had growing up was in Cloverly, and as much as she now despised the town, she also loved it. She sighed and turned when the bedroom door opened.

"Honey, are you okay?" her mother asked, coming into the room.

"Yeah. Just a little tired," Lori said as she crawled onto the bed.

"Okay, sweetie. If you need anything, buzz me," her mother said, reaching for her pillow. "What's this?"

Lori held out her hand. "I don't know. Brid gave it to me." She opened the envelope and pulled out the enclosure cards that could only have belonged to the countless bouquets of flowers she received, which she stupidly forgot about. She was fairly certain Hayden was behind them since her memory was getting better and he was with her at the hospital. She opened the first card. "I love you! Hayden." *Duh! That was apparent by the underlined words.* She quickly thumbed through the cards, and found ten in total. The next card had a one-word message. *Take.* Her brow furrowed as she opened the next card. *Yours.* "Okay, and that makes absolutely no sense at all." She glanced up at her mom and rolled her eyes.

"But it sounds intriguing. Open another," her mother said, taking a seat on the edge of the bed.

"Brid's attempt at being funny, I think," Lori said as she opened another card that had the word *Always* written on it. "I swear, that woman is totally nuts."

"No, wait… that's not what I'm seeing." Her mother opened a card. "My," she said and grinned. "Hurry, and open up the rest of them."

Lori chuckled at her mother's excitement, and continued to pluck the cards out, tossing them on the bed.

"If Brid honestly thinks this is cute, she's so wrong. The woman has gotten so accustomed to talking in riddles; she can't even form a complete sentence."

"Oh, Lori. Give her a break! She tries to be helpful." Her mother laughed. "Okay, maybe she is a bit flighty."

As Lori's mother tried to work out the riddle, Lori opened the last card. "*It*," she said before tossing it to her mother, who practically snatched it right out of the air.

"This is unbelievable. I don't know what to say."

"What?" Lori stared down at the cards. "Take my heart, for it has always been yours. I love you. Hayden." She glanced up at her mom and then looked back at the cards. "That's the same thing Dad wrote on the note he put in the teddy bear's pouch."

"Maybe it was your dad's way of telling you Hayden is the one," her mother suggested.

"Do you believe he could actually do that?"

"I guess that's for you to decide, but I believe in signs as much as I believe in seers."

Great, another decision. She wanted to roll her eyes, but instead, her mind suddenly opened up and everything became clearer. She was a seer, and it was a sign. "Dad must have had a vision of me."

"I think he did. Which means somebody is sweet on my little girl."

"Stop!" Lori pushed her mother's hand from her hair and laughed when she stood up and did a little wiggle as she sashayed to the door.

"I see wedding bells in your future." Her mother's laughter carried all the way down the hall as the door shut behind her.

Lori held the enclosure cards to her chest and lay

back on the bed, her thoughts recalling the night Hayden's wolf showed up at her house. She remembered him, his wolf. His eyes comforted her on the sleepless nights and anytime she was lonely and afraid. *My guardian angel.* That was what she told herself when she was younger—A gift from her dad, a protector to watch over her. "It was always Hayden," she whispered as she looked out the window at the moon.

The moon was in all its glory, brightening the night, and reminding her that Hayden was probably running with his pack. Something she could never do. He deserved so much better. He deserved to have someone that could share his world with him, the way nature intended. Then she remembered Jesse's words. *If Hayden weren't in love with you, he would have never risked his life by phasing.*

A crafty smile spread across Lori's face and she raced into the bathroom, her world instantly a lot brighter. Maybe she was tired of trying to compete when Katherine wasn't really a threat, or perhaps she was finally content with the hand destiny dealt her. Either way, her pity party was over and she was ready to make a stand and claim what was rightfully hers. With her new plan in place, she quickly dressed into warm clothes and pulled on her coat before heading out to the patio.

Thirty-Five

Hayden

Brooding on the back porch, Hayden shoved his hands into his pockets as the family gathered for their run. The night was cold, the sky clear, and the moon much brighter than he could ever remember seeing it. He inhaled the crisp, clean air but it failed to relieve the desperation he was suffering from. His body was healing and he would soon be able to phase again, which was the only thing that stopped him from going after Lori.

He was weary of the games, and determined to make her understand he would crawl through the swamps of hell to have her at his side. She meant everything in his life, and as soon as he could, he planned to go back to Cloverly so he could beg her to bond with him. *Whatever it takes.* However, it was too dangerous to leave his own territory when his wolf couldn't defend him. It wasn't so much a problem in Cloverly, but now that Lori had moved in with her mother and Dean, Buffer County was a little too unfamiliar to him. He shoved his fingers through his hair, tugging slightly to feel the pain. *Hopeless. Just damn hopeless!*

Three weeks passed since the last time he saw Lori. Tucker insisted she was safe but failed to mention Nigel was her guardian. That came directly from Alpha Cooper, which was probably why Tucker never brought it up. He knew Hayden wouldn't like hearing that another male was protecting his mate. Hayden's jaws ached from the constant clenching, and if he weren't mistaken, he also cracked a molar.

"Everything okay?" his dad asked, coming over to stand beside him.

"Yeah, I guess so." Shrugging, he looked up at the moon. Lori would have loved the view of the mountains under a full moon. "I'm just annoyed at myself." It was hard for him to resist the urge to phase and take off across the mountainside to vent his frustration. He couldn't do that yet, not until he was completely healed. "I should have taken my stand when Lori was here. I could have told her everything that night. I wanted to bond with her so badly that I worried I might scare her away. Now, I think I've done just that. Whatever I get now is what I fully deserve."

"Don't be so hard on yourself. You thought you were protecting her. It was your right." His dad squeezed his shoulder before he continued out to the yard where the others were waiting.

Hayden watched the pack with envy as they took off

across the mountainside. Walking out into the yard, he knew Lori loved the mountains as much as he did, but without her at his side, it wasn't the same. He glanced at the sky and wondered if she were also observing the huge moon? He seriously doubted it.

Lori was probably tucked beneath a warm blanket, sound asleep. That was what he hoped for anyway. She went through her own hell from what Tucker told him. He described her near breakdown when she thought he died and how she kept threatening to go after Beth. *She loves us,* his wolf insisted, but he wouldn't allow his mind to believe it.

Honestly, he gave it his best shot. After everything they endured, he had nothing left. He sat down on the ground, resting his forearms on his knees. Surrounded by his family and pack, he was utterly amazed at how lonely he felt—and he blamed it on his jaded outlook. His body was physically exhausted, and his mind wasn't the most stable lately. Even something as simple as a friendly howl in the distance could set him on edge. His wolf longed to tear across the mountainside and challenge anyone that dared to step in its way. That only proved how mentally exhausted he was and clearly not thinking straight.

He squeezed his eyes shut to calm the frustration he felt. It wasn't in his DNA to show his true feelings, but at that point, what the hell did he have to lose? She either wanted him or she didn't. It was entirely her decision. He angrily wiped the moisture from his eyes. He was an alpha, and alphas didn't show weakness. He hung his head. "*I don't know what to do, Lori. We were meant for this life, and the pack. You were destined to be with me to raise a family. I can't exist without you. Why can't you see that? Dammit! I love you."* Weak or not, he sent the message through their bond, and released a fierce growl, which he aimed at the moon. There was no way to appease or placate his wolf—she was his... for life.

"I love you too!"

Hayden's eyes sprang open and he jumped to his feet, stumbling backwards as Sawyer rounded the house and phased. The thoughts in his head suddenly jumbled together, and he stood with his hands out, confused and disoriented.

"Hayden, what's wrong?" Sawyer snapped his fingers and Hayden blinked to clear the haze from his eyes. "MOM!" Sawyer yelled while trying to steady him.

"Hayden, I accept your bond."

Hayden dropped onto his knees, his hands trembling as he wiped the tears from his face. Struggling to catch his breath, he stared up at the moon. *It was Lori! It had to be.* His thoughts became clearer, and he could easily picture her in his mind. "It's okay! I'm fine," Hayden said, swatting Sawyer away. He glanced around the yard and smiled when radiant heat from their bond engulfed his whole body and his connection to Lori intensified even further. He never experienced anything as wonderful and amazing as fate uniting two souls, and he hoped Lori was experiencing the same thing he was.

"Did she deny the bond?" Sawyer dropped to his knees, lines of worry creasing his forehead.

"No. She accepted it!" Hayden looked up and more tears filled his eyes. For once in his life, he didn't care if anyone saw him cry. His mate accepted him and he wanted the whole world to know their bond was complete at last. "*I don't know what I did to deserve you, but I wholeheartedly accept you as my bond mate,"* he sent back to her. He wasn't sure if he imagined it, but he thought he heard a small giggle.

"Yes!" Sawyer yelled as he shot up off the ground, pumping his fist in the air. "I have a new sister!"

"What's all the yelling about?" his mother asked when she and his dad joined them in the yard. She kneeled down beside Hayden, resting her hand on his back.

"Lori accepted the bond," Sawyer said.

"Hayden, is that true?" Lucia looked up at Sam. "Can she do that?"

"Apparently, she can," the alpha said. Helping Hayden off the ground, he pulled him into a hug. "Congratulations. Now go and get your female."

Hayden ran into the house, and if he hurried, he could be in Cloverly by morning. The traffic would be light, and once he cleared the mountains, most of the snow would be gone. Sorting through his closet, he grabbed his best pair of jeans and a white t-shirt. He swiftly changed and even added a red and brown flannel that brought out the color of his eyes. That was exactly how he looked, dressed in the very same clothes he was wearing the day he first met Lori. He wanted her to see the Hayden she fell for, not the Hayden that changed to win her heart.

"Slow down, Hoss, she'll be ready when you get there," Alyssa said, tossing him a pair of socks, but even she couldn't hide her excitement. Smiling, she gave Jaylee a look that suggested they were both holding back squeals of delight.

"Thanks," he said as he sat down on the side of the bed. Putting on his socks and boots, he stood up and looked into the mirror. "What do you think? Should I shave?"

"No!" his sisters chorused, and when he glanced their way, they both grinned.

"Come on, Sawyer, let's go," Hayden yelled as he walked out of his room. He raced down the stairs as fast as he could without tripping. Hearing his truck start up, even Sawyer was one step ahead.

"You all be careful; I'll call Ben and let him know you'll be there shortly," his mother said before she pulled him into a hug, her eyes round with worry.

"We'll be okay, Mom. We're members of the Kinsley Pack by default," Hayden said and she smiled.

"I know. My home pack will be there if you need them."

Hayden waved from the passenger seat as Sawyer pulled out of the drive. It was hard to contain his excitement, and a ton of dynamite couldn't have blasted the grin off his face. It was happening. He was finally on his way to get Lori and bring her home. Everything he dreamed his life could become was all at once within his grasp and he was going to strike while the iron was hot.

Riding shotgun gave Hayden time to enjoy the view while he gathered his thoughts. It was funny how the moon seemed to smile at him as if it were saying, "It's your time to shine." He sighed a thank you to the moon and glanced over and saw the grin on Sawyer's face. Apparently, he wasn't the only one excited to be bringing Lori home. "Thanks for coming with me."

"It's my job. I'll always have your back," Sawyer said and his grin widened. "It hasn't been the same since Lori left, and we've all been holding our breath waiting for her to accept your bond. If she hadn't, I was prepared to fight you. Whatever was necessary to bring her back to the mountains where she belongs."

"Really? You think it would be that easy? That I'd just let you step in and take my female?" Hayden teased with a glare.

"There's no doubt I'd get my ass handed to me, but if it were necessary, I would have at least tried." Hayden's wolf grumbled a warning, which only made Sawyer laugh.

"Can't fault you there." Hayden chuckled. "She's more special than you know which is why we need to get her home. Beth may no longer be a threat, but someone is always waiting in the shadows." That reminder made Hayden's hands ball up into fists as he stared out through the windshield.

"Well, look at the bright side. You have your bond now, and no matter what, that can't ever be taken from you."

It should have eased Hayden's mind, but until Lori was safely back in Tennessee, he couldn't let his guard down. After Brid's warning, he wondered if he could ever allow Lori out of his sight. At least, she accepted his bond, and as soon as she was back on the mountain, his pack would protect her. He closed his eyes, trying to banish the anxiety that kept knotting in his chest. Listening to the low music on the radio, he finally fell into a deep sleep.

Thirty-Six

Hayden

Jolted awake, Hayden stifled a yawn as he eyed Sawyer. He felt bad for falling asleep, but all the worrying had finally caught up with him. "What time is it?" he asked, stretching his back by slowly twisting from side to side. He was still sore from the accident, but would soon be completely healed.

"Just past nine," Sawyer said, nodding towards the *Welcome to Cloverly* sign. "I figured it was better if you fell asleep on me than on Lori." He flicked his brows suggestively and Hayden grinned.

"Yeah, good plan, but I don't see that happening anytime soon." Hayden ran his fingers over the scruff on his jaw and smiled, imagining Lori doing the same. He sucked in his bottom lip to keep from drooling at the thought of taking her to the little cabin after their bonding ceremony. It was pure torture, and he sat up higher in the seat to adjust his jeans while Sawyer snickered beside him. He removed his flannel shirt and rolled down the window, allowing the blast of cold air to cool his jets and chase away his dirty thoughts.

"Tucker called while you were asleep. He and Jesse are helping Lori move the rest of her things from the apartment. Jesse talked her into spending the night with them, so if you wanted to call or stop by."

"Then he doesn't know about the bond?" It wasn't really a question, but Hayden was happy to know Lori would be in Cloverly and he wouldn't have to hunt her down in Buffer County.

"And miss the look on his face when you show up unannounced? No way!" Sawyer laughed, slowing the truck before stopping at the red light. "You ready to do this?"

"I'm more than ready." Hayden looked down the road at the familiar brick building where he hoped Lori would be waiting. "I've waited for this moment my whole life." As the truck inched forward and the light turned green, he drew in a deep breath. Passing the cafe, his eyes automatically went to the street beside the boutique where he noticed Tucker's truck. "Turn here," he said as he grabbed the door handle.

Sawyer cut a sharp right, almost missing the turn, and pulled up behind Tucker's truck. Before he could get the truck into park, Hayden was already out the door and striding up the sidewalk without a second thought.

"Where's Lori?" Hayden asked, sounding a bit out of breath.

"She's upstairs packing." Tucker frowned and looked back at Sawyer, who was just getting out of the truck. "Does she know you're here?"

"She will." Wasting no time to explain, Hayden could hear Sawyer jogging up the sidewalk as he entered the warehouse. Picking up the different scents, he walked between the storage shelves.

Lori's was by far the most appealing, and the sweet, sugary smell with a touch of cinnamon would make any male drool. He cracked a grin, knowing that was exactly what he would be doing as soon as he set his eyes on her.

Traces of coconut let him know Jesse was also there, but the musky sandalwood was not Megan. A low growl resonated through the warehouse and he narrowed his eyes as he continued walking over to the metal staircase that led up to the upstairs apartment. He expected Jesse to be there, and maybe Megan, but a male wolf? He had balls. "I'm here to relieve you of your duties, old man."

Nigel casually glanced up from where he was sitting and smirked. "Don't get too cocky, pup. I'm just doing my job." He stood up, gesturing with his hand for Hayden to ascend the steps.

"About that. We saw how well you did your job the night Beth showed up at the park," Hayden crossed his arms over his chest, glaring down at Nigel, who stood four inches shorter than his six-foot-five stature. His mother would have been ashamed of him, acting like such an ass to Nigel. Especially knowing the relationship between the older wolf and Lori was nothing more than friends. He returned the smirk.

"Yeah, about as well as you did, I'd say." Nigel shoved his hands into his pockets, and leaned against the metal railing. He appeared as if he were not the least bit worried about Hayden's hulking frame looming over him. "Look, I'm no threat. You need to get her away from here as soon as possible."

Hayden tilted his head, his brows furrowed. "So you really do know what she is? I assume you must've known all along." A grin lit up his face when Nigel nodded. "Did you also know Beth was at the car accident site?" He was watching how Nigel responded; it would be the deciding factor as to whether or not he could be trusted.

Nigel glanced up at the apartment, and then at the side door before leaning in to whisper. "Funny you should say that. I mentioned a second set of tracks, but Officer Riley said he didn't notice them. Of course, that was after the police report came out and most of the snow had melted. I had no proof, but I knew the tracks were there, and they weren't yours."

"Wow!" Hayden shook his head in disbelief. "It's my word against a dead wolf's."

"That pretty much sums it up." Nigel shrugged one shoulder.

"Well, I owe you an apology, sir. Thank you for looking after my mate, but as I said before, I'm here to relieve you of your duties." He extended his hand and Nigel did the same.

"You're welcome and good luck! You're gonna need it with that one." Nigel laughed, when Hayden's chin dropped to his chest and he chuckled too. "Tell Lori I wish her all the best."

"I will, and thanks again." Hayden waited until Nigel walked out of the warehouse before heading up the stairs. Clearly, he was wrong about Nigel, but he excused it as having an overly protective wolf.

Hayden locked onto Lori's scent and paused, peeking into the apartment from the door that stood half open. He could never tire of smelling the sweetness that Lori exuded. His eyes flared when he bounded through the door, startling Jesse who was standing at the kitchen sink. "I'm here for Lori."

The scowl on her face was proof she didn't expect to see him there, but he just smirked and continued across the room—Jesse hot on his heels. He stopped at the bedroom door, causing Jesse to bump into him. He grinned when she pinched the bridge of her wrinkled nose before turning his attention back to the bedroom. When the closet door swung open, he leaned against the door frame to watch Lori push a large box across the room, her perfect ass swaying from side to side. He groaned and Jesse rolled her eyes. Snubbing his nosy sis-in-law, he strutted to the center of the room and drew Lori into his embrace.

"Well, hello there, stranger." Lori giggled as she brushed her fingers over the scruff on his jaw. "What took you so long?"

Hayden grinned. He liked the playful side of Lori, probably more than he should.

"O-o-okay. I'll just be right outside... here," Jesse said as she pulled the door shut.

"I would have been here sooner, had I been driving." He stared into her beautiful, blue eyes, which reminded him of a warm summer day. The sadness that he once glimpsed there was gone, and all he could see was the wonderful life they would spend together. "So it's for real?"

"Yeah, my life sucks without you." She wrapped her arms around his neck, and he lifted her off the floor. A frisky Lori promised to be a lot of fun.

"Mine too," he said, drawing her into a slow, sultry kiss. Her soft lips and the sensation of her fingers pushing through his hair caused his eyes to blaze. The intensity made him shudder and as he placed her on the floor, he pulled out of the kiss. "Wow!" What more could he say?

"I love you," she said, her hand lightly rubbing over his chest as tears filled her eyes. "I'm sorry about everything."

"Don't be. It's okay. We're okay." Hayden blinked to clear his eyes as he led her over to the bed and pulled her down on his lap. "I never want to be the reason for your sorrow." He swallowed hard, surprised by the emotion he heard in his voice. "You are my world, and I will do everything in my power to protect you." He glanced down as she worked her bottom lip between her teeth. Something else was on her mind; he could almost see the cogs turning in her head. "What is it?" His heart melted when she smiled up at him.

"You sent the flowers." The rosy hue that colored her cheeks created a surge of excitement in his southern region, and he lifted her off his lap. He placed her on the bed beside him, hoping she hadn't noticed.

"Did you like them?" His voice cracked as he struggled to calm the craving that made his stomach flutter.

"I loved them, but the message… how did you know?"

Lacing his fingers with hers, he stared across the room as if he were seeing his dream play before his eyes. "Take my heart, for it has always been yours." He wasn't a poetic person, but damn! If those words didn't hold true. He cleared his throat and continued. "After talking with that crazy lady, Brid, I had my own vision. It didn't make sense when the dream started, but as it went on, a message came. It was me, writing to you."

"It was perfect... Those words. You have no idea how much they mean to me." She laid her head on his shoulder, and all the tension he had to endure suddenly vanished. He drew in a slow breath, her nearness making him dizzy.

"I know this is kind of sudden, but would you mind having the bonding ceremony on the next full moon? I have sought your attention since the first moment we met. I need to know you will always be mine."

"I don't want to." She tugged at her bottom lip, and he could tell she wasn't sure how to break the bad news. "Do we have to wait? I know it probably sounds stupid, but I think we have something special between us. The man, I mean, not the wolf." She looked down at their entwined fingers. "If you're up to it? I don't want you to do anything that could hurt you," she added as he laid her back on the bed.

"What? You mean, now?" Her nod sounded in his brain, which was louder than any word she could have spoken. He drew in another breath to stifle the heat that burned through his body, but it was too late. "Right here? Right now?" he asked and again, she nodded.

His heart raced as his hand moved up her leg, stopping at the soft, brown sweater that fit snugly across her chest. "This needs to come off." As he pushed up her shirt, she raised her arms. *This is real!* He reminded himself. Because as crazy as his thoughts were, he knew she wanted this. And with her weight gain, she had the most spectacular body he'd ever seen.

He stood up and placed her higher on the bed and stared down at the blue bra that matched her eyes. She was unsure; he could tell by the way her arms shielded her body. "You are the most beautiful female I've ever laid eyes on. I could stare at you forever."

That was all it took to set her mind at ease, and when she smiled, his whole world beamed brighter. He leaned down and trailed a line of kisses to her belly. Before long, it would expand with the life he planned to create with her. His eyes shot up to hers. The emotions that swirled in his head squeezed his heart. She was so gentle and trusting, letting her shield down and exposing her insecurities.

Tugging to unfasten her jeans, his eyes flared with heat that ignited a furnace between them. Fate had finally brought them together, as he often dreamed, but reality was beyond comparison. She lifted her hips, indicating that she was fully onboard with what they were about to do, and holy hell! He slipped the jeans down her legs, his eyes never leaving hers. Then he caught a glimpse of the matching lace panties. *Naughty and nice.* He drew in a long breath to savor her scent, and had to control the irresistible urge to devour her.

"Hayden, I'm not a China doll. I won't break," she said as she grabbed his arm, pulling him down on top of her. "I won't break." Her words brushed over his ear and he closed his eyes at the sweet sound of her voice. *So, so sweet.* She was more than ready and willing to give him her body, and his wolf growled its approval.

He groaned when her hand pushed under his shirt,

and he yanked it over his head. "My sweet Lori, you do not know the monster you are creating." He unsnapped his jeans, and she giggled nervously when he stood up and kicked off his boots.

Her breath was sweet and tempting, and he soon caved to the desire to taste her again. Gentle laps of his tongue, parted her lips, and his body shuddered when she deepened the kiss. She wasn't a wolf, but she had a definite hold on him. The intensity that existed between them was something he never experienced before. Ending the kiss, he studied her attentively as he stepped out of his jeans and lowered himself to the bed, pinning her beneath his huge body. It was something he often dreamed about, and now she was ready to make it happen.

Unable to suppress the growl that climbed up his throat, it vibrated in her ear and sent a wave of goosebumps over her body. She was so tiny in comparison to him, but when she wrapped her legs around his waist, the room faded away and the only thing he could see or feel was her.

Thirty-Seven

Lori

Radiant warmth blanketed Lori as she curled into Hayden's side. With his strong arms securely wrapped around her, she felt safe. He was so gentle and caring, everything she hoped he would be, and nothing like the tough guy she often observed.

Teaching her as he explored her body, how much better could it get? He didn't even make fun of her when she blushed at his dirty words. How perfect she felt in that moment: beautiful, sexy, and loved. It was nice knowing someone loved her so deeply that he gave her every part of himself. It was also unimaginable, yet there he was. She turned her head and kissed his chest, while he, in turn, kissed the top of her head.

"You're mine. I will never let you go." His voice was

firm, and she instantly knew he was talking as an alpha.

"If that's your version of pillow talk, I love it." She giggled when he growled in her ear.

"Do not tempt me," he threatened, before he was interrupted by a light knock on the bedroom door.

"Hayden?"

That was the only word Sawyer got out before Hayden shot back, "Open that door and die!" The chuckle that echoed behind the door caused Lori to blush, but Hayden didn't seem bothered by the fact that there were others in the building.

"Crap! I forgot about them," Lori said as she looked up to see Hayden's grin. Her jaws ached from smiling. He was the most amazing man she'd ever met, and even now, her body was eager to memorize his touch.

"I'm sure they've already figured us out, considering we've been here for at least three hours." His grin widened and she tucked her face into the crook of his neck. "Don't worry, I'll get rid of them, and give you plenty of time to take a shower before we leave."

"Do we have to go?" Lori asked as her hand slipped beneath the sheet, causing him to draw in a sharp breath.

"I love the feel of your hands on my body," he said as he closed his eyes. "But we eventually have to leave."

Lori giggled as a soft moan escaped his lips. "Where are we going?" She loved when he squirmed, especially when she was the reason for it. He was an excellent teacher, and the proof was the tent she instantly created below his waist.

"I'm taking you to the mountains where you belong," he said. His voice quivered and he rolled her over, his knee sliding up between her thighs. His kiss was urgent and possessive, owning her as his body pinned hers to the bed.

A blissful grin spread across her face when he whispered dirty words in her ear, spurring a flame that he slowly stoked into a raging fire that only he could douse. Falling deeper and deeper beneath his spell, her mind went blank as desire exploded throughout her body.

Closing her eyes to catch her breath, *be still, my heart,* she sighed when he rested his head on her chest, his breathing matching hers.

"You are so damn beautiful." His lips brushed over her chin as he wrapped her in his arms and rolled over, pulling her to his side.

"Can't we stay here forever?" She peeked out one eye to see his grin.

"I would love nothing more than to keep you locked inside this room for the rest of our lives. But I can't protect you here without my wolf." His voice, although firm, spoke to her heart, and she nodded her understanding.

"I need to tell Mom first. Will you go with me? I would at least like to introduce you to my family before I run away with you." Lori chuckled when he tweaked her nose.

"I'm sure that won't be a problem," he said, dotting kisses along her jaw. "If that's what you want, that's what I'll do."

Lori's eyes opened to see the contented smile on his face. "Hayden, I love sharing a bond with you and knowing we will spend the rest of our lives together." His eyes opened and she swallowed down her anxiety before adding, "I want to go to college." His brow furrowed and she braced herself for what she was certain would come.

"Really? We have excellent colleges in Tennessee. Sawyer and Alyssa are attending the university, but whatever major you decide on, I'm sure there are several schools for you to choose from."

"You don't mind?" She lifted up on her elbow and stared down at him, unsure that he would actually allow her to go to college without a fight.

Would she be a paleontologist? That was her dream when she was a little girl… until she found out Barney wasn't a real dinosaur. She cried for three days, which resulted in her throwing out her purple fuzzy slippers. *What a sad day indeed.* She rolled her lip to keep from grinning when she noticed Hayden studying her.

"I went to college, and I would be slightly disappointed if you didn't want to go." He gave her a quick kiss before resting back on the pillow.

"Color me clueless because I didn't see that coming." She kissed his thumb that rubbed her bottom lip.

"What do you think we are, a bunch of depraved, wild wolves terrorizing the mountainside?" He tickled her sides, making her squeal.

"No! You just seemed too cool for school." She snickered.

"I have a degree in civil engineering, and Tucker's is electrical."

"So what your saying is: I've bonded with a Brainiac? That's hot."

"No, you're what's hot, and the reason why I have to get dressed." He got out of bed to gather his clothes. He was ripped in all the right places. And the next opportunity she had, she would lick every square inch of that body. He turned and flashed the sexiest grin she'd ever seen, and her face heated.

"I'm enjoying the view, do you mind?" Her snarky comment made him laugh and hell's bells! Her mind went straight to the gutter. Again.

"I like it when you look at me," he said as he oh-so-very-slowly pulled on his jeans.

"Good, because I've dreamed of that fine ass."

"If that's your pillow talk, I'm loving it." He winked and pulled on his shirt.

Lori yanked the blanket over her head as Hayden walked out of the room. Giggling softly, her body buzzed with the memory of his touch. He was hers and their bond was permanent; it would last a lifetime. She pulled the blanket down, listening to him address the others. Gosh, how she wanted to talk to Jesse! But she wasn't exactly dressed for the occasion. She rolled her eyes. Since when did she care how Jesse saw her? She didn't. So doing what only Lori would do, she called for Jesse to come into the bedroom. When the door opened in a matter of seconds, she snorted. "That didn't take long."

"Are you referring to me or to you?" Jesse lifted a brow, but couldn't hold back the grin. "Is it true? Did you accept his bond?"

"Oh, sister, I did a lot more than that."

"Yeah, that was obvious when I walked into the room." Jesse nudged Lori over on the bed and sat down on the edge. "I can't believe you and Hayden. I didn't think you were going to… Lori, you have no idea how truly happy I am for you. You both deserve it."

"So you don't think I'm hateful and nasty?"

"I was just trying to piss you off to get you out of

your head. You are not a hateful person, no matter how hard you try to pretend you are. Nasty, well, yeah, but that's what makes you, you."

"Hey, everyone needs a little nasty in their life. And why the hell didn't you tell me what I was missing?" Lori pinned her with a teasing glare.

"Because words can't describe how I feel when I'm with Tucker." Jesse smiled and patted Lori's blanketed leg.

"Yeah, that's what I thought too... indescribable!"

Jesse wrapped her arms around Lori, both giggling with tears in their eyes. "Oh, I'm supposed to tell you, Randy called and is on his way."

Thirty-Eight

Lori

Lori dreaded the trip to Cloverly that morning, but once the cast was removed from her arm, she still had a few things in the apartment to pack, and then it was goodbye forever. Okay, she wouldn't go that far, but she had no intention of returning anytime soon.

She would miss working at the boutique, but knowing Tracy would be taking her place, made walking away easier.

Satisfied with Hayden's bond, she longed to be back on the mountain to see him again. She fell in love with him sitting in the swing, and no matter how hard she tried to deny it; he always managed to creep back into her head. Now, if she weren't totally crazy, she would have sworn she could sense his emotions. He was thrilled. Just knowing that made the trip more bearable, but Hayden showing up unexpectedly, made it *great.*

Seeing him again, their bond intensified and there was no way she could deny the powerful link between them. He was the total package; better than any book boyfriend. And if she were being totally honest, she couldn't resist her passionate urge to strip him down and... well... you know! She chuckled as her face heated and side glanced his way. He kept his eyes on the road, but the grin on his face indicated he knew exactly what was going through her mind.

"You know, I think this bond between us could get you into a lot of trouble." His voice sent a surge of butterflies to her belly and she squirmed in the seat.

"Do tell," she said, not even bothering to calm her racing heart.

"Well, at times, I think I can hear your thoughts..." He looked her way.

"Then prepare to blush. Because the thoughts I have are most definitely rated triple X." She flashed her pearly whites. "But we'd better save that for the sheets. I wouldn't want to distract you while you're driving." She laughed at the expression on his face and blushed when he made an obscene gesture with his hands.

"So this is where you've been hiding," he said as he turned onto the asphalt drive. It hugged a tree line that hid the house from the highway.

"Yeah, it's not much but we still call it home." She chuckled when he shook his head and if she could have seen his face, he was probably rolling his eyes. He was fun to be around, a stickler at times, which made teasing him that much more enjoyable. But as comfortable as she tried to make him, she couldn't settle her own nerves.

Turning back toward the house, Lori twiddled her thumbs. She had never brought a man home to meet her mother, at least not anyone to whom she willingly offered her virginity. Her mother was an adult, though, and obviously quite familiar with sex. Not too long ago, she even bragged about practicing safe sex—something Lori never actually considered, and apparently neither had Hayden. *Oops!* Or was that a ruse? Would Hayden be black-balled from future family gatherings? Okay, maybe her mother wouldn't be totally shocked to learn that Lori pitched the idea and Hayden scored the home run. Still, talking about her love life with her mother was most definitely out of her comfort zone.

It was a bit awkward when Hayden pulled up in front of the house and shut off the truck. She could see her mom through the large glass windows as she began rushing to the foyer. Yeah, it would be a humdinger of a family gathering, but the sooner she got it over with, the sooner they could leave for the mountain.

She glanced back at Hayden who was struggling to get his seatbelt unlatched. He was in pain if the tension in his body was any indicator, but he played it down with a smile. "Here, let me help." She clicked the button, releasing the belt, and he sat back in the seat and took a deep breath. *That wasn't good.* She popped the handle and got out of the truck, hurrying around to the driver's side as the front door of the house opened. "Are you okay?"

"I'm good. A little stiff is all." He slowly turned until he could slide out of the seat, landing on his feet. He winced with the impact and she scowled.

"You're hurting. What can I do to help?" Her heart

thundered as he pulled her into a hug. With her head resting against his chest, she breathed in his soothing mountain scent.

"Relax. I'll walk it off. Just help me to the house."

Lori did as he instructed, and wrapped one arm around his waist, allowing him to lean on her as they moved around to the front steps. Her mom was standing on the porch, closely watching them.

"Is everything all right?" her mother asked when she noticed Hayden having trouble walking up the steps.

"He's fine." Lori looked up at Hayden and he nodded. "Just walking out the stiffness." That seemed to appease her mom, who hurried to open the front door for them to enter the house.

Once inside, Lori took Hayden's coat and hers, hanging them in the small entryway closet before turning around to make the introductions. "Hayden, this is Linda, my mom, and her husband, Dean," she said when Dean entered the room.

"It's so nice to meet you," Linda said and when Lori flicked her brows, he blushed. "Come in and make yourself at home."

Lori rolled her lip to keep from laughing when Dean offered his hand. "So you're what all the commotion has been about. It's finally nice to meet you. Although I must say, you look like you've taken one blow too many."

Talk about an OMG moment. Lori thought she'd die right there on the spot. Granted, Hayden did look seasoned, in a tough kind of way. His hair was disheveled, thanks to her, and he was dressed like a lumberjack, wearing brown work boots, jeans, and his signature flannel shirt. She was digging the look. Then she caught a glimpse of his smile. Oh, yeah, the beard shadow, along with his height and build? Definite turn-on. She cut a glance at her mom who was enjoying Dean's teasing and Lori rolled her eyes.

"Well, sir, when you get to be my age, you'll understand why they're called hard knocks." Hayden grinned and the strain in the room dissipated.

"Come on, I'll help you into the kitchen." Dean laughed and put his arm around Hayden's waist.

Lori was floored. After meeting Dean, she knew how wrong she was about him, and the way he stepped up to help Hayden was a kindness she would never forget.

"Better get in there before they eat all the food," her mother said, taking hold of her hand. "Dean's been busy in the kitchen all afternoon; he wants to impress you with his special roast lamb."

"You know that wasn't necessary. We would have been happy with a peanut butter and jelly sandwich," Lori said, but once she got a whiff of the roast lamb, her stomach growled. "But I'm awfully glad he went to all the trouble! I'm starving."

The meal was as tasty as she knew it would be, and believe it or not, Dean was a better cook than her mother. He actually teased Linda about her culinary skills, telling her she needed to experiment with new foods and new recipes. Of course, he was right.

Lori sat back and relaxed, rubbing her now full tummy, and listening to Dean and Hayden talk about the mountains. She missed those mountains, as well as all the chaos of his large family. Then Hayden proceeded to tell the story of how they first met. Lori's face heated and she quickly excused herself and headed to the bathroom down the hall. Dean would never let her live that down.

Standing in front of the large mirror, she couldn't help but snicker when she recalled Lily Rose knocking her off her feet. Then the warm fuzzies gripped her insides as she remembered Hayden's eyes and the way they captivated her. He still had a way of making her ovaries swoon, only now, it was for other reasons. She softly giggled and pushed her fingers through her hair as a knock landed on the door.

"Lori? It's me, Mom. Can I come in?" Instantly, Lori thought the worst and pulled open the door, looking past her mother down the short hall.

"Is Hayden okay?"

"Shh, that's what I wanted to talk to you about. Do you all really have to leave tonight? He doesn't look like he's up for the drive, and we have plenty of room." Her mother's eyes told her there was more going on and Lori narrowed her gaze.

"There's more. What is it?"

"Nothing, just..." she paused and closed the door. "Dean's always wanted a family, and you here... oh, Lori, he thinks of you as his daughter. Could you stay a night or maybe two? It would mean so much to him. He already had the pool cleaned and serviced. He was hoping we could bribe you to visit us more often. Please? Humor the old folks, okay?" She smiled and tucked a strand of Lori's hair behind her ear. "You're lucky. I see the way Hayden looks at you. The same way your dad used to look at me."

Lori couldn't stop the tears that filled her eyes, knowing how much her mother approved of Hayden. "I'll see what I can do, but we'll have to call his brother. He's waiting for us to pick him up at Jesse's."

"That's perfect! Invite all of them over. Dean wanted to break in his new grill this weekend, and tomorrow is Saturday. The pool's already heated, and the air temperature should hit the mid-seventies. What do you say? We can celebrate an early spring."

How could Lori possibly decline? The excitement in her mother's eyes was something she hadn't seen in years. It couldn't hurt to hang around for the weekend. Besides, she secretly longed to swim in that big-ass pool. "Okay, if you're sure Dean won't mind having a house full."

"Are you kidding? He'll be thrilled." She pulled open the door and Lori pulled her phone out of her bra. "Thank you."

Was it a mistake not to inform Hayden of their plans to stay the weekend? Probably, but the longer he sat at the table, the stiffer his movements became. Lori dialed Jesse and extended the invitation, knowing they would arrive before dark. Then she washed her face and checked her teeth before heading back to the dining room.

"If you all are finished laughing at my expense, I'd like to give Hayden a tour of the house," she said, walking over to stand beside his chair. Her mother winked, and Lori rolled her lip to keep from smiling.

Her mother was right about Hayden, and Lori nearly panicked when she had to help him out of the chair. He wasn't too pleased either, claiming he was perfectly capable of standing on his own. She ignored him even when she heard the soft rumble in his chest. Wolfy-boy had best watch his tone or come morning, he would be the first victim to get dunked in the pool. She grinned, but felt bad when he stumbled and flinched. "Right here," she said, pushing open the bedroom door, which was across the hall from hers. Unlike her room with a view of the pool, his overlooked the grassy lawn. Lori did a quick inspection of the room as she led him over to the queen-sized bed. Thankfully, it was decorated in blues and burgundies, not the coral and green she adored. "I knew I shouldn't have tempted you this morning."

Once Hayden was sitting on the edge of the bed, he inhaled through his nose. She could tell he was hurting a lot, but that didn't stop him from pulling her down beside him. "I would do it all over again. You have no idea how I felt without you. I needed you." He smiled, trying to hide his pain.

"Well," she said as perky as she could, "I promised Mom I'd help clean up the kitchen, so if you want to rest for a bit, I'll come back and get you when we're done."

"Maybe for a few minutes, but don't let me sleep long." He stretched out on the bed and rolled over on his back.

"I'll be back in a few," Lori said, but as she walked out the door, she glanced back, her heart aching.

Two hours later, Lori stood on the front porch as a vehicle pulled into the drive. The evening was cool, but everyone seemed eager to hang out in the heated pool. It would give Tucker a chance to check up on Hayden. "This way," Lori said, and they followed her into the foyer.

After introducing everyone, she left Jesse and Sawyer to entertain her mom and Dean while she and Tucker went up to Hayden's room.

Standing outside his door, Tucker lifted her chin and wiped the tears from her eyes. "I'll take care of him. He's a mountain wolf. We're tough as steel." Tucker pulled her into an embrace and she sobbed all over his shirt.

"His pain is because of me. I shouldn't have pushed him this morning."

"Are you crazy? You're the reason he's up and moving again. He was lost without you, and his pain is nothing more than a lot of sore muscles. He's going to be fine."

"But," Lori said pulling out of his arms, "he doesn't know we're staying the night yet."

"Dr. Williams said it would do him good to get in the pool, so he can't very well argue with medical advice." Tucker smiled and took hold of the doorknob. "Go downstairs with the others, and let me tend to him. I promise he's going to be fine."

Thirty-Nine

Lori

The next morning, Lori glanced over to find Hayden still sleeping with his arm draped over her waist. She snuck into his room after everyone went to bed, knowing he would sleep better with her there. Who was she kidding? Just lying by his side, she didn't feel alone anymore. She smiled when he pulled her back against his chest.

"This must be heaven." His husky voice brushed over her ear, and she tugged his hands tighter around her body.

"I could wake up like this every morning." She giggled softly as his fingers traced circles over her tummy. "Are you feeling okay?"

"Better than okay." He rocked against her, sending a bout of butterflies to her belly and she shivered. "I could show you."

Yes, please! She wanted to say, but instead she said, "So tempting." She giggled again when he growled. "But first, you're going to get your sexy ass in the shower, and when you're dressed, we'll go down for a late breakfast. Then..." She rolled over to face him, and as she expected, he was sulking. "Dr. Williams said the pool would be good for you. So until you get in the pool, there will be no playtime." She choked out a laugh. "Rolling your eyes will grant you no favors. Now skedaddle your butt to the bathroom. I'll be waiting when you get out."

He spewed a few words below his breath, and had she been a wolf, she would have probably heard them. "What was that?" she asked when he sat up on the edge of the bed.

"You know we can't stay here long. I'm out of territory, and I'm not even sure who the alpha is here."

Lori rose up on her knees and scooted across the bed, behind him. Wrapping her arms around his waist, he laid his head back on her shoulder. "I may not be a wolf, but I have my connections. The alpha knows we're here, and he plans to stop by later to see how we're doing; so rest assured, I've got you covered." In one quick swipe of his arm, Lori was sitting in his lap, grinning.

"You know the alpha here in Buffer County?"

"Not only do I know him, he's one of my best friends." Lori couldn't hold back the snicker when she saw the scowl on his face, nor the laughter when it dawned on him that she was talking about Nigel. Without a word, he placed her on her feet and moved over to look out the window. She suspected he was trying to save face, but she never expected him to turn and match her grin.

"So crow's on the menu tonight... okay. I'm down with that. But just so you know..." His grin turned wicked as he pinned her with his smizing eyes. "You will be the dessert."

Lori squealed and made a mad-dash to the door when his body dived across the bed. "We'll just see how well that works out for ya, hotshot!" She clicked her tongue and slammed the door, his muffled growl echoing in her head.

Once breakfast was over, and the kitchen was cleaned up, Lori was more than grateful to head out to the pool. She and Jesse were the first ones in, and as much as she would have loved to lie on a float, she was still a bit shy about her body. Having boobs was a big deal, and the bikini she wore left very little to the imagination. She tugged on the top as she sat down in the waist deep water while Jesse moved further out to the deep end.

"Hurry and get in. It's warm as bath water," Jesse said when Sawyer bounded out the door in bright orange swim shorts. His tousled dark hair, much longer than Hayden's, whipped about his face but he couldn't hide his grin. Lori laughed when he belly-flopped, splashing water over Jesse.

"This is great," Sawyer said, once his head was above the water again. "We need a pool like this on the mountain."

Lori turned when the patio door opened and Tucker walked out, followed by Hayden. Seeing Hayden's white swim trunks and mocha skin tone, an assortment of dirty thoughts flashed through her brain. The most important concern, however, was if those shorts were see-through when wet. She'd seen Hayden naked before, twice actually, but holy frickin' macaroni-on-a-stick! She stifled a giggle and glanced down to make sure her suit wasn't see-through.

"Care if I join you?" Hayden asked and her eyes slowly trailed up his body, pausing at the swim trunks that hugged his muscular thighs. She nodded and when he sat down beside her, it took all of her resistance not to rub the goosebumps that covered his chest. Dessert was starting to sound pretty damn good. "I could get used to this," he said as he looked at the sky. "And you on a float, naked beneath a full moon? Yeah, that would be the icing on the cake." He chuckled when she smacked his arm.

"Are all your thoughts dirty?"

"Aren't yours?" He winked and moved out into the deeper water. "Come over here and sit in my lap."

"Smooth, real smooth, but that's not happening. No more bed-banging until you are completely healed, mister!"

Hayden laughed at her choice of words and pushed the hair from his eyes. "I didn't hurt myself, if that's what you think. I'm just sore from lack of exercise."

She chuckled and ducked out of his reach, moving around him to the deep end of the pool. It was nice to be swimming in the pool, and it reminded her of all the summers she spent at Megan's house. She glanced over at Jesse, wishing Megan were also there. With the sun shining brightly, and the air temperature warming, it was the perfect spring day. She moved back across the pool as Tucker climbed to the top of the diving board.

Lori squealed when a pair of familiar arms wrapped around her waist.

"You'll never escape me. My wolf has your scent, and it can hardly wait for me to devour you." The soft rumble of his voice zipped through her body and she turned in his arms, wrapping her legs around his waist.

She pushed the hair out of her face, and whispered, "Oh, yeah? Well, I've got something for your wolf."

"Right here?" His brows rose, and she seductively grinned.

"No. Over there." She lifted her hand to point in the direction where Dean and Nigel had just walked out the door. A low growl worked up his throat when he turned and saw the alpha there. "Down, boy. He's on our side."

"Your side maybe."

She dropped her legs from his waist, and took hold of his hand, pulling him to the shallow end of the pool. Waving to Nigel, he walked over to meet them when they stepped out of the water.

"Whoa! Look at you, all spiffy. Guess you aren't planning to go in the pool." She stood with her back pressed against Hayden, his arms covering her chest. It was such a guy move. She mentally rolled her eyes.

"Nah, I'm on my way to an auction. I just stopped by to drop this off," Nigel said, handing Hayden a copy of the police report. "If you have any questions, my number's at the bottom."

"Thanks," Hayden said, stepping around Lori to walk with Nigel to the door.

Lori didn't know what they were talking about, but at least, they were talking. She stepped back in the pool to wait until Hayden placed the police report under a towel to keep the breeze from blowing it away.

"Who was that?" Sawyer asked when Hayden

returned to the pool.

"The alpha; he brought me a copy of Lori's accident report," Hayden replied as he nudged Lori with his shoulder.

"I bet you wore out the pool after your accident," Sawyer said, moving over to join them.

"Actually, this is the first time I've been in it," Lori said to his surprise.

"Oh! I figured with you flipping your car, you would be sore and this is like ahhh." He laid back and smiled at the sky.

"Well, as badass as you make me sound, I didn't flip the car."

"But..." Sawyer looked over at Hayden as a silent message passed between them.

"But what?" she asked.

Hayden twirled her bikini string between his fingers. He was hesitant, but finally answered. "The police report said you weren't wearing a seatbelt when you flipped the car, and that was the reason for the cracked windshield."

"That's not true! I always wear my seatbelt." She thought back for a minute and scowled. "There was a loud thud. Then I slid off the road. I tried to brace myself for the impact, but my head slammed against the window when the car hit the culvert." Lori looked at Hayden. "It was Beth, wasn't it?"

"Yeah, there were tracks leading down to the car, so she probably saw you and the blood, and like me, she thought you were dead."

"But why did they think I flipped the car?"

"Because the top was caved in, and the windshield was busted. It looked like you flipped, but I know the truth and now Nigel does too. It was all Beth."

Lori looked back at the house with a serious frown on her face. "Well, you can bet your sweet ass that will be the last time a flea-bag gets the jump on me." She leaned into Hayden's chest and smiled at the soft rumble she heard.

Forty

Lori

As excited as Lori was to start her new life, she was equally bummed. Saying goodbye to her mom was a lot tougher than she originally thought, and she struggled to keep the tears from her eyes. Everything became final in that moment. She was an adult, in control of her own life, and moving to another state. It was actually scary as hell.

She often complained about her mother never being home, but in the back of her mind, she somehow knew she wasn't far away. Now, though, the six-hour drive sounded like a thousand miles away and she hoped she could find her way back to Buffer County.

She peered over at Hayden who held Tucker in a bear-hug. He had a rough edge about him, but was the most caring man she ever met. He was all about family and even invited her mother and Dean to the mountains for their bonding ceremony. *How insane would that be?* She grinned, picturing Lily Rose taking up with her mom.

Looking back to the disastrous day when her mother pissed her off and left her to spend Christmas alone. It was the start of what Lori now knew to be her destiny, something she could never imagined in a million years.

Thinking her and Steve would always be together she sank into a deep depression once he moved to Oklahoma. Life as she knew it was changing before her eyes. All her friends were moving on with their lives, yet everything about her life was stagnating.

She didn't blame her mom or Brid for keeping secrets, because not only did it keep her safe, but it ultimately led her to Hayden.

Her thoughts wandered back to the first time she laid eyes on him. Actually, it was his wolf, and she was too young to think much into it. Then, that coming summer at the county fair, when she snapped a picture of Tucker and Jaylee. Little did she know, at the time, it was Hayden standing in the back-ground staring at the camera as if he were searching for her soul. Just thinking about it made her heart skip a beat. They had crossed paths; something Hayden said was fate's way of bringing them together. And she liked knowing he had secretly searched out blue-eyed girls, in his quest to find her. Considering she secretly loved her golden eyed guardian angel.

She was positive her dad had sent Hayden to watch over her even if Hayden had no clue he was doing so at the time. And her dad putting the note in the teddy bear's pocket was confirmation that she and Hayden belonged together. Her heart swelled, and she hoped she too would have visions that would lead to happy endings.

"I'm going to miss you," Jesse said, hugging Lori tightly.

"It's not going to be the same, but we still have the phone." Lori swiped the tears from her eyes. "And the greatest thing about us being bonded to brothers is you are now officially my sister-in-law." She snickered and Jesse's eyes widened.

"I never thought of it like that. I have a sister! Oh, I have lots of sisters."

"Don't forget the brothers," Sawyer chimed in, while smiling.

"We could never forget you!" Jesse released Lori to pull Sawyer into a hug.

Lori glanced up and locked eyes with Hayden, and in three strides he was standing at her side. "Are you ready?" He kissed the top of her head and then opened the truck door.

"Call me when you get there," her mother said, she and Dean standing on the top step waving.

"I will. I love you!"

"Love you too!"

Following Tucker's truck out the drive, tears filled Lori's eyes. *So bittersweet,* she thought, looking back over her shoulder to see her mother was still standing on the porch waving. She wiped her eyes and then turned, hearing Hayden's voice in her head. "I'm good," she mouthed, and he gave a slight nod.

"You know, you can visit anytime you like."

"Yeah, I know. But right now I have to do what's best for me."

"And that is?"

"You." Sending naughty thoughts through the bond,

she blushed when Hayden flicked his tongue, and Sawyer snickered.

Lori cut her eyes to the rearview mirror, and stuck out her tongue. “Wake me when we get there.” She winked at Hayden before stretching out on the backseat and closing her eyes.

Forty-One

Hayden

Everything happens for a reason, Hayden pondered, and spending the weekend with Lori's parents gave him more time to talk to Nigel. And believe it or not, they had become friends. It also made Lori happy that he wasn't constantly bristling around the new alpha, and that alone, set his mind at ease. He was finally at peace, and his wolf was ecstatic to be taking Lori home—where she belonged. They could start their life together. She would be safe, and he could walk around with his head held high, so high he could probably kiss the moon.

Getting Lori back to the mountains was the plan since day one, but Lori ditching him at the boutique wasn't part of the plan. She fought the bond and him, thinking he deserved someone like Katherine. If she were ever dead wrong about anything in her life that was definitely it. He was the undeserving one, but that didn't mean he was willing to let her go. He made a mental note as soon as she was safe on the mountain to show her just how special she truly was.

Hayden looked forward to them spending their nights in the small cabin that overlooked the mountainside. Ceremony or not, he wouldn't pass up the opportunity to wake up with her in his arms. He wanted her all to himself, at least for a little while, and he grinned, knowing she would agree.

Glancing over his shoulder to where Lori was buckled up and sleeping on the backseat, he couldn't help but stare. *Just get her home.* That was all he ever wanted—to have her back on the mountain.

With Sawyer at the wheel, the drive made him nervous, and he was constantly checking the speed. But that wasn't necessary. Sawyer was an excellent driver, having been taught by the best. He glanced over to see his little brother following his instructions as directed. He even insisted that Sawyer hang back from traffic by at least four car lengths. It was his over-protective wolf at work, because he knew he would never survive if anything happened to Lori—she had become his whole world.

Hayden turned in the seat and carefully adjusted the small throw blanket to cover Lori's legs. The seasonal warmth held out for the weekend, but Ol' Man Winter apparently had one more trick up his sleeve. Blanketing the mountains with a surprise storm of four inches of snow, it was welcome, but also damn cold.

Turning back to the road as they crossed into Tennessee, Hayden breathed a sigh of relief. It wouldn't be long before they were home. He couldn't wait to start celebrating at Lori's surprise welcome back party. She would be embarrassed, and he would pay for it dearly, but he was so looking forward to that. *Make-up sex.* Was there anything better?

Lori voiced her concern for meeting his parents again and blamed herself for his accident. But had he not been there, he wasn't sure Lori could have survived Beth's attack. *Water under the bridge*, he thought, since dwelling on it only infuriated his wolf.

The tension in his body dissipated when the Tennessee Mountains came into view. They were nearly home, and just thinking about them being alone together, he was glad he wore a flannel that hung down past his waist.

"What are you grinning about?" Sawyer asked when he turned off the highway and onto the narrow mountain road.

"Mom is going to hit the roof when she finds out we've already consummated our bond. You know how old-fashioned she is." His mother knew Hayden would never turn away from Lori if given the chance. He was a horn-dog in that respect, although he credited it with good genes. His mother could say what she wanted, but his dad told a totally different story about their bonding. It was something he would never repeat, and something his mother didn't realize he knew. He couldn't stop the chuckle that escaped. "Do you think she would buy that it was all Lori's doing?"

"With your track record? Fat chance." Sawyer smirked a smile. "Just blame it on the fact that Lori's a feisty human. Man, what I wouldn't give to find a female just like her."

"She's your sis-in-law, so stop drooling." Hayden pinned him with a friendly glare. He couldn't help ragging on his brother, payback for interrupting them by knocking on the bedroom door at the apartment.

Just remembering how Lori wiggled her hips made his jeans tighten. She was so damn perfect, with her one-track mind, and a body that would squeeze a howl from the lips of a dying wolf.

"I'm not drooling, but there will be plenty of males on the mountain doing just that. Not only is she human, and a seer, but in my book, she's a definite ten. Oh, man, you're gonna have your hands full." A low growl filled the cab, and Sawyer laughed.

But he wasn't kidding, and Hayden expected a few males would try to tempt fate. "They best not let me see them ogling or I'll remove their hide and hair." He'd been through hell to get her to accept his bond, and he pitied any male that dared look at her with even a twinkle in their eye. It wouldn't bode well for them. He would have a new head to mount on his wall, and not one with antlers. That, he would guarantee.

Then Lori mumbled from the backseat and he swore his heart fell to his feet, seeing the crease on her forehead. What she was dreaming about, he didn't know, but he was afraid to wake her so he kept a silent watch.

With his finger pressed to his lips, he motioned for

Sawyer to turn down the radio as he cocked his head to listen to her ramblings. Unable to make any sense of the words, he blew out a slow breath when she pushed the blanket off her body and suddenly opened her eyes.

"Where am I?" she asked, squinting against the noonday sun. She looked disoriented as she glanced between him and Sawyer.

"We're on our way to the mountains; we should be there soon." Hayden reached back and cupped her cheek and she leaned into his hand—he needed her to feel safe. "Come up here with me." He couldn't help wanting to hold her when she looked so unsure. It was probably because she just woke up from a bad dream and didn't know where she was.

"He watches from a distance but it will be you who exposes his identity." That sounded so out of place, and Hayden assumed Lori was speaking gibberish until she blinked to clear her eyes.

"What's that supposed to mean?" Hayden asked as he helped Lori over the seat. He was still getting used to her being a seer, and as impressive as that was, it also scared the shit out of him. What if someone tried to kidnap her? *They would be signing their own death warrant.* His wolf agreed. Wrapping her in his arms, her head resting on his shoulder, he inhaled her sweet scent. He briefly closed his eyes, savoring the moment while Sawyer snickered from the driver's seat. He'd deal with him later.

"It was a vision Brid had months ago, and we thought it was about Nigel when I met him in the woods. But it's not. I don't think it was ever about me," Lori said, staring out the window.

"If it wasn't about you, then who?" Hayden tightened

his grip, anticipating what she would say next.

"Tracy."

Acknowledgements

Thank you, Troy. For listening as I went over a chapter for the twelfth time. I really hated interrupting your wrestling. ;)

Thank you, Teri at editingfairy.com. I look forward to working with you again.

Thanks to my beta readers for jumping in at the last minute to get this story out. You rock!

And to the readers, thank you for giving the Cloverly Wolves a chance.

If you liked this story, please consider leaving a review.

About the Author

B. S. Todd lives in a small western Kentucky town with her husband, son, two dogs and a ferocious feline. A nature enthusiast, she has always drawn her greatest inspiration from the natural world around her. Her hobbies include reading, writing, and on certain nights throughout the calendar year, she can be found watching meteor showers or lunar eclipses conveniently from her backyard.

Other books by this author

Please visit your favorite retailer to discover other books by B. S. Todd

The Cloverly Wolves Series

Book One- Looking for Ginseng
Book Two- . Paisley Wolf (July 2018)
Book Three- Always Hayden (August 2018)
Book Four (November 2018)

www.ingramcontent.com/pod-product-compliance
Lightning Source LLC
Chambersburg PA
CBHW020333180626
46812CB00001B/191

9780999116951